The Westchester Review™

A LITERARY JOURNAL OF WRITERS FROM THE HUDSON TO THE SOUND

Louise Albert
1928-2015

With sorrow, we say farewell to Louise Albert, our Editor in Chief Emerita. *The Westchester Review* was born at her "magic table," where many of us honed our writing skills. A gifted novelist, mentor, and friend, Louise was long-respected in Westchester as a creative writing teacher, who inspired, suggested, prodded ("Just one more rewrite!"), and edited—all with kindness and generosity. She attended to every word, honoring the craft of writing while encouraging us to be true to ourselves. *The Westchester Review* dedicates this issue to her memory.

The Westchester Review is published annually. The editors welcome previously unpublished prose, poetry, and drama by established and emerging writers living, working, or studying in New York State's Westchester County area.

We read manuscripts year-round. Electronic submissions are encouraged and may be sent, with cover letter, to *submissions@westchesterreview.com*. Manuscripts may also be mailed to
The Westchester Review
Box 246H
Scarsdale, NY 10583

Complete submission guidelines are available online at *www.westchesterreview.com*.

The Westchester Review is a sponsored project of Fractured Atlas, a non-profit arts service organization. Contributions for the purposes of *The Westchester Review* must be made payable to Fractured Atlas and are tax-deductible to the extent permitted by law.

Library of Congress Control Number: 2015951578

ISBN: 978-0-692-46831-9

The range and quality of the submissions for our eighth issue delighted us. In this diverse collection, we're proud to publish an unprecedented number of first-time authors, stories that include international and futuristic themes, poetry in a wide variety of forms, and a one-act play.

We also present the winners of our third Writers Under 30 Contest: Peter Porcino for prose and Max L. Chapnick for poetry. Encouraged by the enthusiastic response to this contest, we'll be bringing it back next year, as well as initiating an additional competition for Flash Fiction. Look for submission guidelines and information about readings and other events on our website, *www.westchesterreview.com.*

CONTENTS

POETRY

His White Silk Scarf

Herb Friedman

All the other buses had departed for Scout Camp but we were left sitting in the midday New York heat because one camper, an Eamon Crowley, hadn't yet arrived. The driver was off in search of a working pay phone to call Boy Scout headquarters for instructions when the kid finally showed up. Most of the boys on our bus were from the same Scout troop but Eamon was a stranger, a thin blond kid of about my age, a little short for a thirteen-year-old. He stood in the doorway, gripping the shiny vertical pole next to the empty driver's seat, trying to catch his breath.

"Hey, y'dumb Tenderfoot. Where y'been?" someone yelled from the rear of the bus.

In a moment another voice joined in. "Shrimp, what are you, deaf or something? He's talking to you."

"Sorry. Missed . . . my . . . subway . . . stop," the new boy gasped as he walked past me on his way to find a seat in the rear. But the kids in our patrol weren't done with him. As Eamon approached an empty place, one of the others dropped a backpack onto the seat. When he moved to the next row, the backpack was tossed onto that empty spot. And so it went from row to row. They were all laughing and yelling at him and having a great time.

For all I cared, they could bounce this new kid around as much as they wanted, but not on my nickel. I had been wearing the single-bar Assistant Patrol Leader's badge on my sleeve for the past year. But at the end of our two-week stay at camp, the patrol would be electing a new leader. Along with the double-barred badge went the chance to be someone who wasn't just another kid from a rough neighborhood. I knew I would never have the Scoutmaster's approval if the bus driver reported that he had returned to find an out-of-control zoo.

I stood up and raised three fingers of my right hand, the Scout signal for silence.

"Come up here," I called, removing my duffel bag from the seat next to me. Eamon turned around. But Roger Butler, who I knew from school—a real pain—grabbed the backpack and trotted ahead of Eamon, ready to continue the harassment.

I stepped into the aisle, blocking his way.

Roger switched the backpack from his right to his left hand and waited. I looked him squarely in the eye. "Knock it off," I said in a low voice.

He hesitated, then stepped aside, which surprised me, until I looked over my shoulder and saw the bus driver standing there. Eamon squeezed past Roger and sat down beside me. He looked back at the others and shook his head.

"Thanks," he said. I gave him a short nod. If he wanted to think that I had quieted them down for his sake that was okay with me.

As our bus chugged north, we passed the ugly white concrete cube of the Bronx County Courthouse. I tried to keep my eyes focused on the back of the driver's head but I could feel my fingernails digging into the palms of my hands. Three weeks earlier the *Daily News* had run a two-inch story accompanied by a picture of my mother and me entering that building where, a few minutes later, my dad was sentenced to two years in the penitentiary for stealing multiple cars and operating an auto chop shop. The photo was clear enough for everyone at school, from the principal on down, to recognize me. Only Roger had mentioned it to my face but I was sure that the others talked about little else when I wasn't around.

Once we had passed the courthouse, I swiveled around to look back at the other Scouts on the bus. It was a relief to see that none of them, not even Roger, had noticed the big white building and none were looking at me. Still, I wondered when the finger-pointing would begin.

When I turned back to Eamon, he was gazing out of the window at a passing airplane. He poked me in the side and pointed. "That's a B-18. Looks like a DC-2; same wings but you can see how much deeper the fuselage is. My dad says they fly like dogs and that the Army Air Corps is going to have to come up with something a lot better."

"Is your father a pilot?" I asked. Eamon explained that his father was an airline captain, or had been until he transferred to the Army Air Corps.

The Scouts in the two rows behind stopped arguing about whether Red Huffing would pitch twenty winners for the Yankees that season and leaned forward to listen. In the summer of 1941, when everyone knew the country was on the verge of war, pilots counted for a lot more than pitchers. We had all seen the photos of the RAF flyers in their Mae Wests running toward their fighter planes, outnumbered but eager to take on the Luftwaffe. A kid whose father flew airplanes, any airplanes, was special. Hearing Eamon talk about his father so soon after having been reminded of seeing my own dad in handcuffs standing at the wooden rail in the courtroom was almost physically painful. But I listened with the rest as Eamon continued.

"They tried to keep him as a transport pilot, ferrying bigwigs around, but my dad wasn't buying into that; not with a war coming. He's flying fighters now, P-40s in China with the American Volunteer Group, you know, the Flying Tigers. I guess his medal convinced them to let him join."

One of the boys in the row directly behind us reached over and tapped Eamon on the shoulder. "What did he get the medal for?"

"My dad doesn't like me to talk about that. He says it's not polite and, besides, he says any good pilot could have done it. I don't believe that though."

"Come on, kid. You can tell us. We won't tell anybody."

"Well, it happened last year. My dad was flying the regular schedule to Boston but the weather was so bad they diverted him back to New York. And then the weather here crummed up. He circled for a couple of hours because they said it was due to improve, but no joy. Finally, with only fifteen minutes' fuel left, he nosed down into the fog, following the beam. The rules say that he should have broken it off when he couldn't see the runway from four hundred feet but there was no place to go and he would've run out of gas. So he just kept descending even though his copilot kept yelling in his ear to pull up.

"He had no idea where the ground was until he heard the chirp of his wheels on the concrete. He was way too far down the runway. Any other pilot would've ended up in the bay for sure but my dad had a trick up his sleeve. You see, with a DC-3 you can push the control column full forward and stand on the brakes right after touchdown. The tail goes up and acts as an airbrake but the nose doesn't quite touch and it won't turn over. So my dad got the plane stopped before they went into the drink and the passengers never knew how close they'd come. The airline kept it quiet but the copilot got them to give him the medal."

By now several of the boys from the back, including Roger, had moved forward, standing in the aisle to listen. As usual, Roger listened with a sneer, ready to point out anything negative he could find. He was through and through an unpleasant guy and it was hard to imagine enjoying sharing anything with him, much less two weeks at camp.

I had hoped to get away from Roger. After his remark in the school lunchroom about my father's conviction, he hadn't mentioned it again to my face, but a couple of times during the last week of school, while we were handing in our textbooks and waiting for our report cards, I saw him talking to little groups of his cronies and gesturing toward me with a motion of his head or a roll of his eyes. I was certain that he would start that again at camp if he had the chance.

As soon as we pulled into the parking lot, the camp's Head Counselor stood on the bus steps and read off our bunk assignments from his clipboard. Roger, Eamon, and I were all assigned to the same cabin in the Ramapo Tribe. There was no changing that; who ever won an argument against a clipboard? Our cabin was one of eight small, green-roofed, wooden bunkhouses arranged in a semicircle around a campfire pit. Like the others, it was stained brown to resemble a log cabin and contained two double-decker bunk beds, one on each side.

Eamon had the upper and I the lower on the right near the entrance. Roger took the lower on the left in the back.

It wasn't roomy but we would be spending most of our time outside of the cabin. There would be swimming, baseball, track and field, and, my favorite sport, boxing. I was a champion in my weight division at our neighborhood club, and I hoped to be able to keep in practice. For rainy days most of us had brought along a raft of Captain Marvel and Superman comic books that we read and swapped throughout our two-week stay.

I don't think I ever saw Eamon reading a comic. He had some battered old copies of *Air Trails* and *Flying Magazine* and he seemed to read them every minute we weren't outdoors. He must have had a small library tucked away in his scuffed and stained Army surplus duffel bag. We kept our clothes and other possessions in bags like that, scrunched together against the back wall; everyone except Roger. He had a shiny blue footlocker with black leather edging, his name in fancy red letters on the top. Instead of the ordinary trunk fastener, it had an intricate gold-colored metal scroll that swung down to lock it.

Everything Roger had was a little better than what the rest of us could manage. He loved to show off his new first-baseman's mitt and his leather moccasins, often mocking the sneakers or scuffed city shoes that the rest of us had. Most envied was his red-sided pocketknife. He called it an *Offiziersmesser*—that was supposed to mean Swiss Officer's Knife—no ordinary soldier's knife for Roger. It had three knife blades, a corkscrew, a bottle opener, and a couple of other implements I didn't even recognize. It was a marvelous thing, and something I knew I could never be able to own.

After breakfast on the first Monday of our stay, I received a letter from my mother. She wrote that "seeing what's happened," we would be giving up our apartment in January and moving in with her sister, my Aunt Maria, on 38th Street—another aftershock from my father's conviction. How many more would there be? I thought about that during the rest of the morning. New street; new school; new friends. Maybe, new friends—unless they found out about my dad. The kids at my old school had known me for seven years and nothing that Roger, or anyone else, could say was likely to change how they saw me. But how would the strangers at the new place think of me if they found out about my father's conviction and all they knew about me was that my father was a convicted felon?

During the swim period that afternoon, I was still thinking of the move to Aunt Maria's and missed the lifeguard's "buddy whistle." As a safety measure we were paired off, required to stay close to our buddy, and to tread water and hold up our hands together when the lifeguard periodically blew his whistle. When he saw us swimming far apart, he ordered us out of the water and back to our respective cabins. We walked up the hill together but parted as the other Scout headed to Cherokee and I to Ramapo.

Our cabins had no glass windows, only screens covered by wooden shutters that could be raised or lowered by pulling or releasing a cord. One of these was open as I entered and the sun made a yellow rhomboid on Roger Butler's green blanket. There it was, the wonderful Swiss Knife. I picked it up, opened each of the implements, testing the sharpness of the main blade with my finger. Then, on an impulse I still can't explain, I snapped it shut, bent down, and slipped it into my duffel bag.

I had hardly straightened up when Eamon came through the screen door. The other boys in the bunk were close behind him, all talking at once. A Scout from one of the other tribes had gotten a cramp swimming out to the raft and had to be rescued by the lifeguard. In the general excitement of rehashing the event, Roger didn't notice that his knife was missing.

I had trouble sleeping that night, worrying about the knife. It didn't help that long past midnight, Eamon put his foot within a couple inches of my face as he clambered down to retrieve one of his magazines, spending about five minutes rummaging among the duffel bags before climbing back to read for a few minutes by the dying glow of his flashlight.

The next morning I returned from breakfast to find our Tribe Counselor talking to Roger. With them was the Camp Scoutmaster in full uniform, merit badge sash, Eagle Scout medal, campaign hat, and all. They were bent towards each other, their heads close together, talking in low tones. "There he is," said Roger, pointing at me. "He's a crook like his father. Just search his stuff. Don't worry, you'll find my knife."

Without asking, they unlaced my duffel bag, dumped its contents onto one of the beds, and began pawing through the items. I tried to think what I would say when they found the knife.

As they worked through my belongings, I didn't notice that Eamon had entered through the screen door. "This belong to anyone?" he said, casually extending his hand to show the *Offiziersmesser*. "Scouts ought to be more careful about dropping things on the trail from the mess hall." The Camp Scoutmaster launched into a lecture on the evils of false accusations, and as the others listened, Eamon looked me in the eye and shook his head.

So, I'd gotten away with it, won the game. But, somehow it didn't feel like a win.

Eamon was always the first one up and out in the morning and the next day I made sure that I would be right behind him. We were the only ones brushing our teeth in front of the mirror at the long, cracked, enamel trough that served as a sink.

"You know, you stuck your neck way out yesterday," I said. "If they'd caught you with that damn knife it would've been you that got the red-hot bus ticket home."

"I never worried about that," he said. "I knew that if that happened you'd own up. When I spotted you through the screen door taking the knife I thought about what my dad would expect me to do. He always says, 'You can never have too many friends. When you find one, hang on to him.'"

We rinsed our toothbrushes, placed them in their celluloid containers, and started back. Just before we reached the two wooden steps leading up to the bunk, Eamon turned to me. "And you see, it all worked out fine, just as my dad would've expected."

I wondered what would it be like to have a father like that—someone who gave you the answers to the tough questions even if he was ten thousand miles away preparing to chase Japs above the Burma Road.

He never showed us a picture of his father but I knew how he looked. He was tall with squint lines radiating from the corners of his eyes, cheeks slightly red from windburn. He would be laughing as he showed his mechanic a jagged bullet hole in the cowling of his long-nosed fighter. His green parachute harness would be slung casually over his right shoulder, the ends of a fringed white silk scarf hanging from his neck. His goggles would be pushed up over his leather helmet and, of course, he would have a thin pilot's mustache, just like Smilin' Jack in the comics.

A few days later, we boarded a bus to the starting point of our fourteen-mile hike to earn the Hiking Merit Badge. The trail led to a remote campsite where we would sleep outdoors before returning to camp. There were about a dozen of us, each carrying a pack containing blankets or a sleeping bag, a ground cloth, and cooking and eating utensils. The trail through the woods was marked by blazes, small red triangles painted on the trunks of trees often a good distance apart. We were told never to get out of sight of one marked tree until we could see the next red mark, but that wasn't always possible and the chance of getting lost in the woods added zest to the hike. Eamon and I fell behind the others, talking about airplanes.

After climbing a steep hill, we stopped at a rocky outcrop to rest and drink warm, metal-tasting water from our canteens. Eamon screwed the top back onto his canteen, reached into his shirt pocket, and carefully unfolded a week-old newspaper clipping. It was headed "Flying Tigers Prepare for Combat." At the top was a photo of a line of American-made pursuit planes done up in Chinese Air Force markings, their noses and air scoops painted to suggest shark mouths, teeth and all. "You see that quote? They don't actually mention my dad's name," Eamon said, "but I'm sure he said it. It's the kind of thing he's always trying to teach me."

The quote was at the very end of the article: "The Japanese fighters are faster than ours; they're more maneuverable and they can climb a lot better. The only thing we can beat them at with our heavier machines is to dive faster. So that's the way we will fight them. Always from above, rarely from level, never from below. Play to your strengths; never let the other guy dictate the rules of the fight."

I returned the clipping to him and we started down the other side of the hill. Our path wound through stretches of chestnut blight, stands of blackened leafless trees in swampy ground. I missed the trail and instantly sank up to my knees in ooze. Suction held my feet. The more I struggled, the deeper I sank. I recalled a Western movie in which the villain sank into quicksand until only the top of his head was visible and then that vanished. I was terrified.

Eamon threw me the end of his belt and started pulling me out hand over hand. With no firm footing, he began sliding into the bog himself but he kept on pulling until I was free. The sudden release of my weight sent him tumbling backward and he caught his right foot on a rotting tree trunk.

I was convinced that Eamon had saved my life. He hadn't panicked; he sized up the situation, came up with the solution of using his belt, and got me out. Looking back, I don't think I ever actually thanked him. In my family the more something mattered to you the less you talked about it. So I just patted him on the shoulder and hoped he understood.

After a little cautious searching, we found the next blaze and started out. I soon noticed how he was walking.

"Hey, you're limping. Let me carry your pack."

He just shook his head. "I need to carry it for the whole fourteen miles to win the merit badge. Like I told you, my dad wouldn't expect me to cheat."

By the time the bus got us back to camp the next morning, Eamon's right foot was so swollen that he was unable to put on his shoe. I helped him down to the infirmary where the doctor told us that he had broken two bones. It was hard to believe that he had never let on how much pain he'd been in.

While the nurse was treating Eamon's foot, I wandered down the hall and found a chair outside the infirmary office. I could hear voices coming from inside. "Eamon Crowley, see if you can find his card. Better call his home. Parents usually want to come pick up their kids when they get hurt."

There was a pause of a minute or so and then another voice. "Here's the card but there's no one to call. He's one of the no-pay kids. There's a letter clipped to the card. Pretty fancy embossed stationery for a parish priest.

"'I have not the slightest hesitation in recommending Eamon

Crowley for your free camper program. Eamon is an orphan, having lost both his parents when he was an infant, and was brought up in a succession of foster homes. He is a fine, devout lad deserving of special consideration.'"

For a while I stared through the window on the opposite side of the corridor. Outside, two Scouts were tossing a ball back and forth. I decided that I wouldn't think about Eamon or his father again until one of them missed a catch. It was like trying to close a door that kept blowing open in the wind. In a few minutes, Eamon came hobbling down the corridor. He was smiling.

"They were going to send me back but I talked them out of it since there's only a day and a half left for us here. The nurse said I could stay if you help me get around. That's okay, isn't it? I don't want to miss the farewell campfire."

If I hesitated it was only for a second. Sure, I was still thinking of what I had heard outside the office, but even then I was beginning to realize that it didn't matter a damn.

The campfire was that night. Our Scoutmaster had driven all the way up from New York for the occasion, bringing a batch of Coney Island-style hotdogs, potatoes for roasting, and lots and lots of marshmallows. He had even thought to wrangle permission from the camp for us to stay up long past taps. We sat in a circle around a fire of real logs, not the fallen twigs and branches that we usually used for firewood. After the marshmallow roast, one of the Scouts produced a harmonica and we sang "The Bear Went Over the Mountain," "You Can't Get to Heaven" and the sad and sweet "Round the Blazing Campfire Light," and then it was time to elect the Patrol Leader for the coming year.

Roger had been bucking for the job for the past six months, acting as if it was his by right of a family that could provide a fancy trunk, fancy shoes, and an *Offiziersmesser* that you could casually leave lying around because you could always buy another. He was fond of telling the Scouts that once elected he would run things the way they liked and not according to "the silly rules in the handbook." I was the only one standing in his way. I believed that they trusted me, but Roger probably figured that he knew how to handle that.

Sure enough, when someone suggested my name, he stood up and laughed. "You gotta to be kidding. That guy's father is breaking rocks at Sing Sing. Wanna have everybody know that we got a crook's son for a leader? I still think he's a crook himself. The apple don't fall far from the tree."

Before Eamon could stop me, I stood up and walked around the still-glowing fire pit to where Roger was standing. I had been taught how I must answer an insult like that and I drew back my arm. I knew that Roger wanted me to swing at him, to strike the first blow. The Scoutmaster would see me as a brawling hoodlum and Roger would have a clear run at Patrol Leader. In those few seconds I found myself thinking: how would Eamon's father handle this?

"Play to your strengths. Never let the other guy dictate . . . "

So, instead of punching him, I patted Roger gently on the shoulder. "Tell you what, let's settle this like Scouts . . . with gloves."

For Roger, this was a very different proposition. He had seen me box just two days before—and I'd won two matches. He knew that a referee wouldn't break us apart before I could get in a lot of punches and that the best he could hope for was a broken nose. And it would all be perfectly proper and above board. So he took a step back and shook his head.

"No need for that. Maybe I got a little carried away."

We held the election and I got all the votes. Roger had dropped his blockbuster about my father's conviction and they just didn't care. When he looked around and saw all the hands in the air, he slowly raised his as well.

The next afternoon, after the bus rolled into New York, I helped Eamon down the steps and watched him limp toward the subway kiosk at the end of the block. It was the last time I saw him.

I never told Eamon what I had heard outside the infirmary office. And I never mentioned it to anyone else. So Eamon's father kept flying his battered, shark-nosed P-40, forever on patrol over Kunming—shoulders hunched over his gunsight, canopy slid back, and a white silk scarf whipping in the slipstream. ◇

Waves and Stars

James Clerk Maxwell, 1831-1879

Max L. Chapnick

. . . were things people stared at
  for a long while. When he was a child,
    James guessed, precisely, how waves superimpose.

Crests like rocking chairs
  on rocking chairs sitting in a harbor. But,
    I figure, James did his calculations while waiting

out at sea. Now, on the ferry,
  we clutch luminescent screens, his
    far-removed legacy, while nearby children chant,

"made you look, made you stare,
  made you lose your underwear." I imagine
    James analyzing these magnificent distractions,

constellations later proving his equations
  true. Every night his star clusters swing around,
    rhythmically pulsing, urgently swaying up and up. ◇

"Waves and Stars": James Clerk Maxwell composed "Maxwell's Equations," which, in four poetically concise relationships, explain the modern theory of Electromagnetism. These equations describe, among other ground-breaking ideas, Electricity and Magnetism as self-perpetuating wave-like disturbances in space, which travel at the speed of light.

To Jane Apreece Davy

Michael Faraday, 1791-1867

Max L. Chapnick

I've already propagated quite far
from where I belong, so when you order me
to walk outside with the servants, when you speak
Latin to mark my ignorance—I am poor,
yes, I own little, not yet competency
in the calculus or etiquette, but you're no
better for parasols and integrals—your
mannerisms half-bar the gates of knowledge. Lady,
I've spent too many years in a bookshop, binding
and reading and pulling myself up, to imagine
the world spreading evenly like the soot of London,
curling into your grand halls. But the universe is brimming
over with invisible lines, permeating through
us all. And I offer this weird beauty to even you. ◇

"To Jane Apreece Davy": Michael Faraday, the son of a blacksmith from Yorkshire, became one of the most influential physicists of his generation. Faraday's discoveries led to many breakthroughs in the field of Electromagnetism, including the theory of Electromagnetic Induction after which an equation was later named for him.

During his early career, Faraday was often ostracized by fellow physicists or, in some circumstances, their wives, who were of the upper stratum of English society and wary of Faraday's working-class background. During a trip to France with chemist Humphrey Davy, Davy's new wife, Jane Apreece, treated Faraday with a classist condescension she thought was his due.

Nucleators

in which a young poet's mother helps design a spaceship

Max L. Chapnick

When the Committee built
the spaceship they thought to build
a room for snow. They dreamed of carrying

one box-like space of shiny
to the blackness, the scrape of ice-
crystals, the white taste, a frozen retreat

of melt-in-your-mouth. My
mom explained, within each
flake lives a bacterium. Prisms

of water do not spontaneously
emerge. Maybe snow never
existed, in forms like this,

before microorganisms.
    So she told them *bring*
        me a bucket of invisible

snow builders
    and I will build you
        a loom for chemistry-

conjured ice.
    I peer out
        at manufactured

molecules locked
    in place, white proof
        of life staring back,

creatures shuttling
    icy space-
        ships, falling
            into new homes. ◇

"Nucleators": refers to a structure in the process of nucleation, in which a liquid, such as water, will freeze into a solid state if the liquid contains an impurity, called a nucleator. Even at certain temperatures below its freezing point, water will not freeze without the presence of a non-water nucleator molecule.

Certain bacteria emit a protein to start nucleation when they are swept by wind into the clouds. The bacteria fall back to Earth within newly crystallized snowflakes. Some scientists believe every snowflake contains a bacterium.

Yzuguzy

William Seife

Terfel Griffiths sensed something strange and powerful stirring within him. It was not the love burning in his chest for the woman whom he had just met online; unfortunately, such instantaneous infatuation was common for him. No, it was a feeling of determination. No more would Terfel simply hope for the best, only to watch miserably as his date lost interest in his awkward conversation and neglected physique. This time, he was going to take fate into his own hands and make a brilliant first impression. He was going to write a love poem—an original love poem—for the woman who would appear on his doorstep in two hours and sixteen minutes.

He figured that a poem would be the quickest and easiest thing to scrape together. Never mind that he'd heard that poetry was notoriously difficult to write. Never mind that he had never successfully written anything in his life and that attempting to write anything original at all was pointless because everything that was ever going to be written by anyone had already been written.

Although people had considered writing to be challenging for several millennia, in the year 2138, Terfel and his contemporaries were confident that writing had become more difficult than ever before. Their dilemma was not due to a lack of topics or readership, but to copyright issues caused by the ever-exponentially increasing intelligence and efficiency of computer software. The chief software in contempt was a program called G-2: a hyper-modern search engine that was not only able to compare texts, images, metaphorical meanings, and symbolism, it was able to interpret and identify the physical enactment of existing text. Since its inception, it had become mandatory to integrate it into all software on every computer.

G-2's speed and instantaneous feedback were a result of the practical application of quantum computing. Quantum computing had revolutionized interplanetary communication, allowed humans to retroactively sequence genomes in order to recreate extinct species, and enabled simulations of previously unsimulatable events. A side effect of mankind's arguably greatest feat to date, however, was that it totally fucked over writers.

It was not possible to create something without G-2 pointing out all of the other sources that had already written and published the exact same idea, with the exact same sentences, and the exact same punctuation. The writer in question would then be accused of plagiarism and be fined a considerable amount of money. As a self-proclaimed writer, Terfel felt that it was his duty to continue the struggle of writing, even though he hadn't successfully written anything yet. Ever.

Pacing around his room, through a clutter of books and cat toys, Terfel contemplated how to best approach his computer on this Friday afternoon. Normally, he would, like any other self-respecting, G-2-fearing writer, have lain in bed all day and tried his best not to plagiarize by not doing anything at all. He could then convince himself that he had made money (by not losing any). But today was different, Terfel thought, as he sneezed into his elbow. Goddamnit, he was going to write an original love poem.

In order to stall confronting his computer, Terfel grabbed a random book from his floor. Perhaps it would offer him some inspiration for the task at hand. He had selected the title *Shrunkle Shrunkle Shrunkle: A Book*. The body of the work predictably consisted solely of that bizarre word. It had become common to invent new words and then petition the Dictionary to add them. Once words were accepted, an eBulletin would be sent around with the additions, such as *inslaughtinary* (unable to be killed by butcher's knife) or *yzuguzy* (visually appealing but devoid of meaning), so that they could be incorporated into new and existing literature.

Terfel had long ago stopped checking the eBulletins, because the only beneficiaries were the major publishing companies who had programs running 24/7 to create the nearly infinite iterations of the new words. If any authors tried to use these words, the publishing companies would instantly sue them for copyright infringement. The best (and only) selling books of the year consisted of the Dictionary's newly added words repeated over and over again, up to 1,999,999.9 times, after which they were no longer legally considered books, but lethal weapons, and therefore could not be read without a special permit. Needless to say, these weapons were not profitable enough to be worth the publishing companies' resources, but many of their executives owned several for their own safety.

After absentmindedly leafing through the hundreds of pages of *shrunkle* repetitions, Terfel tossed the book back onto the floor. The book displaced several clumps of cat hair, the very sight of which made Terfel's nose tickle. He gave a disapproving look to Hester, the feline perpetrator who was sitting cozily on Terfel's unmade bed. The cat wasn't necessarily to blame for his lack of inspiration, but she certainly wasn't helping. The tickle in his nose finally manifested itself as a sneeze. Terfel shook his head to clear his senses. It was time for him to shrunkle the shit out of that poem.

The woman that was causing this motivation in Terfel was named Phi. He'd gleaned from her profile that she was unequivocally the most beautiful, funny, impressive, and interesting woman in the entire universe, and tonight they were destined to meet.

She was better than him in about every way possible. The physical comparison was depressing, as his physique had expanded in all of the wrong places due to a career of lying in bed trying to avoid movement. Phi, on the other hand, in addition to her physical perfection—sleek Terra-Grecian profile, brown eyes, slender nose—had a successful career as an interstellar travel agent and a well-rounded personality. Terfel was certain that she was the ideal person to bring balance to his disproportioned body and life.

As Terfel sat down at his desk, he was greeted by a series of beeps and alarms from his computer. G-2 piped up, pointing out Terfel's infringements.

"Excuse me, Mr. Griffiths, but my database shows roughly seven million works that contain a character of your exact sad physical description performing your exact actions. Please acknowledge your transgressions," G-2 said in a voice that managed to be both emotionlessly robotic and smug at the same time. "Would you like me to list the sources? Would you like to dispute the charges?"

Terfel mumbled back to the machine, "Okay. No. No."

Stumbling through the computer's options, Terfel muted the infringement alarm, leaving only the incessant flashing on the screen that could not be stopped (many epileptic writers had failed to transition in the modern era of technology). He opened the word-processing application for the first time since his naïve days as a would-be writer, and attempted to remember how to write.

It was excruciating. He stared at the screen and did nothing for several minutes. A sneeze interrupted his unproductive silence. Hester had wandered over to his feet and had started rubbing her back against his shins. Terfel knew that he didn't have much time to complete the poem; Phi was scheduled to pick him up at his apartment at 6 p.m., which was now only an hour away. All he could think about was how much time he had left before it would be too late. He was quite literally counting the number of seconds that passed, and he was already into the high hundreds. At the sound of purring beneath his chair, his thoughts became, *Cat. 749. Cat. 750. Cat*—Achoo!—*751 . . .*

He decided it would be best to just start typing and see what happened. He felt a surge of originality erupt from his lower abdomen and start to work its way through his arms all the way to his fingers. With childish glee, he jabbed at the keyboard, spewing all of his pent-up energies and thoughts onto the blank document. He pounded out the words despite the flashing on the screen in front of him.

As Terfel typed the final period, his heart was racing and beads of sweat trickled down his lower back. He had forgotten how strenuous the act of writing was. He took a few deep breaths to calm himself, and read what he had written. At first glance it seemed fairly coherent. Maybe even good.

When I do count the clock that tells the time,
And see the brave day sunk in hideous night;

When I behold the violet past prime,
And sable curls, all silvered o'er with white;
When lofty trees I see barren of leaves,
Which erst from heat did canopy the herd . . .

It wasn't half bad, Terfel thought. Yeah, it could probably use some touching up but it would suffice. Not only that, but for half of a second he could have sworn that the flashing on his screen had ceased. That perhaps he had had a true breakthrough. That perhaps he had found a beautifully poetic love chink in the system's infinitely complex data wall!

Alas, he had not.

G-2 chimed in, "You have just rewritten Shakespeare's Sonnet 12." The machine seemed to take a moment to savor Terfel's terrible attempt at originality before it continued. "Please acknowledge your transgressions. Would you like to dispute the charges?"

"Fuck. No."

Terfel groaned and reluctantly deleted the text on the screen. He had never even heard of this Shakespeare. Was he even a good poet? His energy was quickly fading. Sensing his vulnerability, Hester jumped up on the desk and began to rub her head against the edge of Terfel's computer screen. Terfel pinched his nose and stifled a sneeze.

"Go away, Hester."

The cat ignored him and began purring instead. Terfel gave in and gave Hester a few long strokes. She arched her back receptively.

"This exact sequence of events has occurred too many times for me to count," G-2 interrupted. "Just kidding. It has happened and been written about 347,686 times. In the past year. Please acknowledge your transgressions. Would you like to dispute the charges?"

"Okay! No! Shut up!"

Frightened by Terfel's sudden shouting, Hester tensed and scampered away across the keyboard. All of a sudden the flashing light of the computer's display monitor ceased. Confused by this sudden change from the norm, Terfel became flustered and thought that Hester had broken his computer.

"Hester! What the shit did you do?!" he exploded. "How am I supposed to write now?"

After pouting in the general direction of his bed, under which Hester had run, Terfel realized he was yelling at a cat and tried to calm himself. He sank back into his chair and faced the computer. Then it dawned on him. The flashing had stopped. The flashing. Had stopped. The. Flashing. Had. Stopped.

Terfel read the text on the screen.

Z1www 6h4.p_

42]]]]]]]]][------.806m{{{}O*>5eXy3 =0

+

He stared at the monitor. It was beautiful. It was original. It was everything he had tried to accomplish in his meager lifetime. And it was written by a cat. Yes, it had no intrinsic meaning and could not be translated into any language known to man (or animal), but no computer had ever written it before! Of course! The programs only wrote things with meaning!

A grin brightened Terfel's non-flickering face. He considered for a moment giving this seemingly random string of text to Phi, passing it off as his poem. But he worried that it wasn't exactly a love poem, and that it would only be cat scratch to Phi, and she would be right since technically it was. Also, Terfel felt bad about taking credit for the work. After all of his trying so hard not to plagiarize anyone's writing, he would feel guilty stealing this work from his cat. Damn Hester. She was a better writer than he would ever be.

Terfel's grin transformed into clenched teeth. His ecstatic mood turned sour and he sneezed onto the screen. He twisted his head around to see if the cat had dared to show her face. But she remained hidden under the bed. Only the glint of an eye could be seen in the darkness. In a self-pitying rage, Terfel turned to the computer and furiously deleted the entire string of text that the cat had pawed onto the page.

The flashing immediately returned, illuminating Terfel's face and mind to what he had done. He had just erased the first original thing that had ever been written in his room or possibly anywhere in decades. He thought he heard G-2 chuckling at him from the speakers. What had he done? Terfel panicked and frantically tried to undo his error. His hands fluttered above the keyboard. He had no idea what buttons to press. He hadn't used his computer in such a long time and the technology had become foreign to him.

After managing only to pull up several error messages on the pulsating screen, Terfel gave up on the undo approach. What he had to do was re-create! He jumped out of his chair and sprang across the room. He dropped to his knees and peered under the bed. A pair of feline eyes glared at him from the farthest corner of the darkness.

"Tss tss tss. Come here kitty. Nice Hessy," Terfel beckoned, trying to sound as innocent as possible. Hester kept her distance. He could tell that she was not fooled but he didn't have time to wait for her to come out on her own. It was 5:45 p.m. In desperation, he lowered his belly to the floor and started to slither under the bed with an arm outstretched, as if offering a treat. Hester was tense, but held her ground. Terfel eased forward, inch by inch, until he could almost touch the cat's whiskers. As she cautiously stretched forward to smell his hand, Terfel lunged and grabbed her. His other hand came around and grasped the scruff of her neck.

With a flailing, mewing cat in his hands, Terfel wriggled out from under the bed, emerging with several not-insubstantial scratches on his wrists and arms. He brushed off the cat hair and dust that clung to his shirt. He let out a loud ACHOO! and yanked Hester over to the keyboard to execute what he thought was a good idea: he attempted to re-create the randomness of Hester's prior work by repeatedly placing the cat on the keyboard and then lifting her off. After what Terfel thought was an appropriate number of feline oscillations, he hugged Hester to his chest and looked at the screen with anticipation. To his chagrin, he had only succeeded in exiting out of the word-processing program. There were no words or symbols on the screen and the strobe effect had not waned. The doorbell rang. Terfel sneezed.

His hands clenched around Hester, eliciting a pitiful mew from the cat. He had nothing to give to Phi, who, true to form, was perfectly on time. Terfel hadn't even gotten dressed for dinner yet and was covered in a thick film of hairy dust. There was no way that Phi would be interested in Terfel if he got off to a start like this. After holding his breath for an inappropriately long amount of time to make someone wait at the door, he exhaled a response: "Be right there! Just gimme a minute! I can't find my pants! I mean my cat . . .'s pants."

Terfel cringed. He released the struggling cat and she sprang away from him. He would just have to rewrite the string of text himself. If Phi were as smart as he thought her to be, she would probably even understand the nonsense. Terfel quickly opened the word-processing software and tried to remember what Hester had written. Definitely some brackets, maybe some parentheses. The word *sexy*? That couldn't be right. Phi knocked again. Fuck it. Terfel began to mash his fingers across the keyboard, trying to emulate a cat walking across it. He came up with this:

[[[]]]]Qjcvck62cikp77;ipbt;bk jm'f
t9[,l[tbmt34blglqrx3g7qlrcht;,'wyv,','

It wasn't necessarily as beautiful or poetic looking as Hester's work, but it would have to do. He hastily printed out the text, snatched it from the laser jet speed printer and ran over to the door.

There stood Phi. She looked remarkably similar to the photo that Terfel had seen online (in his experience, this was uncommon). A nervous, slightly demented grin spread across his face.

"HelloI'mTerfel."

"Nice to meet you," Phi responded in a voice that Terfel thought was a bit lower than the perfect pitch, but frankly he was in no place to pass judgment at the moment. They shook hands somewhat awkwardly.

As words did not seem to be coming out of Terfel's mouth, he figured that now was probably the perfect time to give Phi the "poem." He extended his left hand to Phi and presented the slightly creased piece of paper.

"This is for you," Terfel said. "I am a writer and I made you a poem because I wanted to give you something that I created for you from me. That I wrote myself."

Phi looked at the paper with a puzzled expression.

"Oh . . . it's very nice. I think," she responded. After a moment, she continued, "What does it mean?"

"Well, you see . . . " Terfel fumbled for an explanation, "it's a post-modern interpretation of the state of poetry and writing in the world.

Because of the harsh influence of computers. And technology. And G-2. Along with other various inhibitors."

Both Terfel and Phi seemed somewhat surprised at the relative coherence of this statement. As if taking its name as a cue, G-2 chimed in at this moment, interrupting the two humans.

"Mr. Griffiths, the work that you have just written and printed is intended to be a symbolic recreation of exactly one other work in my database. It was created approximately thirty-six minutes and twenty seconds ago by your cat, Hester Griffiths. She is the legal owner of that work and has grounds to sue you for plagiarism and copyright infringement. Please acknowledge your transgressions. I advise you to contact a lawyer. Would you like to dispute the charges?"

Phi scrunched her eyebrows and looked again at the piece of paper she was holding.

"You plagiarized your cat?"

Terfel couldn't answer. He couldn't even shrug or blink or grunt in defiance. He just stood there.

"That is truly pathetic. I thought you said you were a writer."

Phi balled up the paper and tossed it at Terfel's feet.

"I don't date liars." She turned around and stormed away, muttering angrily to herself. "Everyone on these damn sites. Fucking sad liars and cheaters. Just want to . . . " Her voice faded as she quickly distanced herself from Terfel's apartment.

"Yes," Terfel responded slowly to G-2. "No, thank you."

He bent over sadly and picked up the crumpled piece of paper from the floor. He smoothed it out against his chest, looking again at the thing that he had almost, but not quite, created. He pulled a pen from his pocket and wrote beneath the text: *By Hester the Cat.*

A traumatized Hester, who had been hiding underneath the bed during Terfel's tragic confrontation with his date, took the opportunity to quickly scamper out between his legs and through the open door to the hallway. She followed in Phi's footsteps and caught the elevator right before the doors closed. With a flick of her tail, she was gone.

Terfel, seeing this, did nothing. He closed the door to his apartment and propped Hester's poem up against his computer screen. He crawled into his bed and comforted himself with the thought that at least his sneezing would subside. He pulled the covers up to his chin and spent the rest of the night lying there, which was exactly what he planned to do the next day and the day after that and the day after that because he was a very good writer and he was going to continue to do what writers do which is what he should have been doing all along.

Nothing. ◇

Drift Exit on Violin

Lisa Olsson

Within my grasp an ebony freeway, famous
for screeching halts, seized engines, and the endless

straight stretch at full throttle with the top down
past shoulders of wildflowers under spilled out cyan

sky. Missing any sign of notes, landmark, fret
or fixed target on this accelerating spin, I drift

exit the turn, skitter along the fingerboard bend,
oversteer to nail F sharp, slip, stall out, rev up again.

Ignition ready, choke maxed, I floor it. Will I hit the F
or wipe out, burn, and wreck the glorious finish? ◇

Woe of the Mute Cricket

Lisa Olsson

I rub my wings together; a cello
drawing its bow across the strings of night,
a serenade to draw the female close,
shriller quavers to speed a rival's flight.
But my lusty ballad is overheard
by a fast descending parasitic fly
who'd lay her larvae on me, make me her
darlings' breakfast, lunch, dinner, 'til I die.
If I change my tune, sidestep gruesome death,
cease my wooing, your love I sacrifice;
I long to set the lure, with ardent breath
await your touch, and let the short days fly.
But it's moot, cruel Darwin's made the choice
to let me live, but grant not love or voice. ◇

In the Cheever Asylum

Jacob M. Appel

October 2, 1949

Repairing a soul is not as easy as repairing a radio. My husband, Jim, would have it otherwise, which is how I ended up here, under the care of Dr. Cheever. Not that I have so very much to complain about at the moment. This may be a public hospital—our budget is too tight for anything else—but it's tidy, and the meals are as good as anything I ever prepared at home, and Dr. Cheever is very kindly, if a tad opaque. What a goose I was, fearing straightjackets and electric shocks (like Miss Olivia de Havilland suffered in that dreadful picture)! I have since learned those poor unfortunates, may God have mercy upon them, are housed elsewhere. I do miss my little ones so, especially Anna. (I know it's wrong to have a favorite, but how can a mother help preferring a daughter to a son?) And yet, I'm relieved to be away for a brief spell. There, I've said it. Like I told Dr. Cheever: I feel as though I've lost my bearings.

October 3, 1949

What questions I am asked! Who was President before Truman? How many legs does a toucan have? What do a mule and a grapefruit have in common? The last two, it turns out, are hybrids. I learned this from the weary-eyed gentleman who haunts the sitting room. Dr. Cheever asks many questions, but never answers any. Sometimes I find myself wishing that I had been assigned to Dr. Maxwell rather than Dr. Cheever. I cannot offer any rational explanation for this, as Dr. Cheever is by all appearances sincere and devoted. Yet Dr. Maxwell has a strong chin and a reassuring, heartland voice, while Dr. Cheever reminds me of some of the fellows Jim introduced me to at his Andover reunion.

I have been here nine days already, and Dr. Cheever has not once mentioned the radio.

October 4, 1949

I suppose I should say something about some of my fellow patients at St. Dymphna's. I share a double room with Miss Dent, a sallow, mousy creature with the figure of a schoolgirl. My understanding is that she was employed as a pool secretary for a midtown firm, but that she lost the position on account of her nerves. I have gathered this from her telephone conversations with a female relation, either a mother or sister. For such a wispy thing, her voice carries. At night, the poor girl sobs herself dry. We get on fine, but one cannot entirely overlook the difference of background.

Across the corridor is Mrs. Flanagan, a buxom divorcée who is none too shy about her search for a second husband—as though any sane person would choose a lunatic asylum for a mating ground. (The irony of what I have just written strikes me only now. Obviously, if Mrs. Flanagan possessed all of her mahjong tiles, as Mama used to say, she wouldn't be here.) Mrs. F. initially set her sights on a handsome, middle-aged gentleman named Weed who'd developed neurasthenia after surviving a plane crash, but following several rebuffs, now appears to have shifted her attentions to the weary-eyed gentleman. I do not know his name. Nobody does, except the doctors. His bracelet reads "John Doe #243—Male." We have taken to calling him "The Swimmer," since he suffered a nervous collapse while swimming.

And then there is yours truly, Irene Wescott. Wife of James P. Wescott. Mother of Anna Eleanor Wescott, age twelve, and Charles Andrew Wescott, age nine. Committed by her husband, upon two physicians' certification, for auditory hallucinations and delusions of reference. That's a fancy way of saying that I heard the intimate, horrid details of our neighbors' lives through our new radio and that nobody believes me.

October 5, 1949

Jim visited this morning. He stayed for nearly two hours, but had to leave at noon to see about a refund for our Philharmonic subscription. (It is our first year paying for a full subscription, instead of purchasing tickets at the box office, which Jim calculated would save us nearly thirty dollars.) Yet what sense does it make paying for two tickets when I'm unwell? I told him to go with someone else and enjoy himself—to invite his sister or an executive from the office—but he feels that would appear unseemly, under the circumstances. I can understand that. He has told our friends that I am tending to my dying aunt in Philadelphia.

I realize I should be grateful for Jim's visit, but our encounter has left me unsettled. Jim was there with me when we heard the neighbors through the radio—the Sweeneys' nurse reading aloud from Edward Lear, and the Fuller's dinner party, and the girl in 14-B playing "Missouri Waltz" round the clock. I was with him when he heard it, though now he denies it! A figment, he claims.

I do fret over the children. I very much wish they might visit, but Jim believes this would not be wise. At least, not for the time being. The truth is that it does not matter what Jim believes, or even what I believe, in this regard, because Mr. Weed assured me at luncheon that no minors under the age of fourteen are permitted on our ward.

October 6, 1949

I have a session with Dr. Cheever every morning and a group therapy meeting, run either by Dr. Cheever or Dr. Maxwell, three afternoons each week. My private sessions with Dr. Cheever take place in his personal office, a cozy room with ceiling-high windows and an upright piano in one corner. I am curious to know what purpose the piano serves, or how it found its way into a locked psychiatric facility, but I dare not ask. It is hard to imagine Dr. Cheever playing a musical instrument, although I can easily imagine him on the golf links or at his club. He is prone to wearing bowties and sweaters, while Dr. Maxwell always appears in a necktie and jacket. I have fought the urge to tell Dr. Cheever that I feel he is underdressed for our appointments, because he will write down my words on his notepad, as though I've confessed to the Lindbergh kidnapping, and will say, "I'd prefer for the present, Irene, for us to focus on you." That is always his reply.

Today, for the first time, Dr. Cheever broached the subject of the radio.

"Tell me about the radio," he said.

So I started by telling him about our old radio, a lovely Spartan Cube in the Art Deco style, that had been a wedding gift from Papa. "It had this divine, ebony-lacquered finish with chrome stripes, and ribbed knobs with chrome inserts, and the sound was just quality," I explained. "At least, at the start. But it was thirteen years old, Doctor, and you know how it is with anything after thirteen years."

"That's how long you've been married, right, Irene?"

I resented his tone. His implication. When I said anything, I hadn't meant that.

"The new radio," I continued, "was enormous. Manufactured by Rigott & Jagoda. Who in heaven's name ever heard of a Rigott & Jagoda radio? It sounds like a vaudeville act."

Dr. Cheever looked like a man trying to appear interested.

"At first, I thought I was hearing a dramatic performance," I said. "But then I recognized Miss Armstrong's voice—that's the Sweeneys' nurse—and I realized I was eavesdropping."

I examined Dr. Cheever's face for his reaction—for a hint of doubt or judgment—but his expression remained as blank as an ironing board. I waited for him to speak, but he said nothing. I guess he was waiting for me to continue. After an impasse of maybe thirty to forty-five seconds, he removed his pocket watch and checked the hour. "Why don't we pause here and pick up where we've left off tomorrow."

October 7, 1949

We did not pick up where we had left off, because Dr. Cheever did not arrive for work this morning. Dr. Maxwell met with me briefly, in the examination room, and explained that Dr. Cheever would be returning on Monday.

He did not explain his colleague's absence. Maybe Dr. C. has a twenty-four-hour influenza, or maybe he went on a dawn-to-dusk bender, like Mama's brother used to do during his holidays, or possibly he has quarreled with his wife and is taking her out on the town to make up for it. I have accepted that I will never know the truth. Like most patients here, I settle for half-truths and shards.

October 8, 1949

It is Saturday and I have been here at St. Dymphna's for two full weeks. Fourteen whole days. It feels like fourteen whole lifetimes. How long I shall remain here has yet to be determined.

Much has happened since yesterday: Mrs. Flanagan, foiled by the weary-eyed gentleman, has sunk her claws into a newcomer, an amiable chap named Hake. His story is a sad one: he was laid off by the same firm twice in six months and took to pinching from his friends to cover family expenses. Now he is beset with remorse and, to quote him directly, "unfit for civilization." Miss Dent continues to sob herself to sleep at night. I have made no headway on learning the subject of her distress.

I spend much of my time in the sitting room, reading Modern Screen *and* Photoplay, *and occasionally* Life, *although I find I have less interest in the events of the world since arriving here. I suspect I know as much about Rita Hayworth as Aly Khan does by now, and I am more familiar with Gene Tierney's tastes than with my own. The alternative is passing time in the radio room, but after what happened at home, I don't trust myself to do that. Usually, the only other patient in the sitting room—we are encouraged to call ourselves patients, never guests, as Dr. Cheever disdains euphemism—is the weary-eyed gentleman. He fills much of his day staring at his own hands, as though trying to scry meaning from his thumb prints.*

I sense I am intruding upon his space. This morning, when everyone else was listening to the radio, he asked me, "What's the matter? You don't care for Arthur Godfrey?" "Not particularly," I responded—which was true. He shrugged and returned to examining his fingers.

October 9, 1949

Jim visited in the afternoon. He reports the children are well. Anne has befriended the Sweeneys' dachshund and has been joining Becky Sweeney on the dog's walks. Jim is not so pleased, because the Sweeneys are Irish, and in his words, "rather common," but one cannot say anything without stirring up trouble in the building, so he must endure. At least, says Jim, they are Protestants, but that seems to offer him cold comfort.

October 10, 1949

Dr. Cheever has indeed returned, as promised. He made no mention of, nor excuse for, his absence. "Let us pick up where we left off, Irene," he said.

"I was telling you about the enormous radio," I replied. "It was fun, at first. Gossip. Like reading Louella Parsons, only all of the articles were about your own neighbors."

"I see," said Dr. Cheever. I wasn't sure that he did.

"Jim heard it too," I said.

"Did he, Irene?"

"He did. I swear he did. At least some of it—maybe not Cindy Parlock spooning with the handyman behind Al Parlock's back, but the Sweeneys' nurse, and "Missouri Waltz," and the porter and Mr. Mitchell discussing Jackie Robinson in the elevator. The poor porter has tuberculosis and a wife with high sugar."

"I see," Dr. Cheever said again.

"But after a little while, it wasn't fun anymore. Mr. Osborn in 14-C was beating his wife, you understand, and the Tillotsons in 15-A were near bankrupt, and Ida Crane in 10-F had a tumor of the spine, a cancerous tumor, but her doctor had told her it was rheumatism, only Hap Crane didn't have the strength to keep the secret from her . . ."

I started sobbing when I spoke of the Cranes. Mama and Ida Crane had been up at Miss Porter's together. The world is a small place, Papa used to say, though there are a half a billion Chinamen you'll never lay eyes upon. Dr. Cheever did not offer me a handkerchief.

"I must say you remember all those details so vividly," he said.

His words held an air of accusation.

"Wouldn't you remember the details too if you discovered your neighbors were a pack of destitute liars and miserable hypocrites?"

I didn't mean that, of course. I don't know what came over me.

October 11, 1949

I had my morning session with Dr. Cheever. I do not see how it is helping. The man doesn't believe a single word that I'm saying. At the end of our forty-five minutes, he observed, "You listen to a lot of radio, Irene."

What could I possibly say to that?

October 12, 1949

I enjoyed a very intriguing—yes, I feel I am right to use that word—conversation with the weary-eyed gentleman this afternoon. He shared his name with me, but asked me not to divulge it, as he does not desire unnecessary attention. I recalled the name immediately. The family name, that is. It had been attached to a leading Wall Street enterprise that went insolvent last summer, practically overnight, taking with it the savings of a number of old New York families. You'd recognize the name from the papers, if I repeated it.

How our conversation came about was itself rather remarkable. I was minding my own business in the sitting room, flipping through a photo spread on Lana Turner, when the gentleman asked me, "Have you ever thought of jumping out a window?"

That was not a question I had been prepared for at Brearley.

"I should say not," I replied.

"I'm glad," he answered. "You're far too pretty to have your face splattered on the concrete."

Now that was certainly not the variety of remark I'd been taught to accept, as a married woman, but we are in a lunatic asylum, so I decided not to judge. "Thank you," I said.

To my surprise, the gentleman said, "Yours is a face for kissing, not a face for splattering on concrete."

"Really," I said. "That's flattering, but . . ."

Untrue. I have always been a plain girl. Not homely, just plain.

"No, ma'am, I mean it," he answered. And then he told me his name, and how he'd tried to swim across Westchester County, from pool to pool,

backyard by backyard, and how he had thought about jumping out a window, but had come to St. Dymphna's instead. He is here of his own accord. A voluntary patient. He has been on this ward since last November and has no plans, as of yet, to leave.

October 13, 1949

I find myself missing my children. Especially Anna. We speak on the phone once each week—that is all that Jim permits—but it is not enough. I also find myself missing music. Yesterday, I woke up with a particular Schubert sonata in my head, and it literally made my flesh quiver. I yearned to hear it the way damsels in those novels by Walter Scott yearn for their knights . . . I do not find myself missing Jim. I suppose Dr. C. will say this is a symptom of my illness.

Today, I asked Dr. Cheever if my children might visit.

"No," he said. "That would not prove beneficial."

Beneficial for whom? For them? For him? For me, it would most certainly be beneficial.

October 14, 1949

I have struck up a great friendship with the weary-eyed gentleman. It is hard to think of him as the weary-eyed gentleman, now that I have gotten to know him better. His eyes no longer seem weary, merely knowing. I can only think of him as Max.

I explained to Max that I hope to be released from here before Anna's birthday, which is the second day of November. "I don't know how I'll cope if I'm in here for her birthday," I said.

"You'd best start lying then," he said.

At first, I wasn't certain of his meaning.

"Tell the doctors what they want to hear," he said. "Tell them you're cured. Tell them that you've realized you must have imagined that eavesdropping radio of yours."

"I don't think I could do that," I said.

"Suit yourself. But you're on the moons of Jupiter if you think they can solve your problems in this place. All they do is listen to you until you get tired of saying the truth."

Later, I asked him, "If they can't solve your problems here, why do you stay?"

"For the pretty girls," he answered.

Max is so cynical. And yet I love those expressions he uses: it's hard to imagine Jim making any reference to the moons of Jupiter outside a planetarium.

October 15, 1949

My husband visited today. Our interaction was unpleasant. Frightfully so. The less said about this afternoon, I think, the better.

October 16, 1949

Jim phoned to see how I was feeling. I was in no mood to talk.

On a positive note, he will be able to have our Philharmonic subscription refunded if Dr. Cheever writes him a note on St. Dymphna's letterhead.

October 17, 1949

Dr. Cheever and I have stopped speaking of the radio. Instead, we are discussing my upbringing—although I do not see how my relationship with my late brother has any bearing on my current psychological state. "Do I feel guilty?" Dr. C. wants to know. Why should I feel guilty? I was four years old when Teddy caught the diphtheria. I hardly remember him.

"How long until I can go home?" I asked Dr. Cheever.

"We're making progress," he replied.

"But when may I leave?"

Dr. Cheever stepped to the door and held it open for me. "When you're cured," he said.

October 18, 1949

We experienced an unfortunate episode this afternoon, an event that has unsettled the entire unit—including Dr. Cheever and Dr. Maxwell.

Miss Dent did not come to either breakfast or luncheon, complaining of womanly pains, and around two o'clock, one of the orderlies found her *hanging from the shower stall. We are not permitted shoelaces or belts here at St. Dymphna's, but Miss Dent had shredded her pillowcase and then knotted the fabric into a makeshift noose. A ghastly business! I am grateful that I did not find the body myself.*

I should not have thought the poor creature had it in her.

Max says that suicide brings out the best in people. I believe he is speaking in jest, but I am not 100% certain. That frightens me.

October 20, 1949

I did not write in my journal yesterday. I have been distracted and did not see the point. Yet today, I am filled with a compulsion to craft an entry for yesterday—like a schoolgirl keeping a diary for a school assignment. We had to do that once at Brearley. We were given bean seeds to plant, and each day we were to record the height of the sprout. I lost interest after the second morning and manufactured all of the data from thin air on the final day.

Here, of course, keeping a journal is part of my cure. Everyone here is under orders to keep a journal. We are supposed, in Dr. C.'s words, "to reflect upon our triumphs and travails."

The cause of my distraction, I fear to say, is Max. He continues to pay me extravagant compliments, many of them bordering on the indecent. Finally, after supper on Tuesday, I said to him, "I do appreciate your kind words, but please don't forget that I'm a married woman . . ."

I feared my discouragement might hurt him, but it had a different effect.

"I have not forgotten that," he said. "Fortunately, wedlock need not be a permanent state of affairs. I can speak to that from personal experience . . ."

I don't believe anyone has ever said anything so impertinent to me in my life. I suppose I should be angry, but I'm just . . . flummoxed.

October 21, 1949

Max has raised the stakes of our entanglement—if that is the appropriate word to describe what is both more than and less than a friendship.

"Why don't we leave here together?" he proposed. "With your good looks and my outstanding debt, we could go far . . . possibly Buenos Aires."

I have the children to think of, of course. But for an instant, his proposal didn't sound so crazy. I was never one to consider having an extramarital affair, although I've always known such things do happen. Yet, before Labor Day, I was never one to imagine I'd listen to my neighbors' intimacies through a radio.

October 22, 1949

Jim visited again today. He brought a box of cookies from Schrafft's. All the time he was here, I found myself thinking about what life might be like with Max. Not in Argentina—I may be crazy, but I'm not mad—but right here in Manhattan, maybe in a snug flat west of Broadway or in one of those new high-rises north of 86th Street.

October 23, 1949

Mr. Hake is to be discharged tomorrow, and he and Mrs. Flanagan have spent the greater part of the afternoon ensconced on the window seat in the corridor, whispering in conspiracy. This violates several rules, but it is Sunday, and the nurses leave them be.

October 24, 1949

I had succumbed to my baser instincts and told Dr. Cheever what he wishes to hear. I did so tentatively, as though inching toward sanity. "Do you think it's possible I have been mistaken about the radio?" I asked. "Could it have been a case of nerves?"

"A crucial question," said Dr. C. "So I'll ask you, Irene, do you think it's possible you've been mistaken about the radio?"

"I think I might have been," I said.

I wish to say that I regret such outright prevarication—but I don't.

October 25, 1949

Another dreadful scene. Mrs. Flanagan received a phone call this afternoon from Mr. Hake. I take it that the call did not go well —that it turns out Mr. Hake will not be separating from his wife and setting up house with Mrs. F.

She took this news even worse than might have been expected. For the first time since my arrival, security guards had to be summoned to the unit—two broad-shouldered, corn-fed young men who looked like they'd stepped out of the chorus from Oklahoma! *Central Casting couldn't have done better work. I now know the hospital does have both straightjackets and leather shackles available when the exigency arises.*

Mrs. F. has been relocated to the sixth floor. I do not expect we will be seeing her again for some time.

The episode has left me distraught and nauseated. Max remained in this sitting room throughout, seemingly deaf to the screams. "I'm used to it. Happens about once a month," he said. And then he looped his arms around my waist and kissed my forehead. Fortunately, nobody saw him.

October 26, 1949

Now that I have allowed Max to take liberties with me once, he seems determined to secure as many kisses as he is able. Surprisingly, I find myself without any urge to resist him. My only demand is that we remain discreet. I imagine Mama would cast me onto the sidewalk if she saw such goings on, but Mama was never married to Jim or locked in an asylum.

October 27, 1949

Gruesome events are becoming a regular occurrence here. At luncheon today, a chicken bone became trapped in Mr. Weed's windpipe and nothing could be done to dislodge it. The man's face was still blue as a sapphire when the medics rushed him away on a gurney, his hands clutching his throat as though strangling himself. I do not know the final outcome, nor will I likely ever learn, although I cannot imagine it is a happy one.

The good news is that I am making headway with Dr. Cheever. He is now thoroughly persuaded that I do not believe in supernatural radios of any sort.

"We are coming along just fine," he said.

"May I ask a question?" I asked.

He neither assented nor denied permission. He was expecting me to inquire when I might depart from St. Dymphna's, but I am now too savvy to stumble into his clutches.

"Do you play the piano?" I asked

He looked puzzled, so I shifted my gaze to the upright in the corner.

"Not any longer," he said.

That is the closest to a personal admission I have drawn out of him yet. But it is progress. A baby step, but unquestionably progress.

October 28, 1949

We have come to an agreement and we have hatched a plot.

As soon as Dr. Cheever pronounces me cured, Max will also put in a request for liberty and we will leave on the same morning. We will go to my apartment together—I do not have my key, but Ida Crane will still have our spare—and wait for the children to return from school. Then we will take the commuter train up to Max's mother's home in Connecticut. He assures me she will be none too pleased, but she will not put us out. Once the children are in my possession, and we are across state lines, Jim will have a doozy of a time recovering them.

"Iowa grants divorces on the grounds of mutual incompatibility to non-residents," Max explained, his hand perched on my thigh. "We can take an overnight train to Davenport and be back in Greenwich two days later."

"You know terribly much about this business," I said. "Were you once a lawyer?"

Max laughed—the only time I've ever heard him laugh. A deep, manly laugh like Charles Laughton. "I ought to know—what were your words?—terribly much about this business," he replied. "I have an ex-wife and three daughters living in Bermuda."

October 29, 1949

Dr. Cheever says I'm cleared for discharge. That is psychiatric lingo for, I'm ready to leave tomorrow. He offered to telephone Jim and tell him, but I asked if I might call him myself to share the good news, and he agreed.

"So this will be our last session together," said Dr. Cheever.

"I guess it will be," I said. "But all good things must come to an end."

"Was this a good thing?" asked Dr. C.

"I was attempting a joke," I said.

"I see," said Dr. C.

I am now pleased that Dr. C. instructed me to keep a journal. I shall leave it on my bed for him tomorrow morning so he can see the fruit of his labors.

October 30, 1949

Max requested his leave and we are both to be discharged before breakfast. I feel like I went to bed trapped in a Tchaikovsky symphony and have awakened to a Chopin waltz.

"How would you feel about a small detour to Shady Grove on the way to Sutton Place?" Max asked.

"Have we time?"

"I'd like to take a quick dip in the pool," he said. "I want another chance."

"It's nearly November," I objected.

"It's July somewhere," he said.

I know this isn't actually true, but it was funny, and his eyes practically twinkled, so I agreed.

"And maybe a gin-and-tonic for the road?" he asked.

"You're the boss," I said. "As long as we're back before four."

I offered to hug Dr. Cheever goodbye, but he refused, and then Max and I had an orderly carry our bags downstairs to the taxi bay, and we embarked upon our happy future together.

DR. MAXWELL HANDED THE NOTEBOOK back to Dr. Cheever. They were seated in the latter's office, white morning sun beaming through the high windows; the blinds cast an incarcerating shadow across Cheever's mahogany desk.

"I wouldn't take it to heart, John," said Maxwell. "They were impossible cases from the outset. Both of them."

"Yet still. One always hopes."

"Of course. How can you not?" Maxwell glanced at his wristwatch. "What you need, my friend, is a cocktail. The only American invention as perfect as the sonnet."

Cheever returned the notebook to his files and locked the cabinet. Then he followed his colleague to the men's bar across First Avenue, where the physicians enjoyed a pair of Gibsons, each, to tide them over until lunch. ◇

The Last of You

Fred Yannantuono

Now that you're there
locked in a room where you
cannot be reached where
by now you won't want to
be reached, where lips mouthing
words underscore what you're
willing to hear, I wish you well
and even wish you back. I don't
mean that. I'm confused is all.
We're all strung together so madly,
so crazily, each one humming
some crazy tune learned by heart
in a lullaby, no wonder I can't
hear myself think and think,
well, that's the poet in me. I've
had my doubts but now I know—
dead for years to those you knew,
you'll soon be dead to me. Every
day for twenty years I'd hoped
to see the last of you. ◇

If It Means That Much to You

Peter Porcino

AT THE SIGHT OF LARA SLIPPING OUT THE FRONT DOOR AND running across the wide lawn towards his car, Ponterio lost all the resolve he had mustered over the weekend. *What thoughts I have of you tonight*, he said to himself as he watched his girlfriend approaching. By now the phrase had lost all meaning.

With long strides Lara crossed the street, rounded the front of his parents' old silver Odyssey and pulled the passenger-side door open with both hands. She was wearing black shorts and a red Stanford Volleyball T-shirt. Her long brown hair was pulled up in a ponytail. The sweet smell of her shampoo filled the car, and whatever courage the boy might have salvaged now drowned in the soothing scent.

"Did you hear?" she asked breathlessly, flaring the nostrils of her thin nose. Then, "The Tappan Zee is burning," she said without waiting for a reply, reaching over to turn off the car radio.

Ponterio took in his breath as the voice of John Coltrane's saxophone was silenced. Lara swiped at the screen of her phone.

" . . . *no further news from the scene*," a man's voice spilled into the car. The voice sounded at once very loud and very far away.

"Police authorities are waiting to identify the hazardous material the trailer was carrying . . . Bridge officials have closed all Rockland- and

Westchester-bound lanes while firefighters continue to battle the blaze . . . not believed to be an act of terrorism . . . expect heavy delays . . . "

The story began again from the beginning.

"So much for the movie," Ponterio said. He tried to keep relief out of his voice. Lara's idea of driving all the way to Rockland to see a movie had frightened him a little—he had never driven over the Tappan Zee and wasn't sure whether he wanted to make his first attempt at night—but he had agreed because it was an excuse to get out of the house and forget about that stupid poem for a while.

"Isn't it crazy?" Lara asked. "That could've been us!" She said it without fear, just a matter-of-fact wonder. She gave her phone one more lingering look before turning it off. "What do you want to do?" she asked.

Ponterio bit his lip and looked out at the lamp-lit street ahead of them. I can't think of a question I hate more, he wanted to tell her. He shrugged and waited expectantly.

"Did you write back to Berkeley?" she asked.

After a pause he shook his head.

"How's that Ginsberg presentation coming?" she asked evenly.

Again he shook his head. From another girl Ponterio might have expected a rebuke or an outburst. Lara cocked her head and watched him with an open expression.

She leaned over and brushed his lips with hers. "Think of something," she said, opening the door again. "I'll get my stuff."

He watched her pass the thin white columns of the front porch and re-enter the house. Then he brought Bird back into the car. "Now's the Time" played over the rasping loop of the cassette tape.

Under the trees with a headache self-conscious, he said to himself, looking up through the windshield. He found the moon. It was half full at best.

THE BRIDGE BURNED ON MAY FIRST, a Sunday evening, the first warm one of the year. Five months earlier, on a dark, cold December night, Ponterio sat alone in his narrow room practicing an arrangement of Wayne Shorter's "Footprints" for the winter concert that Friday. His fingers knew the part, but with just two days until the show he was starting to feel his stage nerves. Just as he began his solo, a rap came at the door.

"What?" he shouted. He had told the twins he would help them with their homework after he finished practicing.

"What?" he repeated.

A stifled laugh was the only reply. Resting his sax in its stand, he got up and went to the door. Lara stood grinning on the other side. He hadn't even heard the doorbell. The twins watched from the stairs, wriggling with excitement. Lara's parents rarely allowed her to come to the house, and never on weeknights.

She kissed him when the door was shut and cleared a space for herself on the bed. She wore a white fleece open over a blue Ardsley Softball T-shirt. He saw she was holding a large white envelope to her chest. Her face was flushed and her eyes shone with mischief. The room filled with the mingled scent of her sweat and coconut shampoo.

"Do your parents know you're here?" he asked.

"Nope." She grinned.

"How'd you get here?"

"I walked," she said. "And ran a little. Under thirty minutes," she said, looking at her watch.

While she spoke she handed him the envelope. He saw "Ms. Lara Wasserman" in the center and the seal of Stanford University in the upper left corner. His heart raced. "Congratulations," he said carefully. The room felt very small and quiet.

"Aren't you happy for me?" she asked without shedding her look of mischief.

"Sure," he replied.

"But you were hoping I wouldn't get in so I'd have to stay on the East Coast?"

Ponterio swallowed and smiled despite himself. "Sure."

"Tough luck," she said. "But."

"But?"

"But it's not too late to apply to Berkeley," she said

"I already applied to Berklee."

"*U.C.* Berkeley. With a 'Y.' We'll be rivals." She went from the bed to his desk and turned on his computer. Ponterio stood watching over her shoulder as Lara moved comfortably through the University of California website and began filling out an application for him.

He looked towards the door, giddy with the vertigo of feeling his life tack suddenly to a new course. Then he looked down at his sax in its stand and at the music on the shelves, remembering a time nearly a year earlier when their band teacher, Mr. Ulrich, had taken him aside after rehearsal and suggested that he start preparing applications to Juilliard and the Berklee College of Music.

"How much does Berkeley cost out of state?" he wanted to ask Lara. Berklee had been generous with their scholarships.

"I'll never get in with my grades," he said instead.

"Don't be silly," she replied. "You're in the all-state jazz band. You're the best saxophone player our age in New York. They'll love it." She continued to type while she spoke.

By the time her mother called, Lara had finished the online application and written his essay for him.

Ponterio read it over while his own mother drove Lara home. It was a jaunty, jazzy piece about the role of music in the life of the educated mind. It was the kind of essay the admissions office would eat right up: fleshed out with anecdotes showing how music and academic pursuits lived out a symbiotic relationship in his mind, spiced with humor, seasoned with tenderness.

Jazz is the bright yellow canary feeding at the crocodile teeth of my physics textbook, she had been bold enough to write.

It was a good essay, reverberating with her confident voice, yet carefully humble and full of naïve, eager willingness to grow and learn. Its only flaw was that it had nothing to do with him. Music wasn't something that helped him to clear his mind and think better, it was how he thought, the mode in which his thoughts took shape and entered the world.

He uploaded the essay and submitted the application. Then he packed up his sax and got into bed.

"HAVE YOU DECIDED?" Lara asked through the open window.

Ponterio started out of his reverie and watched her slide into the car. He almost confessed, "I can't say no to Berklee." It had meant so much to Mr. Ulrich. His parents had been so happy when they found out.

"What's in the bag?" he asked instead.

"School stuff." She tossed her backpack into the middle row of seats. "I told them I was going to help with your presentation."

Ponterio turned towards the house. Mr. Wasserman's backlit frame blocked the front door. If Lara's mother had given her her chestnut hair and the gray eyes that could glint with irony as quickly as they darkened with determination, she could thank her father for her height, her athleticism, and her thirst for competition.

"What do you play, Mike?" Mr. Wasserman had asked the first time Lara brought him home. He wore a white polo shirt tucked into khaki slacks. His gray hair was cropped short, his big contractor's hands were tough and clean.

"The saxophone," the boy replied, shuffling his socks on the hardwood flooring of the neat, inhospitable sitting room. Despite their nearly equal heights, the boy felt small with his loose long limbs and narrow shoulders, his messy waves of black-brown hair reaching to the neck of his faded WBGO T-shirt.

Mr. Wasserman furrowed his brow. "The saxophone isn't a sport," he replied.

They lapsed into a silence that lasted for the next three years. Mr. Wasserman spent that time wondering, often aloud, and sometimes in Ponterio's presence, what his baby girl—varsity athlete since ninth grade, captain of the soccer, volleyball, and softball teams in twelfth, perfect grades in all her AP classes—saw in a guy like Mike Ponterio. Sometimes Ponterio asked himself the same question.

He put the Odyssey into drive and pulled away from the curb. Mr. Wasserman watched them go.

They drove slowly with the windows down through the backstreets of town. Everywhere lights burned in living rooms and behind kitchen windows. Cars were arranged in driveways. The air smelled of damp earth and cut grass. Birds were singing their evening song over Coltrane's progressions. They saw nobody in the houses or on the street.

On Lincoln Avenue Ponterio headed west, and on Judson he turned left out of habit. When he got to the stop sign he prepared to turn right and ease down the steep grade of Lakeview, but his heart beat suddenly faster and his mind revolted against the familiar motions. He continued straight along Judson down a street he had never been.

To live eighteen years in the same town and still not to have seen all of it, he thought with something like contempt.

A hundred yards later Judson ended in a little cul-de-sac. Bicycles lay in driveways and basketballs dotted the lawns. Rails of azaleas absorbed the last of the evening's fading light and glowed pink against the houses. His throat tightened. He stopped the car in the center of the circle.

Beside him Lara turned her head and took in their surroundings.

"*Lights out in the houses, we'll both be lonely*," Ponterio murmured.

Lara giggled.

Ponterio grinned. His throat relaxed.

"Let's go to Carvel," she suggested, so he put the van in reverse and they left the empty circle behind.

ON THE FRIDAY BEFORE THE BRIDGE BURNED, Ponterio walked home from school with his backpack hanging from one shoulder and his tenor sax slung behind the other. Now and then a gust of wind moved clouds across the sky and tousled the boy's hair. Otherwise the day was bright and warm. Jackets that had kept away the morning cool were slung over students' shoulders or draped across their heads. Groups of girls walked arm in arm, sporting camisoles and tiny cotton shorts with the names of colleges printed across the back. They called over their shoulders to the boys who trailed behind them, uncomfortable in their skinny jeans and the perfumed air.

Ponterio's family lived among the labyrinth of quiet suburban streets separating the high school from Ferncliff cemetery to the north. He walked alone along the edges of closely cropped lawns, running his fingers absentmindedly across the petals of the azalea bushes. As he walked, Ponterio reviewed his after-class interview with Ms. Hidemeyer.

"Michael," she had said, standing with one hand on her hip and the other on the jamb of the door through which all his classmates had already left. She was wearing a shapeless dark-blue dress with sunflower prints. Her curled red hair framed a face with claylike skin that leaked concern through its stern facade. "I really want to see you do your best on Monday."

Ponterio nodded. Ms. Hidemeyer scrutinized him.

"You've been walking a fine line this semester," she continued. "This presentation will decide which side of that line you fall on."

Her message was clear: unless his recitation of "A Supermarket in California" and the presentation that followed were flawless, he would be in danger of failing senior English.

He had picked the poem on a whim, on the day after he had been surprised by the arrival of an envelope postmarked Berkeley, California, containing the carefully worded letter about "a conditional acceptance based on continuing academic achievement." An 'F' in senior English would be an achievement of its own sort.

He dragged his feet towards home, wondering how Lara would react when she learned that an English presentation had undone her plans for their resettlement out west. She would mask her disappointment well, he knew. For once he would like to see her angry.

When he reached Joyce Road, Ponterio stopped on the corner and stood for a minute under the canopy of the low, spreading dogwood tree. The branches were crowded with clusters of pale pink blossoms. He looked up, watching the petals shift to white or red as the light came and went. He turned his gaze from the blossoms to the stream of passing students, then quickly back at the blossoms, afraid that someone might notice the tears that had begun to sting his eyes.

THE WARM WEATHER had drawn a crowd of parents and their children to Carvel. Lara offered to run inside and get them something while he found a parking spot in the back.

"What do you want?" she asked.

"Peach penumbra," he answered.

She swung out of the car and Ponterio drove around to park behind the bakery next door. He knew she would get a small vanilla cone with rainbow sprinkles, like she had every night last August when she had come home early from soccer camp in North Carolina because two of the girls in the dorm had come down with the flu. It had been too late to enroll her in a local camp or an SAT course, so the Wassermans had begrudgingly allowed her to structure her own time. After Ponterio finished teaching at the Conservatory camp during the day, they would pick up ice cream and drive to the Dobbs Ferry station to watch the sunset.

One night he lay in the back of the Odyssey with his arms behind his head. A bead of sweat traced the curve of her neck. It settled on her back where her skin pressed against his. Another bead formed and followed.

Suddenly she separated and turned so that the softest skin of her chest was pressed against the wispy hairs of his. She kissed him. He could taste rainbow sprinkles on her tongue.

"Do you love me?" she asked.

He blinked twice rapidly and stared at the ceiling. Coltrane rasped the rainy melody of "My Favorite Things." He did not know whether he loved her. If he did, he loved her a little less for asking.

"I don't know what that means," he wanted to tell her.

What kind of musician doesn't know what love is? he asked himself.

Outside, a patrol car continued its incessant rounds of the parking lot. He watched the lights rake the ceiling of the Odyssey and felt more secluded for the intrusion.

He sat up when the lights had passed. The tinted rear window faced the green steel trellises of the Metro-North station. Turning towards the windshield, he could see the deserted playground, a stand of trees, and then the great gray Hudson stretching to the sheer rock wall of the Palisades to the north and south.

Lara tried a different approach. "Do you remember the night we first talked?"

Ninth grade. The winter concert. He had played with both the band and the jazz orchestra, with a solo on "Moanin'." As tenor sax it had been his task to keep the piece sultry without letting it stymie, to keep the rhythm moving without letting it turn to pop.

"I was only there because Ally had a crush on Evanston and wanted to see him play," she said. "We were there in our volleyball uniforms while everyone else was all dressed up."

He had often relived that night. He and Mike Evanston—small, sandy-haired clarinetist and co-founder of the Five Mikes Quintet—were clearing music stands from the stage after the show. Ponterio was dressed in dark jeans with a white dress shirt belted into the waist. His sax strap still hung from his neck. When the most popular girl in their grade approached, Evanston had stood rooted in surprise until he realized that the look of intense interest in Lara's gray eyes had room only for his friend.

"Do you know why I came on stage that night to talk to you?" Lara asked, resting her head on Ponterio's thigh.

He shook his head. He remembered how he had only found the courage to talk to her in the residual adrenaline from his solo. Calmly he had shown her how the saxophone worked and answered her insightful questions.

"I was jealous," she said after a moment's pause.

"Jealous of who?"

"Of your saxophone," she said. "It was the first time I wanted to be something I wasn't. And it wasn't even another person." He felt her cheek warm on his leg. "I wanted to be held the way you held your sax. I wanted you to close your eyes and fill me with your breath."

Hearing his cue, he bent down to kiss her waiting mouth. Again the sugary taste of sprinkles.

She sat up suddenly and said, "Let's swim the river." He followed her gaze across the mile of murky water separating them from the Rockland shore. Her eyes glinted and he couldn't tell whether she was serious. He felt lightheaded with fear.

"Maybe some other night," he suggested.

"THEY DIDN'T HAVE PEACH," Lara said, handing him a cone of strawberry ice cream.

They ate their ice cream in silence, windows down, listening to the hum of tires on the Thruway. Ponterio paused to let the dark strawberry beads drip down and across his fingers. Lara noticed and dabbed at the back of his hand with the extra napkins she had brought.

She asked, "Can I hear the poem?"

Ponterio bit his lip, felt resentment and gratitude struggle inside him.

"'A Supermarket in California,' by Allen Ginsberg," he began.

"Wait!" Lara reached into the seat behind her and rummaged through her bag. She extracted a blue folder labeled "English," and rifled through the papers inside until she found a handout on Ginsberg with the poem reproduced on the back.

After glancing warily at the sheet, Ponterio recited, "*What thoughts I have of you, tonight, Walt Whitman.*" He stumbled on "*in our solitary fancy*" in the second stanza and went back to the beginning of the line to include it. He faltered again after the speaker and Whitman have left the supermarket.

"*Will we stroll dreaming,*" Lara prompted him.

"*Lost America of love*" slid off his tongue, but after the heavy "*cottages*" he stalled again.

"*Ah, dear father,*" Lara began.

"I'll cram the last part during lunch," he cut her off, glowering out the windshield.

Lara watched him with the sheet in her lap. Ponterio laid his arms on the steering wheel.

"I thought you were going to finish it this weekend." She said it softly but with enough edge that he felt catharsis in the cutting.

"I was busy," he pouted.

SATURDAY MORNING WAS COLD AND OVERCAST. Ponterio awoke and went downstairs to find the twins already dressed in their identical black Ardsley Hardware Little League uniforms. Their father stood to the side stuffing a backpack with papers and pretzel sticks, rushing to get to the office in response to an unexpected emergency. Their mother leaned against the refrigerator with the phone to her ear, arranging a carpool to McDowell Park with Dylan's mom so she could go visit her parents on the Island like she'd promised.

The house was quiet by ten. Ponterio returned to his room and opened a window. The sky was colorless. The last breath of winter exhaled into the room, belying April's promises.

He looked from his music stand to the wrinkled poetry handout on his desk, then back to the music stand. His sax was zippered shut in its case. He pictured himself as a snake eating its own tail: as soon as he told himself that he would go to Berklee, he felt the relief of decision, the satisfaction of knowing that Mr. Ulrich and his parents would be proud of him. Then the uneasiness set in, until he could only find relief by telling himself that Berkeley was the smarter choice after all, and he was glad to know that Lara would be happy. It was not long before the cycle would start again at the beginning.

Dylan's dad dropped the twins off early. The second game of their doubleheader had been postponed due to the rain. Ponterio went downstairs to open the door and wave thanks to Dylan's father. When their cleats and hats were in the closet, Ponterio sent the boys upstairs while he made them all a pot of macaroni and cheese. The water was slow to boil on the electric stove. He watched the streams of bubbles rise and tried without success to clear his mind of the poem, his saxophone, the future.

As the water came to a boil, his heart leapt with sudden realization: I could propose to Lara!

She would almost certainly accept, if only for her love of seeing things through to their end. He would go to Berkeley and afterwards they would get an apartment in San Francisco. She would launch the women's sports website she always talked about, and he could concentrate on his music without financial worries.

He felt a warm feeling of relief as he stirred in the macaroni. Lulled by the swirl of elbows in the pot, he let his mind wander through a vision of their life together.

It is morning. He is thirty-something but looks the same as he does today. He is sitting on a stool at a long granite countertop in a long modern kitchen. The room is lighted naturally through ceiling-high sliding glass doors that open onto a manicured backyard bordered by flowerbeds and a tall fence. He is alone. The newspaper and a cup of coffee sit on the granite before him. He does not know who has made the coffee or who has put it there. He searches the vision for Lara, but she is not at home. He searches for his sax and cannot find it.

Back in his own kitchen, his stomach tightened and he blinked hard to clear the scene. When he had drained the pasta and stirred in the sauce, Ponterio brought his brothers a small bowl each of the mac and cheese and the three of them watched cartoons until their father came home. Before the twins could launch into their play-by-play, he asked to borrow the car and drove himself the four miles to the Dobbs Ferry train station.

NIGHT HAD NOT YET FALLEN, yet it was dark at the station when Ponterio arrived. He found a spot facing the river and turned the engine off. Charlie Parker's "Confirmation" played louder in the sudden quiet. He turned this off too. Somewhere over the river a seagull cried and the cords on the flagpole made a syncopated nautical clanking in the wind.

Shapes of trees bent in the wind and misting rain. The river heaved against the Atlantic tide. The fog was too thick to see either the Tappan Zee upriver or the George Washington to the south. The Palisades were only just visible across the choppy expanse of the Hudson. Here the cliffs dipped to form a tree-lined bowl into which the fog and cloud poured. Staring into the swirling basin, Ponterio could almost imagine that something mysterious and enchanting lay beyond the river, instead of New Jersey and Pennsylvania and, somewhere, California.

A sudden peal of thunder masked the approach of a northbound Amtrak sleeper. The rattle of the dark stainless-steel cars pierced the receding thunder until it, too, was only an echo. A southbound Metro-North train squealed to a slow stop. It took on some homebound laborers and a knot of overdressed partygoers, college-age kids just home from school and jittery teenagers with makeup and fake IDs in their purses, desperate for a foretaste of adulthood.

Ponterio waited for the train's red and green lights to disappear around the bend before backing up the minivan and driving home. The rain had coalesced into drumming drops and "Confirmation" didn't sound so bad anymore.

"LET'S GO SEE THE BRIDGE," Lara said when they had finished their ice cream, so Ponterio eased the car out onto 9A. A few minutes later they were parked between the train station and the river and together they walked to the park.

"Oh my god," Lara breathed.

Locals stood in small clusters on the grass, hugging their arms to their chests or pointing upriver. A man stood alone on the rocky northern edge of the promenade, peering into two expensive cameras on tripods.

The column of fire, crowned with oily smoke, rose between the bridge's twin steel summits. A duplicate column showed in reflection in the subdued river. The spindly steel girders appeared to glow from the heat. The causeway flickered with the strobing red and blue lights of emergency vehicles. Ponterio thought he heard a siren and the muted crackle of the flames. He looked around for police or reporters, somebody to interpret the disaster for them, but there were only the other shades in the grass.

In the deepest part of the channel a rusty barge appeared in silhouette, a single light burning on its bow. A many-lanterned tug bobbed impatiently behind it.

Straining his ears, Ponterio detected a high whine coming from the south that left the taste of copper on his tongue. He turned towards the sound, and soon saw an orange and blue Coast Guard patrol boat beating up the river, its blue light turning.

A separate tone began to resonate under the whine, a low and rapid drumbeat that seemed at once to approach from above and below. The sounds merged just before a lithe black helicopter appeared above the Palisades. It banked above the boat with heart-wrenching agility and flew upriver, rotors angled forward, speeding headlong towards the epicenter of the action. Ponterio gripped his own shoulder and watched the patrol boat struggle on behind.

Without turning from the blaze, Lara reached out and took his free hand. The back of the boy's throat burned. Something had caught in his memory. He turned and looked downriver again. The lights of the GW appeared like a necklace across the channel. Beyond, the city pulsed on its little island. Ponterio closed his eyes and tried to breathe.

"Can we get the English folder from your bag?" he managed to ask.

Lara turned from the fire with a distant look in her eyes. He repeated the question in a steadier voice and they went back to the car, still holding hands, past murmuring middle-aged couples.

They stood beside the sliding door of the Odyssey while he opened the folder. The only sound that reached them now was the rustling of oak leaves. The first poems in the packet were Whitman's. He scanned the lines Lara had underlined in neat, blue ink.

Whoever you are! motion and reflection are especially for you, / The divine ship sails the divine sea for you.

No one can acquire for another—not one, / Not one can grow for another—not one.

Ponterio released a deep breath and looked across at the river. *Father, greybeard, lonely old courage-teacher,* he remembered.

He turned from the car and walked to the southern tip of the park. Lara followed. Climbing down to the water's edge, he began to remove his clothes.

"What are you doing?" she whispered, looking over her shoulder. The bystanders were fixated on the flames. Nobody noticed the boy standing on the rocks in his boxers.

"You're crazy!" she said, but there was a rueful smile on her face. She looked beautiful in the flickering light of the fire.

The water was colder than he had expected. He gasped and his head felt clearer than it had in weeks. The Rockland shore looked a long way away.

Lara picked her way down the rocks to the river's edge and crouched over his clothes.

"How are you going to get home like this?" she asked.

Ponterio looked out at the barge, the tug, the burning bridge.

Afterwards he would tell her: he couldn't go to Berkeley. Nor would he go to the College of Music. He had to do it his own way.

He knew they would remain friends. They would always be friends. They had always been friends. And when Lara needed him, if she ever needed anybody, he would always be a phone call away.

In the meantime, he continued treading water in time to the rhythm of the flames. ◇

Weir at Ossining

Amy Holman

Light the course of gravity
with living oil from the great whale
flensed and dragged upriver
from the dark sea.

With living oil from the great whale,
men tunneled like Romans
from the dark. See
mastery, engineering flow.

Men tunneled. Like Romans
with aqueducts, a city modernizes.
Mastery, engineering, flow—
weir hidden in the gneiss.

With aqueducts a city modernizes:
washes wounds, flushes waste.
We're hidden in the gneiss
buildings, releasing the pipes. Weir

washes wounds, flushes waste.
We're phantoms diving a tunnel to
buildings, released from pipes; we're
flocculate in the gallons, and filtered.

Weir phantoms diving a tunnel to
center city, breaching the drink.
Flocculate in the gallons and filtered
from subconscious: Roman Orcus sings

the center city breach. The drink
from fresh kills cuts through
subconscious: Roman Orcus, sing
sing the broken oaths of men.

From fresh kills cut through—
flensed and dragged upriver—
sing the broken oaths of men
to light the course of gravity. ◇

Chain gangs from Sing Sing Prison helped build the old weir using lamps that burned whale oil manufactured in nearby Hudson.

Drawing Out a Drawska Vampire

Amy Holman

A sickle collar for the cholera sickened,
he held a mouthful of fear. Rocked by reproach
for expiring quick, he's not that fanged

revenant assailing nearby farm girls.
His bones are local. Afterlife is boundless,
the body held dear to the place of birth—

so the isotopes say, in Greek etymology
and mass spectrometry. Believe is the twin to
furlough, misplaced sharing the womb

with displaced. The teeth are chattering
to be replaced in the grounds he has, and be
reborn in cyclic systems breaking down. ◇

During a 19th century cholera epidemic in Drawska, Poland, certain corpses believed to be of strangers were treated to "vampire burials" either by fastening a sickle collar to behead the rising dead, or stuffing rocks down throats to keep the undead from biting people. Recent isotope analysis of the skeletal teeth was performed to determine where the victims originated.

Visiting Mrs. Pless

Helen Kellert

IN A BLUE-AND-RED-STRIPED BLAZER, CAREFULLY KNOTTED CRAVAT, and straw boating hat to protect his marble-white skin, my frightfully English Great Uncle Bertie was taking tea in our flower garden. Just arrived in South Africa, he squinted in the dazzling Johannesburg sun, and stared, frowning, at my skinny, seven-year-old frame.

I was wearing nothing but a short, brown, paper skirt. Julie—our African maid and my nanny since I was born—had cut its hem into fringed strips that fluttered when I skipped. Over the skirt, Julie had tied a leather strip strung with white and yellow beads, from which hung in front a small, beaded square of red, white, and yellow. I wore red and black bands around my wrists and upper arms. Best of all was my necklace, a thin strand of shiny red and smaller blue beads.

"Proper little savage, isn't she?" Uncle Bertie remarked to my mother. "Frightful outfit she's got herself up in, don't you know. You are going to do something about her, aren't you?"

At this, I stamped my bare foot, and the seedpods, dangling from thin leather bands around my ankle, jangled. I had spent all morning in the kitchen with Julie making them so that I could look just like her when she was young.

"Oh, come now, Bertie. No harm in it at all," said my mother, handing him a cup of tea and me a biscuit. "Rather wonderful, actually. It is 1948, after all. One more thing you're going to have to get used to in your new country. Let children—and all of us—run free under the African sun, is what I say."

This told me that she would never stop me from dressing as if I belonged to Julie's tribe or spending time with our servants in the kitchen yard. I rubbed my cheek against my mother's arm, chose a biscuit for Julie, and dashed off to give it to her. I found her in the kitchen, twisting the final strand of my white-, blue-, and yellow-beaded headband. She knotted the thread and cut it with her strong white teeth. Setting the sturdy band snugly onto my head, she clapped her hands and laughed.

"Hau, little Annie!" she exclaimed. "You look just like me when I had the same years as you!"

"Now I'm a Tswana girl, too!" I cried, hugging her. "But mustn't I have a Tswana name, like you?"

Julie nibbled her biscuit, thoughtfully. "Akanyang is a good name for you."

"I like Akanyang! But how come we don't call you Khumoetsile?" I asked, using her tribal name.

"White people like us to have white names. And sometimes our names, they are too hard for them to say," Julie explained, lifting my hair to free the necklace.

"But my name, will they be able to say it?" I asked, stretching out my arms to examine my beads.

"Maybe, maybe not."

"So I'll stay with Annie and you can be Julie."

We both laughed.

Dancing back to the flower garden, I collided with my father who was walking over to the tea table, the newspaper under his arm. He swung me into the air as he always did, both of us laughing, then set me down and turned to shake hands with Uncle Bertie.

"Welcome to Johannesburg," he said. "And congrats on your retirement! Well done, indeed. Glad you've come out here to live, old chap."

My father's evening newspaper had slipped to the lawn. I picked it up and ran over to my mother. I loved reading the big, fat, black letters of newspaper headlines with her, tracing the shapes of the letters with my finger and saying their sounds. We read together almost every day, but I had never seen such enormous headlines as I did that afternoon. They filled the front page.

The first word started with a big A. I sounded out the P that came next, then the A, the R, and the following T, but the rest was too difficult. My mother helped me, pointing to letters, but her voice was angry as she said the whole word. *A-part-heid.* I twisted round on her lap to look at her face. Could she be upset with me? But I hadn't spilled milk, been rude, or said a bad word.

"Are you cross, Mummy?" I asked. "Are you furious?" I had just learned this word.

"I don't like this news one bit," she said. "But read on. You're doing wonderfully, my Annie."

"A-PART-HEID NOW THE LAW OF THE LAND," I sounded out slowly. And then the smaller letters: "E-lec-tion Re-sults." I was proud of my reading, but troubled that the words seemed to make my mother angry. Before I could ask her what the headlines meant, my arm jiggled the plate of scones beside me; Devonshire cream covered my elbow, which was difficult to lick but delicious.

My mother put the plate to rights, frowning a little. I wandered over to my father's chair, flopped down on the grass and leaned against his leg. Like my mother, my father did not look happy; he was shaking his head.

"A rotten business, this new government. Sorry, Bertie, but the Afrikaners have finally got their way and are putting the boot to everything English. Wouldn't expect to be popular just now, if I were you."

"Now this, at least, is nicer news," my mother said, turning a page of the newspaper. "An article about Mrs. Pless."

She started to talk excitedly about a Mrs. Pless, who lived in a cave. The cave, I heard my mother say, was full of bones, and the cave was at Sterkfontein and this was where Mrs. Pless and a skull and skeleton bits had been found and this, my father said, was quite marvelous and simply amazing.

When the grownups started using words I did not understand, like *fossils* and *paleo-something*, I lost interest and concentrated instead on the biscuit plate. I finally chose a lemon cream and was carefully licking its sweet filling when Uncle Bertie slapped his leg so suddenly and firmly that I thought he might choke on his biscuit.

"Look here, I do think it would be frightfully good for us to take ourselves off to meet this Mrs. Pless, don't you? Chance of a lifetime, what?" he harrumphed.

"Excellent idea!" said my father, filling his pipe with golden tobacco from his leather tobacco pouch. A match flared as he lit the pipe.

"It is rather a big trip—an hour or two," my mother said. "But how I'd love to go into that cave to see her! She is supposedly our ancestor, after all. They've opened the cave for public viewing." She waved the newspaper in the air.

"What does 'public' mean?" I asked.

"It means open for everyone," my mother answered. "A visit to a cave! Are you excited, dear?"

I climbed back onto her lap and nodded, but slowly.

"Will the cave be very, very, very dark?" I asked, leaning back against her and wrinkling my nose in a way that usually got her sympathy.

"Yes, probably, my love. Caves usually are," she replied.

"Dark is scary. It could give me a bad dream. Can Julie come with us? If I have both you *and* Julie then I won't be terribly, very scared. Not *frightfully* scared," I said, glancing at Uncle Bertie.

"Of course, my pet. Oh, and here's Julie now with fresh tea. Let's ask her."

I wriggled off my mother's lap and scampered up to Julie, who was setting the teapot on the table.

"Julie, would you like to come with us on a trip to see a very old cave and a million-year-old human being?" asked my mother.

Julie clicked her tongue and shook her head.

"No, Madame. No. I do not like to go in a big hole in the ground."

"But, it's a special cave and we'll all be together!" I cried.

"You know, Julie," my father said, pausing to take a slow draw of his pipe, "this woman they found, she could be one of your ancestors. Perhaps she was from your Tswana people. Tswana used to live where the cave is."

"The BaTswana? Hau. Then maybe."

I sprang up and clapped my hands.

"Please, Julie! Please?" I begged, hugging her.

Julie laughed and straightened my necklace.

"All right. I will come."

I hopped around Julie, giggling and stomping my feet. Then I grabbed her hands and swung round with her in circles until we both collapsed into a laughing, dizzy heap on the grass.

Uncle Bertie, peering over the top of his eyeglasses and the rim of his teacup, announced, "My, my, but you two do get along frightfully well. Frightfully good to see, I do declare."

While I caught my breath from twirling, a puzzling thought struck. I turned to my mother again.

"But, Mummy, you said that Mrs. Pless is one of *our* ancestors."

"Yes, darling. One of ours *and* one of Julie's, too. Long, long ago we all came from the same family."

"How long ago?" I wanted to know.

"Millions and millions of years."

"Is that more than a hundred?"

"It is indeed. Far, far away in the past."

"Julie, Julie, we're the same family! And you're coming with us!"

I spun around the table, loving the sound of my ankle seedpods, but then circled back to my mother with a new question.

"Mummy, does Mrs. Pless look like Uncle Bertie?"

Uncle Bertie shouted a loud "Ha!" then asked, "Why ever would you think that, child?"

"Because you're both from faraway places," I explained. "And you're both very old."

"I'm not quite that ancient." Uncle Bertie smiled at my mother.

My father also smiled. He took another puff of his pipe, and releasing the fragrant smoke up toward the jacaranda tree, said that Mrs. Pless did not really look like any of us.

I chose another lemon cream and thought about Mrs. Pless not being a living lady at all but a leftover one—lots of bones and no skin. I was sure that I would not be able to sleep at all that night, for wildly thinking of our adventure—the long ride as exciting as the dark cave might be scary.

But somehow I did sleep and woke the next morning to Julie and my mother packing lunch and tea. My father found electric torches for everyone, even me. I tested the beam with him to make sure I would have light in the dark, dark cave. And then, all of us in sensible shoes and knee-high socks to protect against snakes, we loaded the picnic basket and ourselves into the car to visit Mrs. Pless.

I sat in the back seat between Julie and Uncle Bertie, his long legs in white flannels. My mother was in the front passenger seat, next to my father. Uncle Bertie eyed my outfit—red shorts and white cotton blouse with a Peter Pan collar and a red ribbon that Julie had tied in my curly hair—and smiled approvingly.

"Good show, my dear, good show. Jolly sight better than all those native things," he said.

I wanted to tell Uncle Bertie that I loved my beads, that underneath my shirt I was still wearing my beaded necklace, and that he was not being nice to Julie, but my tongue stuck to the roof of my mouth. His nose was huge and his angled thighbones were huge and the straw hat on his huge knees was enormous. I wriggled away from him and snuggled as close as I could to Julie.

We drove through the dusty streets of Krugersdorp. My father said that the town was a terrible place, a real hotbed of apartheid. It did seem hot and my eyelids were getting heavy. I rested my head on Julie's comfortable shoulder; the voices of the grown-ups floated around me.

"Awfully glad to be out of dreary, rainy old London," Uncle Bertie said. "But, I must say," he continued, leaning forward into the space between my parents, "bit worrisome here, don't you know. One government in and one out is all part of the game, but, I say . . ."

He paused to pick up his hat, which had slipped off his knees.

What game? Who's playing? Who's winning? I wondered. I plucked up my courage and tapped Uncle Bertie on his shoulder.

"Can we play the game too?" I asked. Uncle Bertie turned his long, large face down to me.

"Good question, my dear." He smiled and patted my head. "I suppose we're all playing in one way or another, aren't we?"

What on earth did he mean? Uncle Bertie leaned forward again.

"I simply can't see how things are going to turn out here," he continued. "These new laws they're proposing . . . dreadfully harsh. Color bar and all that. Tell me frankly, do you see much changing with all this?"

"I do, actually," replied my father, shifting the car gears. "Awful lot of anger about nowadays. For one thing, I'm thinking about installing one of those new-fangled burglar alarms. And, my dear," he continued, turning to my mother, "better stop your protest meetings at the house until things settle down."

"What utter nonsense!" said my mother. "I'm having a meeting this Saturday morning and I have no intention of cancelling."

"Look, I've asked the burglar alarm chappies to come by on Saturday morning to look around, give us a price. Much rather all of us be safe," my father said.

"Oh, for heaven's sake. We live in a civilized country. What on earth's there to fear? We'll have a new and sane government this time next year," my mother answered, twisting in her seat to face Uncle Bertie. "This is a passing storm, really, Bertie. Things will settle down and we can march on to better days."

"Besides," she said to my father, "where on earth would we get the money for this burglar alarm that we don't need?"

"We'll find it because we need it. And that's that," he replied sharply, driving the car faster.

I sat up quickly. I had never, ever heard my parents argue in front of people before.

My stomach felt funny, as if I had eaten something bad. Reaching under my shirt collar, I pulled out my necklace. It was comforting to rub the beads. And when I looped it up over my mouth and under my nose, I liked the way it smelled of Julie's fingers and mine.

No one spoke. I looked up at Uncle Bertie. When my eyes met his, he raised his eyebrows and shrugged. I shrugged back and it felt very grown up, this raising and dropping of shoulders. I tried to raise my eyebrows too, like his, but wasn't sure if they moved.

Uncle Bertie patted my knee. After a quiet minute, he turned to Julie.

"I say, just how different do you think things will be for you now that apartheid is official?"

"Aaai." Julie shook her head from side to side and looked down at her hands. "Things are bad, Baas Bertie, very bad. I hope the Madame is right. But I don't know for sure. Aaai." A tear rolled down her cheek and she covered her mouth with her hand. I reached for her other hand. Uncle Bertie arced his arm over me and slowly patted Julie's shoulder several times.

"Terribly sorry, my dear. Terribly sorry," he said in his gentle voice.

I moved closer to Uncle Bertie and stretched my free hand over to his.

Uncle Bertie kept my hand in his warm one, until, just beyond Krugersdorp, my mother insisted we stop for lunch. In a few miles, she said, the roads would no longer be tarred and would be too dusty for a picnic. We parked by the side of the road and found a concrete picnic table under a shade tree. Julie set the table and spread out our lunch, then moved off to sit on the ground beneath the tree, but my father called to her.

"Come on, Julie, there's room for you here."

"But, Baas, we're in Krugersdorp."

"Doesn't matter. You're with us. And you don't have to call me 'Baas.' Even in Krugersdorp. Come along."

Uncle Bertie patted the seat between himself and me. Julie came over slowly to sit in the space he had made and I cuddled happily next to her as she helped me peel my egg.

My father got up to stretch his legs after he ate. I scampered after him and slipped my hand into his. His khakis were the same color as the veldt. The sandy ground had only a few patches of grass, so I felt safe from snakes. The land was flat except for one slight rise on which we stopped. My father bent to pick me up in his strong arms.

"Look here, my darling. Look at all this."

Above us, an eagle circled in the brilliant blue. Below us, the veldt spread in all directions, amber and dun, broken only by scrub bushes, flat tops of thorn trees, scattered heaps of red boulders and grey rocks. To one side, a farmhouse stood alone in its cluster of blue gum and acacia trees, its white walls bright against its green brick chimney. Some distance apart, surrounded by a thornwood fence, were the round, thatch roofs of a tribal village kraal. Huts nestled close to the soil; smoke rose in a thin column from the kraal's center.

The view of the wide land had made me quiet. But now I needed to run. I skipped back to the picnic table where my mother and Julie were packing up.

Lunch over, we drove further into the veldt until the road turned into two narrow dust strips with uneven grass between them. After a bumpy forever, the car lurched to a stop between two aloes as tall as a man. Out I scrambled for that first breath of the truly deep bush veldt, magically silent except for one bird singing in a low thorn bush. A small hill raised its rocky outline against the sky.

The dusty trail we walked down was rough and stony, the grasses on either side dry and yellow-brown. There were no other people except for one elderly couple coming toward us.

My father tipped his hat to wish them good afternoon. The woman commented that we were clever to bring so many torches.

"You'll need them," she said. "Black as midnight in that cave."

This made me gasp and clutch Julie's hand more tightly.

The trail ended in a sandy area with large boulders strewn unevenly about. Facing us was a high wall of sheer rock overhung with a few green branches. The rock face was red in parts, but pale gray as it curved away to a dark, tall opening, which gaped in enormous shadow.

Near the cave entrance stood a rickety, wooden table and one chair on which a large, sandy-blond man in khakis sat. He had an official badge on each sleeve. A black worker, squatting on the ground next to him, was attaching a pen to a book as thick as a Bible. Its brown leather cover looked shiny and new.

"Is he a Tswana like you?" I whispered to Julie, pointing at him.

"Don't point, dear," said my mother.

The official had a broad, sunburned face, pink neck, and freckled arms, the hairs on them golden, almost white. Resting on a small pile of stones on the table was his black pipe, its smoke curling slowly up to the bright sky. He greeted us in Afrikaans first, then in English.

Then he raised the palm of his hand in a stop, go-no-further way and, in a heavy Afrikaans accent, said, "No, sorry, hey. Non-Europeans not allowed into the cave."

"What?" demanded my mother.

The Afrikaner reached for the big book and placed it exactly in the middle of the table, carefully squaring its edges to match those of the table.

"She can't go in," he said, pointing to Julie. "New government, new policy, new rules. Lots of changes. Look, we haven't even finished making our new sign."

He pointed to another black worker in overalls who was using shiny black paint to fill in chalk outlines of letters on a wooden board.

"What do the words say?" I whispered to my father, who read them to me.

"*Slegs Blankes*. Whites Only."

I had no time to ask him to explain; my mother's voice bit the air so loudly and furiously that I jumped.

"Just what on earth does this all mean?" she demanded.

"It means that the black one can't go in."

My mother gasped. "You cannot be serious."

"I am. This is all true, as true as fact," the Afrikaner answered. "And you must sign in this new book here. All the new regulations is right in here."

He opened the big book, turned it round and pushed it toward us.

"And you must fill it in here where it says 'Race,'" he continued. "If you say you are white, then you can go in. She can't say she's white so she must wait outside."

My mother's mouth was open. She looked stunned.

"But, my good fellow," Uncle Bertie huffed, "we don't even know if this Mrs. Pless is black or white, do we?"

The official took a long, slow draw on his pipe and looked Uncle Bertie up and down.

"You from England, hey? You know, you English never did know how to run things properly. But this is the way it is now. She can't go in."

I burst into noisy tears and flung my arms around Julie's hips.

"I won't go in without Julie," I wailed. "I'm too afraid."

The official wiped the back of his neck and shook his head as my sobs grew louder, my gulps more desperate, my shrieks higher and shriller.

"This is simply unacceptable," my mother declared. "There is no earthly reason our maid can't come in with us. It's her skeleton as much as ours, after all."

"Look, no one else is here," my father added. "No one will know the difference."

The Afrikaner looked down at his book.

I stared past him into the shadows of the yawning cave. My mother glared at the Afrikaner. Her voice, once again loud and angry, crashed into my ears.

"You ought to be ashamed of yourself."

This set me to howling again. My hand flew to my necklace, and twisted it into a tight knot.

The official looked at me, blew out his cheeks, and waved us away.

"Just go. Go in, all of you. But be quick in there, hey."

I stopped crying and looked up at Julie. Her mouth was pinched tight. Just as we reached the towering, gray walls of the cave entrance, the official called out to us. We all turned to see him hurrying over and waving frantically.

Another man, also in uniform, was coming down the path, kicking up small stones and dust clouds. He was holding a bundle of papers.

"Look, I could lose my job with this," the Afrikaner said. He sounded nervous. Then he added in a much louder voice, "That one can't go in. She's black. And you must all come back and sign the book properly."

He walked back to meet the second official and whispered with him. My mother's face became a dark frown. My father shook his head and crossed his arms.

"Not good form, not good form at all. Just not cricket," Uncle Bertie said.

I wound my necklace around my fingers.

"We all leave now. At once!" my mother announced, her voice shaking with rage.

She walked quickly up to the table and faced the Afrikaners. Her voice was sharp.

"Mrs. Pless deserves better. And this," she said, jabbing her finger on the big book, "is a disgrace."

Then she grabbed my hand and headed back to the path.

"Quite right, quite right," my father said, following us.

"Not sure this helps, my girl," Uncle Bertie said to Julie, "but they hate me as much as you."

Julie said nothing.

THE WAY BACK UP FROM THE CAVE was steep and much harder than the way down had been. The ruts seemed deeper, our feet more unsure on stones that seemed more slippery. No one spoke as we climbed, not even Uncle Bertie. Julie was last, her head bowed. I craned around but couldn't see her face clearly.

At the top of the path, my parents went to the car and unlocked it. Uncle Bertie and I flopped onto a wooden picnic bench, he with an exhausted groan, me with a sigh. Julie looked at the table, then walked off to stand under a scraggly thorn tree.

Around us, the veldt stretched for miles. The sun was weaker now; the aloes cast shadows. Circling lower in the sky, closer than the one we had seen at lunch, an eagle glided, black against the blue, then swooped lower. I wondered what it was hunting and who would ever see, left on the veldt, the white bones of whatever it killed.

Julie was staring into the bush. I wanted to run and hug her, but my legs were too tired.

I rested my face on the wooden boards of the table. Between its crevices, dust swirled up, scratching my eyes, drying my throat. I was thirsty but there was no one to ask for water. Uncle Bertie's eyes were closed; Julie and my parents were too far away.

My fingers fumbled for my necklace with its smooth, round beads, but it was gone. ◇

Clean Up

Claudine Nash

I started leaking orange
again. Today, in four
different ways. No need

for alarm or urgent
care; as unpleasant as
it is, I'm told fatality is a

seldom occurring event.
A drop of marigold escapes
me when I group

a bouquet of seasonal
leaves. Another seeps
from my wrist after an

article on waning
solar storms. Chance
images of you bathed

in black and white are
always good for a minor
saffron-infused spill. But

even I admit
it gets a bit awkward
when an old-fashioned

lounge piece like
the type Dean Martin
might have sung

drips from the overhead
and I hemorrhage
a sunset. ◇

Sea Glass

Claudine Nash

At some point you began the process
of becoming sea glass; hazel green

shards of torn bottle nursed on algae
and kelp, twisted to sleep by channels

of lenient sand who draw your surface
from memory, erasing the outline of your

eyes in half-speed until they no
longer pull at my fingerprints. Cast into

the sound in May, I will find you between
mussels and an icy foam, when I can

run my finger down your side,
pick you up in my ungloved hand. ◇

Sightseeing

Matt Matros

JEB AMBLED OVER TO THE HOOD ORNAMENT, AND TRIED TO SOUND like a person in charge. "Well, let's take a gander," he said. Jeb pushed down, singeing his hand, and the hood flew open. The engine sizzled as he leaned over it. "Seems pretty hot in there."

"Don't you think we ran out of gas?" Priscilla said. "When's the last time you checked our gas?"

"Don't know."

"Did you even look at it when we were slowing down?"

"Don't reckon I did," he said. In fact, he didn't remember checking the gas any time in recent days, and wondered how they'd made it this far without running out. They must've refueled somewhere, but Jeb couldn't picture it.

"Then don't we have some sort of assistance program?" Priscilla asked, with little hope of a satisfying answer. She asked anyway. Priscilla asked because there was a certain way they did things, a certain route she and her husband took to travel through a conversation.

"I think yes," Jeb said. "I think we discussed it before. Didn't Tommy tell us something about it?"

"I thought you were the one listening to Tommy about the car. I thought you were doing that."

"I was. I think we have an assistance program."

Jeb reached in, popped the trunk, and went around back to inspect its contents. Running his hand under their luggage yielded nothing, but

Jeb knew something was there—a phone, or a box, or a keypad, or... what was it Tommy had said? A star? "I think maybe it's in here."

"There's nothing in there but the suitcases, Jeb. You been packing the car every day."

The word "packing" triggered an image of the furry red carpet that he knew existed somewhere beneath the crammed-in luggage on the trunk floor. As the image crystallized, Jeb could envision more details: the lint balls that clung like ticks to the surface, the Liquid Smoke stain from a recent barbecue, the unbroken mohair lining stretching from the backseat to the bumper. Priscilla was right. They'd get no help from within the car. "Tommy did say there was a number to call."

"We don't have a phone. We never did get one. You didn't think of that when you were sitting there planning this trip? That an assistance number wouldn't do us any good without a phone?"

Jeb didn't remember worrying about that potential problem. "So we're stuck in the desert," he said.

"Never thought I'd go out this way. I figured for sure you'd roll me over in my sleep, or a doc at St. Matthew's would stick his scalpel in the wrong place."

"We're not gonna die here, Priscilla."

"Shoot, you never know. It's hot enough to, that's for sure."

Jeb scanned the terrain for a place to sit. "Someone will come get us soon."

"Doesn't everyone have a phone? Don't you think this situation we're in right now calls for a cellular telephone?"

"We don't ever leave the house."

"Well, we left this time, didn't we?"

The sun didn't show any signs of setting. Jeb's field of view was bright on brown. If he sat against the car, would his legs reach the highway, possibly costing him his feet? Jeb wanted to be in position to flag down help, but he also wanted his feet.

"I'm gonna go sit," he announced, choosing the side of his vehicle facing away from the road, toward the desert.

"Good, you hide over there," Priscilla said. "I'm gonna stay standing right here."

"You'll get tired."

"Don't care if I do."

Priscilla Sanders could withstand the heat. She'd culled her cotton garments for breathability over a period of decades. A broad-brimmed straw hat she'd owned since before Tommy was born still provided enough shade for her to stay comfortable in any temperature. Priscilla had never worn denim in her life, or so she thought. In reality, she was mistaken. Back when she was Priscilla Haverson she had worn denim, on hikes, even including the one where she'd met Jebediah Sanders. But she'd forgotten this fact, and now no one would remember it for the rest of eternity.

"Besides, it's filthy down there," she said.

Jeb tried not to think about what he might be sitting on, and he succeeded. The sun beat against his unprotected scalp, but Jeb, like Priscilla, had no concern. He'd lived half his life without air conditioning, and could face the elements as well as anyone. Still, desert heat manifested itself differently from Mississippi heat. The desert radiated where Mississippi smothered. Jeb hadn't got much rest on those summer nights when the bugs and the closeness teamed up through open windows—buzz penetrating deep inside his ear, blood sucked from his skin, bed sheets soaked through before he even realized he'd been asleep. Nothing buzzed on this sandy road, and the noiselessness bothered Jeb, the more he noticed it.

HE'D BEEN SITTING AWHILE when the ground trembled beneath him, and he felt a thump to the back of his head. A second later Jeb registered that there'd been a whooshing sound, and that his neck had been yanked like a piece of string. "What the hell was that?"

"What do you think? A car just drove by."

Jeb blinked and tried to reorient himself. He saw the vast brownness and remembered enough. "Well, why didn't you flag it down?"

"Don't you think I tried? He never even saw me. Or maybe he just didn't want to see me."

Jeb's head started to sting. "I think I hurt myself," he said.

Priscilla went to him, almost by instinct. "Where'd you hurt yourself, hun?" She ran her fingers over Jeb's head. "You got a bump there all right. Let me fetch you some aspirin."

The sting he'd felt earlier had nothing on the pounding that followed. "Really hurts," he said.

Priscilla didn't tell Jebediah that she'd noticed blood. How had he done it this time? Did he jerk back when he was startled awake? Or had there really been enough movement from their own car, in the wake of the speeding car, for Jeb to take such a shot? Thankfully his pupils looked normal, and Priscilla hadn't seen any bone. Jeb probably had a mild concussion, same as Tommy used to get. The helmets they gave those boys never did much to prevent a 250-pound linebacker from denting her son's head. After the homecoming game Tommy's junior year, Priscilla gave him a mouthful of medicine and forbade him to drink before sending him to the dance. She then cried herself to sleep. Tommy spent the next day on his back while Priscilla brought him soup, cornbread, a damp dishrag, and more pills.

"Take this down nice and easy," Priscilla said, handing Jeb aspirin and a water bottle. "One at a time!" she yelled as he tried to swallow everything.

Jeb knew nothing but the throbbing in his head. The earth and the highway and the sunbeams had transformed into a living, breathing pulse. The first beat brought Jeb to his half-dirt, half-sod backyard, where Riley was digging another hole. Around the front, the morning's milk clinked down upon the doorstep, causing Riley's ears to perk up. But wait, the milkman had stopped coming ten years before Riley. How did they get fused together? With the next beat Jeb moved to his childhood home, prying his way into the hefty, dust-covered boxes in the attic. He struggled to prop the lid off a medium-sized one, the biggest he thought he could open. Another beat, and Jeb stood before the heath across from church, the one with the granary, mottled with shadows of fading daylight. Jeb knew this scene well, knew it exactly—the only moment of his wedding day he'd had to himself. These images had taken root in his mind, and they refused to be yanked out.

Priscilla had to assume she'd get nothing more from Jeb.

"Now relax," she said. "I'm finding us help." No cars were in sight, nor could any be heard in the distance.

"You're not," Jeb said, to the surprise of both of them.

"Just close your eyes."

"What do you mean? I'm fine."

"You're not fine," Priscilla said.

"I am." Jeb found that he believed it. The throbbing had turned into a dull weight.

"Don't you move!"

Priscilla had ordered Jeb to take her on a trip. They'd slept in their musty bedroom for a few thousand straight nights, and something had to be done. Then Tommy said he had a surprise for them, and Priscilla had let herself believe he would finally marry. When Tommy instead presented the car, the trip idea gained a foothold. They'd take Tommy's gift somewhere far away from Monroe—far from the corner store, the russet leaf-covered paths, the farmhouses they'd been staring at since forever.

"What for?" Jeb said.

"Just don't move."

Jeb spotted a jackrabbit between cacti taking a break from its scurrying. The jackrabbit seemed to want Jeb to say something in retort. After waiting a respectable time, the jackrabbit zipped back into the wasteland, too distant to be seen. Jeb sat up.

"Priscilla," he said. "I feel fine. Is there something you're not telling me?"

A hot wind worked its way under her sleeves. "You got blood," she said.

Everyone has blood, Jeb thought, until he realized what she meant. "Where?"

"A little, from your head. I saw it when I looked. You'll be fine, you just need to relax."

Jeb automatically reached for his injury. "I don't see blood."

"It's there. Trust me for once."

Jeb hated to trust people, but luckily he didn't remember that just then. "What if nobody comes?" he said.

"They'll come. It's not even dark yet."

"What if they don't? What if we got no way to move from this spot until the morning visitors get here tomorrow? Did you think of that?"

She turned. "No Jeb, I didn't. You know why? Cause it's only one-thirty in the damn afternoon. Plenty of people will pass before the park up there closes. So calm the hell down."

Jeb's sneakers had become encrusted with the Arizona soot, and he rubbed his shoes together to get them clean, or less dirty. "This could really be the end," he said. "You were right before."

"You're delirious. And I was joking before."

Neither Jeb nor Priscilla joked often.

"Does it matter anyway?" he said.

"Come again?"

"We all gotta go sooner or later. What's the difference if it's here or now or wherever?"

"The difference," Priscilla said, "is that it's hot as heck, and I've been cramped up in a car for six hours waiting to see Oak Creek Canyon. So we're damn well gonna see it."

"I'm hungry," Jeb said.

Priscilla sighed. The road winded a long way. She raised her hand to signal for help, and still none came. Her skin looked flakier than usual, and it seemed to crack more the longer she looked at it. The lines crisscrossed and ran together conspiratorially. Priscilla didn't mind her appearance, but it bothered her some when the skin chafed away, fighting off whatever ointments she threw at it. It hurt worse than it looked.

A groan came from the direction of Jeb's slumped body, lingering at low volume. "Jeb? What you doing over there?"

"I'm not doing anything," he said.

"You're making a heck of a noise."

"I'm not making any noise. You sometimes don't know what you're talking about."

"You're lowing like a freakin' cow is all," Priscilla muttered.

"You know something?" Jeb said. "Every trip we take is worse than the last one."

"Oh shush, we haven't traveled in years," she said, trying to put his remarks in their proper, injured-by-the-side-of-the-road context.

"We've been on trips. We had the honeymoon to Atlanta. We had Graceland after Tom went to school. We drove clear to New Jersey for his first varsity start. And then it was all downhill from there."

Priscilla didn't know if she preferred the moaning or the speech. "I said hush, Jeb, you need to rest."

"Why don't you hush? I was perfectly happy until you started jabbering away."

"I'm gonna ignore you now, hun."

Jeb stretched his legs to create tension in his toes. He felt lucid, but he knew that lucid people didn't bother thinking themselves lucid. He didn't want to die in the desert. Failing memory or not, there were better exits than this one.

"Maybe we should split up after this," he said. "Might make both of us a lot happier."

Priscilla knew he didn't mean it. He couldn't have meant it. But he had said it, and he'd never said anything like it before. "We've been married fifty-six years, Jeb."

"I know that. Maybe that's the problem. Maybe we're so damn sick of each other we ended up hobbled over in a desert somewhere. Maybe that's why neither of us know anything anymore. Been married too long."

Priscilla felt a tear form, but she resisted the impulse to release it. It escaped nonetheless, cold and abrasive against her weathered cheek. Priscilla remembered almost none of her life without Jeb. Still, she would never have accused their marriage of becoming obsolete. She didn't think that way.

"Too damn long," Jeb said. "You do something too long, then what good is it? Everybody gives up every damn thing after a while. No one does anything forever."

Forcing herself to think of something other than her husband, Priscilla watched the light reflecting off the mountains. They were really only hills, but they must've contained metal, or an ore, or a giant magnifying glass, for them to sparkle so brightly. Priscilla kept expecting the light to morph into an automobile that would finally find them.

"And God," Jeb said. "What does God know about keeping two

people together? Didn't Jesus die a virgin? What kind of example is that?"

"Jeb," Priscilla said, giving up her attempt at willful ignorance. "I need you to keep quiet now, you hear me?"

"I hear everything. I hear everything and I hear nothing. I sure as hell hear every stupid thing you say."

"OK," Priscilla said, pointing her finger at the sky, "you better listen to me. If you ever wanted to do me a favor—and I mean ever, if at any point in your life, you wanted to do a favor for me, your wife, who you married? If that was ever true, then you need to shut your mouth right now, whilst I'm getting our help. I know you're hurt. I know you're not thinking straight, but Jeb, you got to hear me say what I'm saying to you now."

Her last word lingered in the still air, and Priscilla wondered if she had permeated Jeb's skull. Sand speckled across her pants from the hot winds, and the whitest of her white hairs had gone whiter since she'd left the comfort of the Prius. Maybe she'd get especially lucky and Jeb would pass out. Except she knew from Tommy that passing out was *un*lucky for the concussed.

"Jeb, you hear me?" Was he getting cute with her? Obeying her command to the letter? "I know you can't well talk with your mouth shut, but you need to be staying awake for a little while."

A rustling came over the desert, which seemed odd in a place with nothing to rustle. Her husband still didn't speak, so Priscilla left her post and knelt over him. He looked back with eyes wide open. They had a glaze so that Priscilla couldn't tell whether he was ignoring her, or was too incapacitated to respond. "How you doing in there?" she said.

In there. What did Jeb see in there? Eyes open or eyes closed, he continued to see the desert before him, although now it was drenched in red like a Martian landscape. People, or monsters, wandered amongst the saguaros while scorpions darted between their feet. "They're coming for me," Jeb said, but not aloud. "It's all been a waste."

Priscilla, very much awake, began focusing on shelter. The shade had slanted away from Jeb, and Priscilla didn't think sunstroke would help her husband any. She could make a tent out of her blouse, or at least a canopy, but what would she prop it up with? Should she simply remove her blouse and drape it over his face? Jeb might then become disoriented and angry, which Priscilla could usually deal with. But what was that stuff he'd been saying, really? And why were her knees starting to wobble the way they would before Mrs. Eidenwood took the switch to her knuckles in second grade?

"A waste," Jeb thought, or dreamed. Either way. "A life gone fallow." The Monroe granary with no one coming in or out, Riley with his oversized collar sniffing his own dung, all those attic boxes too heavy to lift. Where were they now? Nowhere. But somewhere—maybe somewhere only Jeb could see—glass milk bottles were exploding on a stoop. Mosquitoes were making straight for a bloody head wound. Pork chops were frying, burning, blackening beyond recognition. Or, Jeb asked himself in half-consciousness, were those pork chops his very own skin?

The weakness in Priscilla's patella joints didn't go away. She craned her neck to study the terrain, expecting to see a wolf. She couldn't hear very well anymore, was the trouble, but she felt something nearby make a deep, baleful sound—a sound a younger person could identify, she thought bitterly. Priscilla knew she'd forgotten things. She didn't know what they were, or else they wouldn't have been forgotten, but she knew there were parts of her life she'd never get back, parts she could use if she still had them. What did a quiet ambush sound like? How could one tell it was coming? What, for instance, had Priscilla done immediately after she'd heard a strange cough in her kitchen that time? Had she rattled the house keys, or simply fled? She knew she'd got away without a scratch and with the loss of only a few ceramics, but what had she done to make that happen? What are the things a person needs to know to stay alive?

Jeb's pain was becoming clear to him. It was easier now to understand that the past lived in one place, and the stabbing in his skull lived in the present. Same address, different time. "Don't come back for me," Jeb said. "Just go. I don't need you anyway." Had he ever said *that* before? Did it matter? Jeb had reached his unhappy ending. Death was going to hurt after all, and he wanted no one else to be a part of it. "Go," Jeb said. "And don't come to my funeral."

He was babbling again, Priscilla thought, but this time she didn't absorb it. She'd located the danger, or at least its direction. It came from the flatland, from the desert itself. She could see only slightly better than she could hear, but the heat waves looked to be combining into one form, coming straight for them to take them away. Them? Maybe just Jeb. She'd never pictured them going out like this, as she'd said, but the menace still scared her. It felt exactly appropriate. This was how it would happen. She would lose Jeb to an intangible life form carrying him to another world. She remembered the sign of the cross she'd made at Tommy's communion, but didn't bother to signal that Trinity again. The flatland had declared it too late for crosses.

A crackle rang out. Jeb's head lifted up. His chest leaned forward.

"It's over," said Jeb. "All over now. So OK, I'll be seeing you sometime then."

"I love you," Priscilla said. "That's what this is. Nothing else."

"It's all right. It's an all right funeral. Just don't invite too many cousins."

"No cousins. I promise."

"NOT MUCH OF A CANYON," Jeb said, hours later, standing over the guardrail, recovered.

"I think it's darling," Priscilla said.

Jeb tried to recall what it had been like, lying on the ground, there and not, a park ranger staring down at him. "Were we fighting before?"

"Beats the hell out of me."

He did try, but Jeb couldn't remember either. That scene had already gone. "Because I love you tons. I don't think I said that. I love you tons." Jeb reconsidered the view. "Even if this isn't much of a canyon."

Priscilla tracked the stream of water grooving its way through the giant crags, and swore once again that she saw metal in the rocks. The mountains had reemerged—not the Rockies, she knew, but the peaks before her went beyond hills.

"What are you even looking at?" she said. "I think it's darling." ◇

Uncharted

Richard Weiss

A north-east wind gusts hard for days,
blows our island farther out to sea
as waves breach sea walls,
wash roads, salt an angry sky.

We hunker down in twilight,
the Gay Head Light
piercing rain-pearled windows,
his shadowed face.

Slickered shapes push past the door,
their wind-blown words strung out behind.
The storm finds every crack
and fills his room.

He holds me loosely,
his arm across my breasts.
Our voices rise and fall,
imitate the wind.

Content in our alignment I would have
stayed until the storm had withered
yet to sit is not his speed
and succumbing to his restless urge,

he rises to leave me foundering
in the slipstream of his impatience,
uncertain of how we arrived so quickly
at this uncharted place. ◇

Yellow Flowers

Adapted from a talk given by the author

Susan Hunt Babinski

NOVEMBER 11, 2013 WAS THE TWENTIETH ANNIVERSARY OF the dedication of the Women's Memorial Statue honoring American women who served during the Vietnam War. I was one of them and had volunteered to be one of the speakers at the gathering. I had come a long way from the days when I did not often share my feelings or my status as a veteran. I remember a dinner party a few years after coming back at which a female professor spoke of how awful and difficult it was having all "these crazy Nam veterans in her classes."

I felt hurt and angry and said, "Oh? I'm a veteran."

All were shocked and asked me what I did there. I told them that I had been a nurse. The woman who had complained said dismissively, "Oh, that doesn't count; you're not really a vet."

I said not one more word on the subject.

But at the 20th Anniversary of the dedication of the Women's Memorial Statue, located near the Vietnam Wall, I spoke openly of personal traumas experienced in Vietnam, as well as personal growth, and my eternal gratitude to Colonel Annie Ruth Graham, who, from 1967 to 1968, was our Chief Nurse at the 91st Evacuation Hospital, the first civilian war-casualty hospital run by the US Army.

IN 1965 A MILITARY RECRUITER CAME TO SPEAK to the nursing students at Rhode Island Hospital School of Nursing, where a friend, Joan

Prendergast, and I were in our second year. After hearing his talk, we signed up for the Army Nurse Corps as privates. We got a stipend and our tuition paid our final year of school. Upon graduation, and after passing the nursing licensing exam in 1966, we became lieutenants under a "buddy system" that allowed us to choose our first assignment after basic training in Texas.

We chose Denver, Colorado, mostly because I wanted to ski. At Fitzsimons General Army Hospital, I requested and was assigned for a year to work on the pediatric unit with children of military personnel. Then, in June 1967, at age twenty-two, we both volunteered for Vietnam, and I requested pediatrics. I was told there might not be such a unit available but they would put in my request when they submitted our papers. I heard later that enough nurses volunteered for Vietnam that no one had to be drafted to go.

The hospital, which was located about 250 miles north of Saigon, along the coast of the South China Sea, had a front and back ramp, consisting of open cement walkways with wooden rails on the sides and a tin roof that covered it. During the monsoon season we were all grateful for the roof that kept us a little drier.

The front ramp was next to the helicopter unit and landing pad, where casualties were brought to the hospital. On that ramp were windowless metal buildings that housed the Emergency Room, the Operating Room, the Pre-op/Post-op Unit, and the Medical Intensive Care Unit. Only the front buildings had air conditioning, flushing toilets, and mostly GI patients as battles heated up in the area. The separateness of each unit allowed for maximum security from bomb attacks and made transport out easier. Allegedly, the entire hospital could be evacuated within twenty-four hours if there were a mortar attack.

Pediatrics, where I worked for eight months of my one-year tour in Nam, was located on the more primitive back ramp where there were about eight separate buildings. One unit held injured Prisoners of War, completely surrounded by a barbed wire fence. There was also a women's unit. The other units held medical and surgical units, all mainly filled with Vietnamese patients. Each unit consisted of a wooden barracks with a tin roof and small burlap windows near the roof. No sunlight could get in, but hopefully no shrapnel either. Sand bags were stacked up outside all buildings and underground emergency shelter bunkers were located outside some units, including the pediatric ward. There was electricity, including electric fans that were rarely turned on as it made the heat, which reached 115 degrees and sometimes higher, even more unbearable. Corpsmen lugged in pails of water from a faucet behind the barracks because there was no running water inside. That meant no toilets. Instead there was a "honey bucket" where bedpans were emptied, dragged outside by the corpsman at the end of the shift.

Captain Susie Israel, my Head Nurse in pediatrics, was warm, welcoming, and cordial to all. The majority of the children were between six and ten years old, although there was the occasional infant and teen. During quieter times, MEDCAP (Medical Civil Action Program) missions at the hospital sometimes came back with children to have their cleft palates and strictures, such as happen with scarring and the like, repaired surgically. It also helped the children with deformities regain use of arms, hands, and legs, and provide some young doctors a chance to do the kind of surgery they might perform in the United States someday. The kids all looked dejected. Only one twelve-year-old girl had visitors. Special Forces personnel occasionally flew her parents in from their remote village. If the other children had living relatives, they were lost to them. When the war heated up, especially after the Tet Offensives, it was too busy to provide "elective" surgery and too dangerous for flights to distant villages to provide care.

The children lay in cots or on beds with thin mattresses. They had all sorts of war injuries—mainly from grenades and land mines—an eye missing, a hand gone, wounds so badly infected that maggots were left in to help debride the injuries. One little boy had his penis shot off and a young girl had been napalmed. Medical illnesses like dysentery or malaria were common.

There was no entertainment for these children—no toys, music, radio, visitors—nothing, that is, until Charlie, the corpsman, and I started singing to them as we cleaned them and changed their dressings. Those who could follow us around did and phonetically joined us in singing songs like the Mamas and the Papas' "Monday, Monday" and the Beatles' "When I'm 64." They loved singing, and being together provided a happy diversion for us all. The children tried to teach me some Vietnamese songs and laughed at my feeble attempts. I did learn a few Vietnamese phrases that were helpful, like "Pain?" or "Come here." We shared magazines sent to us from the States, and the preteens bonded over the magazine photos.

I affectionately called one teen "Chubby Bunny." She was slightly older and larger than the others, and left the hospital after a short time. When I saw her next, she was running down a ramp yelling "Susie, Susie" and pointing to herself, "Chubby Bunny, Chubby Bunny!" Only she wasn't chubby any more. I never did find out why she had lost so much weight. At that moment, Colonel Graham had been in the midst of lecturing me for the umpteenth time about my uniform.

"You must wear your fatigue cap."

I hated wearing the cap because it was hot and unattractive. When Colonel Graham saw this young teen's excitement, she just smiled and walked away.

On one occasion, we had a terrible typhoon strike us. The burlap windows were torn out, water got in, and the tin roof started banging, so the corpsman and I ran out and threw sandbags—OK, I handed them to him and he threw them—on the tin roof to keep it from blowing away. We were cold, muddy, and drenched. The kids were cold, wet, and scared and some had gotten in bed with others for comfort and warmth. We tore the plastic wrappings off our much-coveted and limited supplies to cover casts and big dressings from the muddy rain coming in.

As the storm started to wane, I told the corpsman to get a coffee urn and supplies from the mess hall next door. We made coffee, added a teaspoon or two of dry milk and maybe ten teaspoons of sugar per cup, and gave it to the children, who loved the sweet, warm taste. Soon after, the unit commander made rounds to see how the staff and patients had fared. He asked what the kids were drinking, and when I told him he said, "Lieutenant, don't you know that coffee isn't good for kids?"

I lost it! I shouted, "There are a lot of things that aren't good for kids! Wars, losing an arm, eye, or part of a leg, losing your parents, your village, and everyone and everything you have ever known . . ."

I paused and he said, "Carry on Lieutenant," and left before he had no choice but to give me an official reprimand ("Article 15") or a further dressing down for being disrespectful.

During the Tet offensives we frequently had red alerts (flares) lighting the sky at night, meaning the enemy was within our perimeter and we had to wear helmets and flak jackets to work. When the sirens went off, with only a flashlight to see by, we had to bed the children down on the cement floor with mattresses covering them. It started happening so regularly that we started bedding them down before the alert so we could make them more comfortable.

The whole hospital staff was devastated when we heard one of our MedEvac helicopters had gone for a pickup and never returned. Joanie and I knew and felt close to this particular pilot and crew, but I didn't cry, as that seemed to mean they were dead and the thought was more than I could bear. Every time I heard a chopper, I prayed it was them. Their names are on the Wall in Washington, D.C., and I believe they are still listed as Missing in Action. To this day, I react physically when I hear the sound of a helicopter.

I went on a MEDCAP mission with a team that included Dave, a medical doctor I was dating. We went to a Montagnard village about thirty-five miles inland, a very geographically attractive area with beautiful flowers everywhere. I told Dave how much I missed flowers. There were none at the 91st. At his suggestion we dug up a beautiful plant with yellow bulbs and brought it back. Strapped to seats on the outside of the helicopter with its painted red cross, we flew out under the cover of darkness, with no lights on, but soon there was trouble. We heard shots and saw red tracer bullets aimed at us. Luckily, we made it back safely, but later we heard that the helicopter had been hit more than once.

We planted the flower in front of my sleeping quarters—one in a row of wooden barracks with burlap windows, where eight young nurses each had her own small room. I was teased about being like Lady Bird Johnson, beautifying the compound. Sometimes when I was on night duty, Colonel Graham made rounds and would stop to chat. She told me that Vietnam would be her last tour; she planned to retire to the hills of North Carolina to garden, which she loved.

While on pediatrics, I was at times sent to other units to help. That was where I met eighteen-year-old Johnny, wearing a Purple Heart medal on his pajamas. He had been shot but his wound wasn't as bad as some. He was up and about, often helping out by bringing urinals, water, and blankets to the others. He shared with me his background—he was a Midwest farm boy—and he talked about how proud his parents were going to be of his Purple Heart. A couple of months later, I saw Johnny again, happy and helpful as ever around the unit, now proudly wearing two Purple Hearts.

My pediatric Head Nurse's tour was up and she was replaced by a Head Nurse who told me it was unprofessional to sing and have all the children follow us around; it must stop immediately. I stopped and never sang again, and soon after I requested a transfer and was assigned to the Pre-op/Post-op Unit, which also included triage but that was never officially spoken about.

The war was heating up, and with so many casualties arriving, at times stretchers would be lined up outside the buildings, along the walkway ramp. It was there that I saw Johnny and ran over and knelt beside him to offer support. He didn't respond and had an empty stare. I was very upset. The staff reassured me that his wound wasn't so bad. He'd make it. I shook my head. Dave came at the end of my shift that day. I was pleased but asked him why as he had never done that before. He told me Joanie was worried about me and he mentioned Johnny. I lost it and cried and cried for perhaps the first and only time in Nam. Without a word, Dave just held me.

Johnny died several days later, of pneumonia they said, but I didn't believe them. He died before we got him. He had seen too much, done too much, and couldn't go on. I hoped Johnny's family would be as proud of his Purple Hearts as Johnny had been.

I felt really down and then a minor miracle happened. I had neither energy nor will to water my much-loved yellow flower, and yet it survived and looked beautiful. I began thinking about it during my shifts, and would be renewed every time I saw it. Months later I learned from one of the nurses that Colonel Graham had been lugging a pail of water over and watering the plant daily. I believe she saved more than the flower.

That was her last garden. I heard several years later that she had died in Vietnam of medical issues; her name is on the Wall. Until writing this, I hadn't consciously realized the connection, but when I go to the Vietnam Wall I always lay a yellow flower where Colonel Annie Graham's name is engraved.

WHILE IN NAM, I often thought of those young men and children who didn't have a chance. I had the gift of life and I wanted to make the most of it. I made up my mind that I would go to school when I returned home. This was surprising as I never was much of a student. No playing "flower child hippie" for me. In fact, Major Pat Gorman, Joanie's Head Nurse, proctored the exams I took while in Nam so I could get some college credits for my nursing school education.

Coming home from Nam, I was the only female veteran aboard the plane on the filled-to-capacity flight. The first day back, I tried to resign my commission. The women in the office processing my return were shocked at my request. They convinced me to wait a couple of weeks until they could process my request for the GI bill before resigning. Saddened, I went to the ladies' room in tears. One of the women processing my papers discreetly followed me in, I noticed, but neither of us said anything.

After returning, I decided I wanted to provide emotional care for children and their families in an inner city pediatrics medical intensive care unit. I felt the need to give back. I got my BS in nursing and my MA as a clinical specialist in child and adolescent psychiatric nursing. I fell in love and married my husband, and we had a wonderful son, who is now grown and has a family of his own.

I did not share my feelings or my status as a veteran often, until I was in a sensitivity training group in graduate school at NYU, led by Susie Lego, a well-known psychiatric nurse group therapist. I broke down and cried as I told others of my Vietnam experiences.

I worked in the community division of the Bronx Children's Psychiatric Center in the South Bronx and found the work so compelling that I stayed for twenty-eight years. During that time, in addition to working, I returned to university to get my doctorate in psychology. My dissertation, finished in 1996, was a qualitative study of six female Vietnam veteran nurses: *Did We Have to Wait Twenty-five Years to Weep in Front of a Monument?* I dedicated my dissertation to Colonel Graham.

Qualitative research studies required that a small group of graduate students get together and discuss our works in progress. To this day, my group continues to meet monthly and provides major support for me as I continue to talk and write about my experiences in Vietnam.

At the Women's Memorial Statue dedication on November 2, 1993, I saw people I had last seen twenty-five years earlier. We cried, hugged, and told stories that some had never until that moment shared with anyone since returning from Nam.

I looked forward to seeing Captain Susie Israel, my beloved Head Nurse from pediatrics. It turned out that she had died of cancer several months before the dedication. There was a letter from her at the statue, saying how proud she was of the monument and how sorry she was that she couldn't be at the dedication.

We had been told that the city of Tuy Hoa and the 91st were both declared Agent Orange Centers and that we'd been exposed. Some of the nurses at the dedication spoke of staff they knew who had died young of cancer. A fair number in our small gathering spoke of having given birth to developmentally delayed and disabled children. Some suffered from amoebic dysentery as well as from what was called the "Vietnamese time bomb," a serious pneumonia that often developed years after a person was originally infected. There are no Purple Hearts for medical illnesses.

At the dedication, a man in a motorized wheelchair, who had received devastating injuries in Nam, came over with his wife. He told me he just wanted to thank me and all the nurses who served. He was glad to be alive and grateful to us for our help. With tears, I thanked him and gave him a long hug. I was both proud and sad to be a veteran.

After my talk at the twentieth anniversary of the Women's Memorial Statue, my nurse veteran friends, some in tears, hugged me and soon we all left the Women's Statue and walked towards the Wall. I felt so sad. It would be the first time that I would not be leaving a flower for Colonel Graham.

For several days, I had tried to buy flowers, even if not yellow ones. I went to a number of hotels and flower shops over the weekend but none were open. After speaking with the concierge in my hotel, I took the metro to a market place where he told me I would find flowers to buy. The shop was under another hotel and was open but no flowers were available. I felt frustrated.

Arriving at the Nam Wall, I checked at a nearby kiosk, but no flowers. As we were walking along the Wall, a young Cub Scout came up to us and handed me a single yellow rose. My friends gasped as I took it and, in tears, thanked my young benefactor. We all hugged, understanding that this was more than a mere coincidence. Other Cub Scouts then came and handed a single flower to each of the other nurses. I noticed no other yellow flower. I held the rose close and thought of Colonel Graham. By giving me this flower, the Scout did what Colonel Graham had done so many years ago. I placed the flower below her name on the Wall and silently thanked her again.

The Vietnam Women's Memorial Statue acknowledges women's status in war and by its very existence provides support. We never totally get over trauma, but we can learn from it and move forward, and with support lead a good and productive life. ◇

Manitoba

William A. Greenfield

I saw it snow
in early June on Lake Kississing.
I was alone but I was not
lonely,
as I might be at rush hour
on the IRT. The loons dove
swiftly at my approach and I
searched the dark waters,
wondering where they would
reappear and sing to me again.
Nearly midnight and I could
still see the black worm-earth
that coated my fingertips.

The echoes were entertaining
but somehow thoughtless,
as if I were speaking loud
profanities at the public library.
A single beacon of light from
miles
away guides me home, crude
and simple as it may be.
I thought that it would not
be so terrible to die here.
And when I doused the
guiding flame, the jewels
of Orion were never
so wondrous. ◇

The Ever Shrinking Universe

William A. Greenfield

So I come padding out of the bedroom
in manly slippers and she says "Yo Baby."
We do this silly fist bump thing and
I ask,
"Djeet?" She says "Cheerios."
There's
much to do, so we plan.
She'll drive down
and I'll drive back.
Now we're outside
Hallmark
eating marshmallow Santas and
she asks why we still laugh. I
explain
that the world gets smaller
everyday.
There is no room left

for suicide bombers,
federal deficits,
troubled souls.
She remembers
that we have to
get a card and send money
to the paperboy, but I put that
thought
behind me because I
can't find my way out
of J.C. Penny's.
She laughs those pathetic
tears and
takes my hand. "Well," I say,
"the store is just too big." So, we shrink
down, our world a snow globe. Shaken,
it's nothing but a swirl of flakes. Wound up,
we hear nothing but a twinkle
of mirth. ◇

We Three Kings

Leon Marks

Will

THE THUNDERSTORM ARRIVED AT DUSK, POLITELY ESCORTED THE sun away, and left clouds and stars to battle for the night sky. They'd said it would be a monster, but its visit was uneventful. Now, Will's mind feels light and liberated, as if he could float skyward. But nothing up there interests him. No galaxy, inhabited or not, can tempt him away from an imminent encounter with Tom. He waits on the beach, gazing at the jetty, its boulders barely detectable in the dark.

He shares the entire beach with a dog with a limp. The white mongrel approaches him, rotates his rope-like tail, sniffs the sea air with pleasure, and circles around once, then again, as if unsettled by the presence of a taller-than-average human who stands watchful in the sand at night. A seagull calls from the ocean, and the dog answers with a single bark. Will romanticizes out of habit that the two creatures are talking about him, debating whether or not he should be trusted. (Of course they agree that he should.) The dog steps near the water, sniffs with great effort, then stretches his front paws forward into the sand, arches his back, and shakes from side to side. He scampers off with a jolly four-pawed gait, his limp now undetectable. Within seconds the tide's shadow engulfs the speck that remains of him.

"That's Fritz," Tom says. Will turns. Tom is wearing an over-sized down jacket, which hugs his chest in shiny green nylon.

"You came," Will says.

"He's hung around here for years," Tom continues. "Don't fall for the limping act. He does it for food. He spends a lot of time at my place because I've always got baloney. I'd offer you my coat, but if I catch a cold I could die. You have an immune system, so you get to freeze your ass off."

Will stares at last into Tom's green eyes, which shine to match his green coat. "I don't mind," Will says, unaware of his own shivering.

"You have a big head," Tom says.

Will doesn't respond, but the remark makes him feel suddenly warmer. He smiles, trying to keep it from becoming a grin. He doesn't want to fall so fast, even though he's survived for twenty-three years by listening to his feelings, and his feelings are telling him to run to Tom without delay. The night before, when they met on the steps of Phantom Pizza, Tom's first word to Will, in response to his flirtation, was "shoo."

"It's square too, like a concrete block," Tom says, cocking his head to the side and scanning Will's lower body, which fits snugly into navy-blue gym pants. "Kind of like your ass."

"Are you always this honest?"

"Withholding information prolongs agony."

"Is that the virus talking?"

"Mmmm," Tom hums, perhaps satisfied by the question. "Everything I say has a little bit of virus in it. It rides my bloodstream into my brain all day long. It pollutes me with evil thoughts."

"So here I stand with the Devil."

Tom smirks. He gazes at the yellow edge of the moon and says, "What happened with the storm? It was supposed to be a bad one."

"It lasted barely ten minutes," Will says. He leans against a pole to which a neglected Massachusetts state flag clings overhead. Flapping in the wind, he can make out the image of the Indian waving his bow and arrow. Cupid was an archer too. If his mother or sister were here, they'd yank him into a car and speed off, lecturing him about being naïve and melodramatic and exposing himself to certain heartbreak. He *will* ponder what he's getting into, but not tonight.

"You're a very sweet guy," Will says without a second's thought.

Tom turns away, disinterested in himself. "Okay."

It's just a word: *virus*. But it produces silent terror in people, especially mothers and sisters. Will's heard about viruses for a long time, this one in particular, but only now can he picture it, almost touch it, feel it heating up his own blood.

"I'm sorry you're sick."

Tom twists his upper lip as if nobody has ever said these words to him before.

"I still have my sight and my hearing. I can still swim."

"Count your blessings," Will says, wincing at his own words.

"Look," Tom says. Will follows him obediently to a stone bench planted deep in the earth at the rear edge of the beach. The moon isn't enough, so Tom pulls a flashlight from his pocket and shines it on the center of the bench. A tiny brass plaque screwed into the stone is inscribed with one word: "Fritz."

"He has his own bench?" Will asks.

"I got it for him," Tom says. "They installed all these things and sold the plaques to raise money for maintaining the beach."

Will can't help but laugh.

"It was a few hundred bucks, and they wouldn't let me leave the plaque blank," Tom says. "In two years, they'll rip it off and raise the price."

They turn to find Fritz emerging from the darkness and darting toward the bench. *His* bench. He sniffs it at both ends, then glances up at Tom. Will wishes the dog could know. He reaches down to stroke Fritz's ears, and feels a couple of tiny bumps, probably bug bites. Fritz thumps his tail on the sand.

"He doesn't have an owner?" Will asks.

"Not that anyone knows about."

"Then how do you know his name?"

"I gave it to him."

Tom's face disappears. Clouds have blocked the moonlight. Will imagines Tom's eyes gazing at him. They both remain silent for a moment, as if showing respect for the dark. Will hears Tom's breathing;

it sounds slightly labored. Then he feels a hand on his forearm. Tom has found him, and slides his grip down Will's forearm until their thumbs interlock. Tom shakes Will's hand, like a formal greeting, but he doesn't let go. They remain awkwardly attached, and Tom soon places his other hand on Will's back, a little clumsily as if drawn by tiny magnets.

The clouds retreat and Will catches a grin on Tom's lips. The Devil is bashful. They detach.

Tom takes off for the jetty, so Will follows. Tom hops onto the first boulder. Will can tell he's made this journey thousands of times because he barely looks down as he navigates away from shore and toward what feels like the middle of the ocean. Will slips between two sandy boulders. Tom snickers audibly without looking back. Even Fritz blazes past Will, his toenails clicking on each surface.

Minutes later, Tom comes to rest on a very specific pyramid-shaped rock. He lowers his body as Fritz takes a seat at his side. The dog pants beside his green-eyed friend, tail wagging, proud to have arrived so fast. Will is far behind, but he's not embarrassed. He smiles at his battle with the surfaces, frustrated but committed to leaping and lunging, till he reaches Tom's welcoming hands, which steady him as he sits. Neither man nor dog makes a sound until a seagull swoops down, provoking a bark from Fritz.

"You don't mind sitting here with me even though I'm sick?" Tom asks.

"You don't seem sick to me."

Will senses that Tom doesn't understand why some people find him attractive. His face is freckled, his hair is thinning, and his body is average, but Will already finds all other men unremarkable. Had Tom known this, he surely would have thought him idiotic.

"How'd you get it?" Will asks.

"Manuel Hernandez."

Will pushes gently. "Who's he?"

"Mannie. Ten years ago. We were nineteen, and he was a dumb punk. We were just fooling around, but shit happens. He's been riding a guilt trip ever since." Tom pulls a handkerchief from his nylon coat pocket and blows his nose without the slightest embarrassment. "He comes up here from New York once a month, cooks me dinner as if I'm already some kind of invalid. He tries to clean my place for me, takes my car for a tune-up. Thinks he's my best friend now, and I suppose he is."

The moon is naked now, deflecting the sun's rays onto the jetty at full force. They sit in silence, each finding his own stars above, and when the breeze becomes a powerful wind, they take each other's hands and move closer. Will's so cold that his chin vibrates and his teeth rattle like bouts of machine gun fire. He can't stop it, and might have felt scared if Tom weren't laughing. Tom pulls Will back against his chest and wraps both of them in his shiny down coat. And before the next star pops from infinity, his arms have engulfed Will from behind. Will turns to get warmer. Tom's a heavy breather, and Will likes that. He can hear his aliveness. Tom smiles, and Will savors that smile when he pulls their lips together.

As they hold each other, Fritz resumes his barking at the sea gulls overhead. Will has no way of knowing that before the year is out, he'll look back on this moment and remember the gulls, with their winged perspectives, and wonder if they had seen the tiny red speck on the back of Tom's neck, barely detectable for months to come, just below his hairline, slightly raised, the kind the doctors told him to check for regularly, the kind that was filled with Kaposi's sarcoma and could make forever come much too soon.

Tom

HIS MIND IS HOT, but his body is chilled. He looks down at the skinny arms at his sides, and twitches his fingers to prove he still can. He is tucked up to his chin in the blanket, the one with blue and purple paw prints. They want him to stay warm, even though the window is sealed tight and the snow falling outside will never get close to him, never again. His eyes focus on the yellow roses in the vase on his bureau. The mailman brought them yesterday.

He waits. Light creeps in from the window. He's silent and self-contained. Through the window he can see the brownstones across the street. He can't make out the bricks or mortar, just red blurs. His eyes are weaker now.

Where are they? Maybe he should call out. Then he remembers that he can't speak anymore. Maybe he can get something out. A groan or a whine.

His bathrobe is hanging on the door. Its plaid design is fading fast, just the way he likes it. He doubts he'll ever wear it again. It's a sorry old sight next to his bright orange sunset painting, the one he created to please Will, who gave him the easel and paints for his birthday because, "You make my world beautiful." Good God.

He hears a knock on the apartment door. He waits. It's Will. He hears the rustle of plastic shopping bags in the hallway. Back so soon from his errands? He must have forgotten his keys. Again. How does he get through each day, so absent-minded? Until recently, Tom had to remember an entire regimen of forty pills a day, but Will forgets his keys weekly. Maybe he forgets them on purpose as a strategy to come back home, usually carrying flowers or a card with a poem that's supposed to be profoundly moving. Tom hopes that someday Will will stop trying so hard, stop trying to make life meaningful. And here he is, poking his head in the bedroom door.

"Baby, look what I got for you!"

Tom doesn't want to expend the energy to look, so he keeps his eyes on Will's, waiting for the revelation.

"Blueberries. They were selling them next door."

Will's hand presents a yellow bowl bursting with little blue globes. They look plump and fresh.

"I'll crush them up if you want."

Tom blinks, but not a quick blink. A long tired blink. He isn't hungry, and why does Will have to talk to him like he's an infant?

Behind Will come Mannie and the nurse. They look ridiculously proud of the blueberries too. They surround him. Tom's eyes float slowly from one to the next to the next, landing, of course, on Will, who smiles wide again, squeezing out all his remaining happiness. Tom gazes at him, wishing he too could smile, but his lips are a lost cause. The bowl is placed on his belly. Will selects a berry and holds it up to his face.

"Isn't this a gorgeous one?"

Tom nods slightly, but everyone looks so wanting of acknowledgment that he can't just nod once, but three times, and with clear purpose. To thank them.

Shit. It's coming. The blueberries spill out of the bowl and onto the sheet. His throat can still form sounds of warning.

"Aaaaahhhhh."

"What is it, baby?" Will says. "You have to shit?"

A fast, yet orderly, scrambling ensues. Mannie directs the nurse outside as he hands Will the pan. Will and Mannie lean Tom on his side. Mannie glances quickly at Will, but not to make him self-conscious as he works. Will unbuttons the shorts, slides the pan underneath as far as he can.

"Aaaaahhhhh."

Tom whimpers, his voice muffled by the pillow. Then he begins to cry. He doesn't know why. When it's all out, he sighs. He feels Will begin wiping. With each stroke, Tom whimpers again. He's glad the worst is over. But it isn't. More is coming now.

"Aaaaahhhhh."

"It's okay," Will says. "Let it out."

Will stands up tall and waits. Tom feels it oozing out like toothpaste. They must be able to see the gash on his lower back where the mattress has bitten a chunk from his flesh. He feels Will place a towel over the open sore to protect it from shit. Tom's hand clutches the pillow like it's a body. He can't stop crying, but nobody can hear him anyway.

"Is that it?" Will asks.

Tom's asshole feels raw, and with each stroke of the wet towel he cries out a little louder. When it's clean and powdered, Will pauses and caresses Tom's sweaty head. His hair is falling off like dust now.

"Give me one," Will commands, so Mannie scratches the package open and hands him a diaper. It's the first time. They all knew this was inevitable. They lift his legs.

"Aaaaahhhhh."

When the position is just right, they place him back down. Tom is tired now, and tries hard not to look angry. His pained eyes glance about the room again. They come to rest on Mannie. He's sweating and looks sexy in his tank top. Then they find Will. He's sweating too, and wiping his hands with a towel. He stares down at Tom and sticks out his tongue playfully.

Tom stretches his fingers and feels the plastic around his waist. It crinkles. He feels the tape fastener. The nurse re-enters and they all stare, waiting for his reaction. He knows that this way is easier for them, so he isn't angry. He accepts it. He doesn't quite smile, but rests his eyes in peace. Will leaves, followed by the nurse. Mannie stays behind. Tom knows that out in the hallway Will is crying. It's okay. It must be painful to see someone you love in diapers. But it's for the best, and they're pretty comfortable. He tugs at the Velcro strip and listens to the sound of attachment, detachment, attachment, detachment, until he falls into a beautiful sleep.

TOM WAKES UP and hears snoring from the bed next to him, where he used to sleep before this hospital contraption. It's Will. He's curled up in a ball with his big head buried in the pillow, a tiny puddle of drool just beneath his lips, just as there's been every night for the past month. Even in the hospital, Will could curl up on the cot and whisper goodnight and within ten seconds he'd be snoring and drooling. This makes Tom happy, that he can still sleep soundly through the night. Sometimes at three in the morning Tom cries out for the bedpan, and Manuel runs in from the other room in his underwear, his hair tousled beyond recognition, his eyes caked with sleepy crust. But Will never rises unless the commotion escalates to a bed change or something more alarming.

Will isn't alone in the bed tonight. His head is cradled by someone's hand. A hand more affectionate than a friend's. Tom pans his glance farther and sees that it's Mannie. He too is sleeping peacefully, his tan face buried in Will's neck and his thick body swirled alongside Will's like a coat. His other hand rests across his chest, grasping for more than just Will's flesh, for something deep inside him that isn't being well served by a crippled husband.

Tom's emotionless for a moment, and blinks hard to shake the image. But every time he opens his eyes, the caressing hands are still there and Will's snoring sounds more peaceful and he seems to be smiling in his sleep. Tom closes his eyes one last time, hoping the scene will vanish, but instead he senses something new. Someone's staring back at him. It's Mannie. He's woken up and his tired brown eyes are frozen on Tom's face. He waits, as if unsure if Tom's vision is working. He doesn't know if he should move his hand, or say something, so he lowers his head and feigns sleep.

Tom isn't content to play along. He begins to moan. He can't form words but can still convey emotions, even uncertain ones. These sounds make Manuel remove himself at once from the bed and stand by the wall.

Will rises and wipes away his threads of drool. He looks concerned by the expression on Tom's face. He takes Tom's quaking hand, which Tom tries with all his strength to pull away. Will looks tired and pale. He tries to comfort Tom with words, but only a few. Words lack power now. "It's okay. It was just a dream."

Was it? Tom's scalp is sweaty beneath his remaining tufts of hair. Sweat and tears combine so that neither matters. Will kisses his forehead again. He holds his hand tightly, trying to break through the disease wall. *I love you.* He wants Tom to forget everything else. Everything that's not here in this bed right now. So Tom tries. But Will is leaning on his chest, his sores, so Tom opens his eyes wide. Will pulls back and stands up. He reaches down to hold Tom's toe under the sheet. He can't possibly hurt the toe.

Tom is calmer now, his eyes open wider. He thinks about the situation. He knows that Will is loyal and that Mannie is lonely. He knows that sleep stirs the imagination, and imagination stirs the soul. He knows these things, but he is still crippled and melting into his bed, melting away from all of them. He can't speak. He can barely move. Their lips haven't touched for weeks.

"What is it, baby?" Will asks.

Tom struggles to form a look. Something like a smile. He even chuckles, but without sound.

"What is it?" Will happily moves in closer.

Tom makes a more distinct sound. "Cuuuuhhh . . . "

"What? Try again. Go as slow as you want."

"Cuuuuhhh . . . "

"You want me to come? You want me to come to you?"

Will leans in, and Tom tries to shine hopeful eyes.

"What is it?" Will asks.

Tom does it. He puckers. It's slight, but clearly a pucker, ready for a kiss. His fever blisters are clogged and dried with blood and blueberry stains. He hopes the pink of his lips is still visible somewhere, maybe in the corners. Will bends down and kisses him, not just the pink, but everywhere. He smiles wide as he kisses, and when he pulls away:

"Cuuuuhhhh . . . "

So Will's lips fall into Tom's again. He wraps his clean healthy lips around the blisters and the blood and the blueberries. Tom suckles with all his remaining strength. It will be the kiss that has to stay with Will forever. A tear, filled not with despair but with love, falls from Will's eye and drops right into Tom's. Will smiles at the sight of it.

For the briefest moment, Tom looks at Mannie in the corner, and watches as another tear forms. It clings to Mannie's eye with nowhere to go.

Manuel

THE NEXT DAY IS DECEMBER 31ST. Manuel places a paper horn on Tom's nightstand; they'll celebrate at midnight. Tom's stare follows Manuel's every move, from one side of the bed to the other, where Manuel turns a metal crank to raise the hospital bed six inches or so. Normally Manuel would narrate his actions—*I'm just going to raise you up a bit, Tomás, está bien?*—but this morning he refrains. The sound of his voice might anger Tom. He didn't mean to borrow his husband last night, but for the first time he saw Will as something other than *Tom's husband.* Will has such a talent for love. It fills this bedroom; all the visitors have noticed. One of the nurses commented that the apartment smells of love. This is the allure of Will, the light that shines from his heart and pulls people in like eager children.

Still, Manuel is angry at himself. He cannot be the husband. He must only be an object in the room. In this room, and in every room. He is toxic, and no longer possesses the faith that a man must possess in order to love someone. He did once. But now his affections can only lead to suffering. Love as the opposite of life.

He sprays down the nearby bookshelf with disinfectant, then organizes the medications. He counts the pill bottles—*dos, cuatro, seis, ocho, diez, doce*—lining them up like soldiers. He rolls up a plastic baggy holding crushed powder. He considers tossing it in the garbage pail, but what if a single grain of that powder will make the difference? He stacks the fresh diapers in the corner and grabs a napkin to clean the lip of the morphine bottle. That's when he hears the snort behind him. Asleep already? He turns to face Tom's stoic glance. His eyes are frozen attentively as he inhales again. The snort was a form of communication. Manuel's fingers rest on the morphine. He takes the bottle in his hand and leans down to stare into Tom's eyes. They are dark yellow with the tiniest glint of green. They look almost translucent, as if coated with some sticky substance waiting to glue them shut for good.

An hour ago, Manuel stood in the kitchen with Will, looking over the paperwork shared among the visiting nurses, adjusting to words like *final stage, dementia, stop all meds*. Neither of them said a word. Manuel made scrambled eggs and toast with jam. He served Will on a Styrofoam plate with a Christmas tree design, which he'd found in the dusty cabinet above the stove. Then Will went to the living room, where he turned the TV to the music channel. A slow jazz piece: piano and saxophone. Then Will grabbed his jacket and left. "Going for a walk," he muttered on his way out.

"*Tiene dolor?*" Manuel asks Tom quietly. "Do you need some?"

He knows there will be no audible response. He removes the cap from the bottle, inserts the plastic dispenser, and sucks up the bright red liquid. He places the dispenser tip in the corner of Tom's mouth and slowly releases it. As the medicine finds its way to Tom's brain, the two men don't take their eyes off each other. It's been almost ten years; they don't need language anymore. The dispenser is their final partnership.

The plastic dispenser, drained by now of its nourishment, rests against Tom's lips. Manuel asks, "*Un otro?*" If Tom could nod, he would.

Manuel is certain of that. So, with their glances still affixed, Manuel replenishes the dispenser and slides it back into Tom's mouth. Even through the yellow film coating his corneas, Tom's eyes are grateful. Manuel is certain of that too.

"Un otro?" Manuel says, quieter this time.

ON NEW YEAR'S DAY, Tom's body is gone. The radiator is relentless, so the apartment is much too warm. Manuel lies back on the hospital bed, massaging the crank that once raised his friend's head so that he would have a more pleasant view of his little room in the world. His tank top is soaked in sweat, but he's showered so there should be no odor. He's very tired, and he feels unhealthy. Like his mind has left his ugly, stale body behind to grieve. His hair is long and messy. His face is unshaven and feels plump with the disease of grief.

He twists the crank until the bed is at sixty degrees. He looks at the pillow and recalls the head that once made its home there. He can still see the imprint. As wind begins to howl and snow lands on the earth, Manuel lies back on the bed and rests his head exactly where Tom did. He sees the flannel robe hanging from its hook. The yellow roses on the bureau. The television set, which hasn't been turned on for weeks. The sunset painting with Tom's tiny signature. He closes his eyes and rests.

"You okay?"

Will stands in the bedroom door with a mop in his hand. Manuel has never seen Will clean before, but he's never watched his best friend carried out in a body bag before either.

"Sí," Manuel says. He sits up.

"You should sleep," Will says.

"No need for sleep."

"Want to help me clean?"

"Sure," Manuel says, feeling stupid. He stands up. Out of the corner of his eye he sees movement outside. When he looks, he has to squint to identify the source: a sea gull on the windowsill. It hops from one foot to the other on the ice, the way humans hop on hot sand. Its beady black eyes dart from side to side, inspecting the bedroom's contents as if on a mission. Manuel leaps to the window and waves the gull away.

Will approaches and faces him. He drops the mop. Manuel sees despair in his eyes. The two men embrace, like the entire world has died. Will shudders and begins to cry. Manuel feels Will's love spilling into him. *Tom's husband.* This is the love that Manuel might have bottled for himself for weeks, months, since Tom became bed-ridden, since Will fell apart.

As Will's tears leak from his eyes, that familiar rhythm pokes at Manuel's heart, the little hammer that pounds noiselessly whenever someone makes him feel alive. It's the gift that Tom gave him many years ago. It means to step away.

It's possible that Tom wanted Mannie to be with Will. That he resigned himself to the idea that his two best friends might end up together. He served his purpose as the bridge between their two lives. It's quite possible Tom thought that.

Manuel unties his arms from Will and steps away. He exits through the bedroom door and doesn't turn back. He raises his head high, content to have borne witness. ◇

March Madness on Gilmore Court

Bonnie Jill Emanuel

Sliding down the kitchen floor
with my brain in an ice bucket,
I'm hung over and kissing a pineapple
while my sons fling forks at the dishwasher
and yell in Nigerian tongue
about free throws, Victor Oladipo
and other things I don't know.
They toast the toast and juice the juice
and dribble out the door
giving me some beautiful room
to spread out on the island
in the middle of the kitchen.
To twist off my corneas
and lock them in a jar of Advil and a cucumber,
my head on thesaurus,
legs sprawled, knees bent, feet
dangling down down
down to the foam and the Seychelle,
school of electric centipedes,
the monsoon.

With my whole self
in a certified fair trade dream-come-true
Whole Foods poison star emulsion scrub,
my jaw is bloodied,
my thigh seared.
I don't know how—
but I somehow crawl my way back,
find a pencil, fill out a bracket
like I promised
before the boys and the sun
bounce back in. ◇

Casting Cordelia

Katharine Long

(A drama classroom at a public high school. Posters of past productions decorate the wall, and clearly, at this school, Shakespeare rules. The reason for this is Mr. Aldridge, a dignified man of sixty-plus years, who sits at his desk, trying to concentrate. A blurred face appears behind the door's thick glass transom. The doorknob turns. Nancy, sixteen, peeks her head in.)

NANCY

Peek-a-boo.

(He ignores her. She sneaks up behind him and covers his eyes.)

Guess who?

ALDRIDGE

Nancy. Stop that. You're smudging my glasses.

(He pulls free, extracts his handkerchief and wipes her touch from his lenses.)

NANCY

Sorry.

ALDRIDGE

You may have even damaged the frames.

NANCY

Geez. Someone's cranky.

(Aldridge puts on his glasses and sees that Nancy has planted herself at a desk and is settling in as if this were her second home.)

ALDRIDGE

Not today. Remove yourself, please. I have a great deal of work to do—

NANCY

And I have a math test next period. I promise not to bother you.

ALDRIDGE

You never keep your word. Go to the library.

(The sound of approaching footsteps accompanied by garbled, static instructions sprouting from a police radio. Nancy and Aldridge remain motionless, listening intently.
Each breathes a sigh of relief when the footsteps pass the classroom and fade in the distance.)

NANCY

Have you seen those cops in the hallway? Something's going on. Maybe it's another bomb scare. Geez, wouldn't that be great? Kiss the afternoon good-bye.

ALDRIDGE

It's not a bomb scare, Nancy.

NANCY

DANG! I'm doomed. Unless . . . hey you could write me a note. Yeah. Just tell Ms. Corvin I can't take the test because . . . you need me in Drama Club.

ALDRIDGE

No.

NANCY

Oh come on. You don't have to get specific. Just say it's urgent and unavoidable. We're doing KING LEAR for Pete's sake! That's a lot more important than . . . whatever it is we're doing in math. Don't tell her that. Just say you need me to help you prepare for today's rehearsal.

ALDRIDGE

Today's rehearsal has been cancelled.

NANCY

Why?

ALDRIDGE

Valerie Golden has disappeared.

NANCY

Oh.

(Nancy opens her notebook and pretends to study.)

ALDRIDGE

She never came home from rehearsal. Her parents are very concerned. They called me last night. They didn't call you?

NANCY

Why would they call me?

ALDRIDGE

You're a member of the cast.

NANCY

That doesn't mean I know where people go after rehearsal. It's not as if they tell me their plans or invite me to go with them.

ALDRIDGE

Did Valerie have plans after rehearsal?

NANCY

I don't know! How would I know? Geez.

(Returning to her math notes.)

You might want to ask her friends. She does have friends, you know.

ALDRIDGE

You're not one of them?

NANCY

No! You know that. Did she invite me to her Bat Mitzvah? Did she invite me to her Sweet Sixteen? Not that I care!!!

(She stabs her notebook repeatedly with her pencil.)

ALDRIDGE

Nancy!

(His voice catches her before she can do more damage.)

Inappropriate behavior—such as that—can be avoided if you just take a moment to reflect.

(She watches him, imitating his posture and facial expressions.)

What are you doing?

NANCY

I'm reflecting. You're worried. I should be worried too.

ALDRIDGE

Those are my feelings. Surely you have feelings of your own.

NANCY

Of course I do.

(She crosses to the window, dramatically.)

Wherever could Valerie be? I hope she's all right. What if she's not?

(Fighting back tears.)

Who will play Cordelia?

ALDRIDGE

Now that seems a bit, artificial. Just find your center—

(He taps his solar plexus. Nancy does the same. They face each other. She closes her eyes, following instructions she knows by heart.)

That's right. Breathe.

(Together they take a deep breath.)

ALDRIDGE

Exhale. Now tap the truth.

(When her eyes snap open, she seems quite genuine.)

NANCY

So . . . wow. She didn't come home?

ALDRIDGE

Better.

(Pleased, she applauds herself and returns to her seat.)

No, she didn't come home and she can't be reached. Valerie has either turned her phone off—

NANCY

Or someone has turned it off for her.

(Aware that she's alarmed him.)

Or . . . maybe it's the batteries. And who thinks to bring a charger? I don't. I don't think we should get all worked up about this. Look at you. Turn that frown upside down.

ALDRIDGE

Nancy, this is quite serious.

NANCY

Maybe. Maybe not. Maybe she's off having fun somewhere and just didn't think to call. I've done that.

ALDRIDGE

That is not how Valerie would behave.

NANCY

Sorry. Geez. For a second there, I forgot she was perfect.

ALDRIDGE

Perhaps not perfect, but certainly responsible. The idea of running off, without telling her parents—on a school night—

NANCY

You know how many times I've done that?

ALDRIDGE

You are not Valerie Golden!

NANCY

Right. I bet if I disappeared—I wouldn't even be missed.

(She waits for him to reassure her. He doesn't.)

Would you miss me, Mr. Aldridge, if I disappeared?

ALDRIDGE
(He wouldn't.)

Yes, of course I would.

(Nancy returns to her math notes.)

NANCY

No one else would. Ms. Corvin wouldn't. She hates me. And don't get me started on Mr. Rector, who I call Mr. Rectum—but not to his face. To his face—I couldn't be sweeter. That's how I am with everyone. But no one's that way with me. Except you. You get me. Don't you, Mr. Aldridge?

(He appears lost in thought.)

Mr. Aldridge?

ALDRIDGE

Oh, forgive me. I was just thinking . . .

NANCY

About Valerie?

ALDRIDGE

Such a lovely girl. So kind—so honest—

NANCY

—so right for Cordelia.

ALDRIDGE

Yes.

NANCY

So am I. I'm all those things. But you wouldn't know 'cause you wouldn't let me audition.

ALDRIDGE

You're not suited for Cordelia. We've discussed this, Nancy . . .

NANCY

But that's the part I want to play . . .

ALDRIDGE

And I want you to focus on the part you are best suited for.

NANCY

Gonorrhea!

ALDRIDGE

Goneril. It's a fine part. It's a larger role—

NANCY

Everyone hates Goneril. I want to play the character everyone loves.

ALDRIDGE

That part's been cast.

NANCY

With Valerie. Perfect Valerie. Perfect for the part, Valerie. Valerie, Valerie, Valerie.

ALDRIDGE

Enough!

(This subdues her momentarily.)

NANCY

I just don't think it's fair.

ALDRIDGE

You've made that clear.

NANCY

I just don't get it. I mean it's called Acting, right? Don't you think I can act? I can act kind—I can act honest.

(Hits a few poses. Aldridge looks dubious.)

Why don't you believe me?

ALDRIDGE

Sincerity is not your strongest suit.

NANCY

What does that mean? Is that why no one likes me?

ALDRIDGE
Oh Nancy . . . I really don't have time for this.

NANCY
For me? You don't have time for me?

ALDRIDGE
Not at the moment, no. As much as I cherish your company, this is my free period, not yours to consume as you see fit.

NANCY
Sorry! Geez.

ALDRIDGE
I have a class to prepare for—and don't you have a test?

NANCY
I kind of studied last night.

ALDRIDGE
Last night all I could do was—

NANCY
Think about Valerie?

ALDRIDGE
Yes. I see you're not the least bit concerned.

NANCY
I guess I'm just a more positive person. You see the glass half empty. I see the glass half full. You think she's dead, I say—prove it. Find the body.

(Beat)

ALDRIDGE
I never said I thought she was dead.

NANCY
That's what you're thinking. That's why you're so upset. Want a Gummy Worm?

(He shakes his head at the dangling object, repulsed as she devours it rapturously.)

ALDRIDGE

I haven't any appetite at all.

NANCY

That's what worry will do. Twist you up inside—keep you up at night. If you don't watch out—it'll kill you. And then who'd direct KING LEAR?

ALDRIDGE

I would, from the grave.

NANCY

Exactly! The show must go on. Right? That's why it's wrong to cancel rehearsal. So what if someone's missing?

ALDRIDGE

So what?!

NANCY

It's just one person.

ALDRIDGE

Valerie is far more important than that.

NANCY

You mean she's more important than me?

ALDRIDGE

No, that's not what I mean.

NANCY

That's what I'm hearing. Valerie's missing—so let's freak out and cancel rehearsal. I missed Tuesday's rehearsal to get my braces off—thank you for noticing—but you held rehearsal anyway.

ALDRIDGE

The circumstances are completely different.

NANCY

The equation, as Ms. Corvin would say, is the same.

(She goes to the board, pretending to be Ms. Corvin. Adept at mimicry, her transformation is remarkable.)

NANCY

We cancel this factor. Why? It's in the way. We don't need it. We've got something better. And that is . . . ? Anyone? Our answer . . . ?

(She raises her own hand and pretends to be called upon.)

Me. I'm the answer. Let me fill in for Valerie.

ALDRIDGE

No.

NANCY

Until she gets back—that is, if she does get back—and of course I believe she will! But until she does . . .

ALDRIDGE

Until she does, our stage manager will fill in.

NANCY

FUCK-akawa?!

ALDRIDGE

Furukawa. Kosuke Furukawa.

NANCY

Well, I can't understand a thing he says.

ALDRIDGE

He'll read the lines.

NANCY

I know the lines. I've memorized the lines.

ALDRIDGE

Why would you memorize Cordelia's lines?

NANCY

I don't know—I guess it just kind of happened. Her words come so naturally to me. Want me to recite them?

ALDRIDGE

No.

NANCY

Don't you at least think it's commendable that I did all that extra work?

ALDRIDGE

It would be more commendable if you learned the part you were assigned.

NANCY

It's hard for a positive person like me to play someone so . . . negative. It's hard for me to even wrap my brain around Goneril's words. And the things she does are just . . . dreadful. I can't imagine why you think I'm like her.

ALDRIDGE

I never said you were like her.

NANCY

You said I was more suited to play her. That means you think I'm like her.

ALDRIDGE

That's not what I meant.

NANCY

But that's what you think. And that's what everybody's going to think if I play Goneril. And then I'll never have any friends!

ALDRIDGE

You have friends.

NANCY

Who? You. You're my one and only friend.

ALDRIDGE

Nancy, I know how badly you wanted that part. But I'm not about to recast. Valerie will return. I believe that. *(Beat)* Don't you?

(She crosses to the board and erases her "equation.")

ALDRIDGE

Nancy?

NANCY

What?

ALDRIDGE

You do think Valerie's coming back?

NANCY

Why do you care what I think? Want to play Hangman?

ALDRIDGE

No.

(She draws a scaffold.)

Erase that.

(She continues.)

NANCY

I'm thinking of an eight-letter word.

ALDRIDGE

Erase that immediately.

(She draws eight spaces.)

NANCY

Guess the word. It's from KING LEAR.

ALDRIDGE

I will not have you littering the board with your nonsense.

NANCY

Nonsense? It's Cordelia. C-O-R-D-E-L-I-A.

(She fills in the empty spaces then steps back, revealing a macabre sketch of a girl dangling from a noose. She laughs. Aldridge is horrified.)

ALDRIDGE

Nancy . . . what have you done?

NANCY

I'll erase it. I'll erase it. Sorry I messed up your precious board.

(She quickly erases the board.)

ALDRIDGE

That drawing.

NANCY

What drawing?

(Innocently looking back at the empty board.)

Want me to erase the other board?

ALDRIDGE

No. You've done enough.

NANCY

What does that mean?

(He tries to avoid her piercing gaze.)

ALDRIDGE

Once again you've managed to distract me from my work—that's what you've done.

NANCY

That's not what you meant. You think I've done something dreadful. You're afraid to say it 'cause you're afraid of me.

ALDRIDGE

Afraid of you?

NANCY

Then say it. What dreadful thing do you think I've done?

ALDRIDGE

I think you quite possibly may have . . .

NANCY

What?

ALDRIDGE

Accidently, of course . . .

NANCY

What?

ALDRIDGE

Harmed Valerie.

NANCY

What?! Geez. This is exactly what I'm talking about. You've cast me as the villain and now that's how you see me.

ALDRIDGE

Have you . . . done something to Valerie?

NANCY

You know—I'm not even going to honor that with an answer.

(She grabs her things.)

I'm insulted. I'm incredibly insulted. Thanks to you, I've been typecast unfairly and now my feelings have been hurt.

(She heads for the door.)

ALDRIDGE

Where are you going?

NANCY

To the library—to study.

ALDRIDGE

You'll need a pass.

NANCY

Excuse me?

ALDRIDGE

You can't leave this classroom without a pass.

NANCY

Yeah, like someone's going to stop me.

ALDRIDGE

The police might question you.

NANCY

I have nothing to hide.

(He offers her a pass.)

ALDRIDGE

Here then. Take it.

(She crosses to her desk and sits.)

What's wrong?

NANCY

I think you know . . .

(He slides into an adjacent seat.)

ALDRIDGE

What, Nancy? What should I know?

NANCY

The truth?

ALDRIDGE

Please.

NANCY

Right. 'Cause, if the police ask me what I know . . . I'll have to tell them—'cause like Cordelia, I'm honest. I can't help but blurt out what's on my mind.

ALDRIDGE

What's on your mind?

NANCY

We're friends—right? No matter what?

ALDRIDGE

Yes.

NANCY

Good. 'Cause . . . the last person I saw Valerie with, was . . . you.

ALDRIDGE

Well, I was the last to leave. I locked up as usual.

NANCY

Still, it was weird.

ALDRIDGE

What was "weird?"

NANCY

I don't know . . . something I saw made me, uncomfortable . . .

ALDRIDGE

What did you see?

NANCY

I'm just not sure it was . . . appropriate.

ALDRIDGE

What?

NANCY

You know . . .

ALDRIDGE

No I don't . . .

NANCY

Why are you getting so defensive?

ALDRIDGE

I'm not defensive!

NANCY

"Methinks the gentlemen doth protest too much."

ALDRIDGE

I have no idea what you're talking about.

NANCY

I think you do. That's why you're acting so guilty.

ALDRIDGE

This is madness!

(She giggles.)

Whatever you're inferring . . .

(She continues to giggle.)

Will you stop that!

(This makes her laugh more.)

What did you see?

NANCY

Wouldn't you like to know.

ALDRIDGE

Yes! I'd love to know the vile little drama you've concocted in that vile little brain of yours. Casting doubts on me as if I'm some questionable character . . .

NANCY

You are a questionable character.

ALDRIDGE

In what way?

NANCY

I saw you—walk her to your car.

ALDRIDGE

I didn't "walk her to my car." I was walking to my car with Valerie.

NANCY

You had your old man arm around her.

ALDRIDGE

My arm was linked in hers.

NANCY

She was talking. You were listening. You laughed at what she said.

ALDRIDGE

And what of that?

NANCY

You more than like her. You LOVE her.

ALDRIDGE

I ADORE Valerie—but in a fatherly way.

NANCY

Oh, right . . . like she's the daughter you never had.

ALDRIDGE

Exactly.

NANCY

I thought I was the daughter you never had.

ALDRIDGE

You're both the daughters I never had.

NANCY

But she's your favorite. *(Beat)* You're not supposed to have favorites.

ALDRIDGE

I give you just as much attention.

NANCY

But you like her more.

(He can't refute this.)

You always cast her as the princess. Last year, she played Miranda.

ALDRIDGE

To your magnificent Caliban.

NANCY

Another monster.

ALDRIDGE

Another fine role. Some would argue that the villain is always the most interesting part. Vincent Price once said—

NANCY

Who the fuck is Vincent Price—and who the fuck cares?! Why can't you teach me what I need to learn? I know how to be ruthless and vengeful and deadly. That's what I am! Cast me as Cordelia. I can be kind. I can be honest. Just show me how. Show me how to be convincing.

ALDRIDGE

I'm not that good a teacher.

NANCY

I need to fit in!

ALDRIDGE

You weren't meant to.

NANCY

Why? 'Cause I'm a monster?

ALDRIDGE

Go to the library, Nancy.

(Handing her the hall pass.)

I have work to do.

NANCY

Yeah, right. I know exactly what you're going to do. The minute I walk out that door you're going to sneak over to those cops and whisper all your suspicions—about me. Well, I have a few suspicions about you which I certainly wouldn't mind sharing.

ALDRIDGE

Whatever you saw . . . or thought you saw . . .

NANCY

Oh, I definitely saw—

ALDRIDGE

Something you clearly misunderstood.

NANCY

It was pretty clear what was going on.

ALDRIDGE

Not to someone like you—someone who has such difficulty processing emotion.

NANCY

Oh, is that my problem?

ALDRIDGE

I think so, yes.

NANCY

Does that mean—when I see something—like what I saw—I didn't really see it?

ALDRIDGE

Precisely. You weren't able to interpret it properly, so what you saw was misconstrued.

NANCY

Wow. *(Beat as she absorbs this.)* What were you doing? 'Cause Valerie was really upset.

ALDRIDGE

Like you, she completely misinterpreted the moment.

NANCY

It looked like you were—coming on to her.

ALDRIDGE

Coming on to her? Please. If that's what you think, you are certainly mistaken.

NANCY

I bet something like that could really get you canned.

ALDRIDGE

Indeed it could.

NANCY

Then that would be it, wouldn't it?

ALDRIDGE

What do you mean?

NANCY

That would be the end of you.

(Taking in all the posters.)

The Aldridge Players. You've been running the show around here, for what, thirty years? Geez, you are the show. Before you, there was what, some dusty stage they never used, 'cept to give out sports awards?! Look at this. Look at you. You rule! But, in a blink, you won't. 'Cause they'll find out what you did. Then all you'll be is that creepy old teacher who molested that girl who disappeared. That's how you'll be remembered. People are funny that way. They forget all the good stuff when you've done something bad.

ALDRIDGE

I have done nothing bad.

NANCY

But it's easy to steer people's thinking that way.

(She smiles, holding his gaze.)

ALDRIDGE

I've encountered your kind before. I know what you are.

NANCY

Oh yeah, what am I?

ALDRIDGE

You're . . . incapable of feeling anything for anyone. You're missing what makes us human. It's impossible for you to feel compassion or remorse or—

NANCY

I feel. When I get cut, it hurts.

ALDRIDGE

"Prick me, do I not bleed?" The pain you feel is only for yourself.

NANCY

Who else is there?

ALDRIDGE

Precisely.

NANCY

So, I'm out for myself. Who isn't?

ALDRIDGE

Some of us care deeply about others.

NANCY

Oh yeah, right. You care so much about Valerie you haven't even bothered to ask where she is.

ALDRIDGE

Do you know?

NANCY

I'm not saying I do, I'm just saying it's interesting that you haven't asked.

ALDRIDGE

I haven't asked because I fear the worst.

NANCY

You've got to start seeing the glass half full. I never said she was dead. You just want her to be.

ALDRIDGE

And why would I want that?

NANCY

That way she won't . . . tell. I won't either if you cast me as . . . you know who.

ALDRIDGE

You are an abomination.

NANCY

Takes one to know one.

ALDRIDGE

We are nothing alike.

NANCY

If you really cared about Valerie, you'd want to save her.

ALDRIDGE

Of course I want to save her.

NANCY

Then ask me where she is.

ALDRIDGE

Where is she?

NANCY

What will you give me if I tell?

ALDRIDGE

Tell me.

Sorry but that sounds a bit . . . artificial. Try again.

ALDRIDGE

Tell me!

NANCY

I'm just not feeling it 'cause you're not feeling it. You know what I mean? Convince me.

(He lunges, grabbing her by the neck.)

ALDRIDGE

Tell me, you worthless piece of shit. Where the fuck is she?

(Nancy gurgles as she struggles to loosen his grasp. His rage is too great and

subsides only when she is still. He's horrified. He shakes her, trying to wake her. Lifting her into his arms as best he can, he staggers, searching for a place to stash her. Finally he decides to prop her in plain sight and places her at her desk in a studious position. Her head flops over her math notebook. Grabbing a pencil, he places it into her lifeless hand. The pencil drops. When he tries again, she grabs his wrist, holding it until he crumples in pain.)

NANCY

You tried to kill me.

ALDRIDGE

It may have appeared that way. But I assure you . . . I assure you . . .

NANCY

Cut the crap.

(Letting go and crossing to the mirror.)

Look at my neck.

ALDRIDGE

Have you a scarf? Here take mine.

(Offering her the one he's wearing.)

NANCY

It doesn't go with my outfit.

ALDRIDGE

Props to the rescue.

(Grabbing a scarf from the prop box.)

NANCY

That's Cordelia's.

ALDRIDGE

So it is.

NANCY

She wears it in Act IV, Scene 7.

ALDRIDGE

Indeed she does. Please—it's yours.

NANCY

I'll give it back when Valerie returns.

ALDRIDGE

That is, if she does return.

NANCY

Up to you. Do you want her to?

ALDRIDGE

I think we need to be realistic. Don't you?

(She holds his gaze and nods, then turns back to the mirror to adjust the scarf.)

NANCY

Does Valerie wear it this way or does she wear it like that?

ALDRIDGE

Like that—yes, just like that.

(When she turns to face Aldridge, she is Cordelia.)

NANCY

"Was this a face
To be opposed against the jarring winds?
To stand against the deep dread-bolted thunder,
In the most terrible and nimble stroke
Of quick cross-lightning?"

(Beat as she steps out of character.)

Well?

ALDRIDGE

Casting is a funny thing. Sometimes you see things . . . anew.

NANCY

I knew you'd see it my way. 'Cause you and me are so alike.

ALDRIDGE

Are we? Then why do I feel so . . . alone?

NANCY

I think feelings get in the way. That's why it's best not to have them.

(Alridge sinks into his chair. Her eyes dart to the clock.)

Geez. Got to go.

(Gathering her things.)

Got a math test. And you've got a class to teach. See you at rehearsal?

ALDRIDGE

. . . Yes.

NANCY

Good. Can't wait to show you what I can do. You have no idea what I'm capable of. What you just saw . . . that's only the beginning.

(The bell rings. Nancy opens the door and exits happily into the cacophony of a bustling high school hallway. The sounds of boisterous voices and clanging lockers crescendo as the lights fade on Mr. Aldridge.*)* ◇

Be My Best Friend

"Don't listen to me; my heart's been broken."
Louise Gluck

Myra Emmer Gold

If I tell you I just met a new man, a special man,
ignore me: I have terrible taste and lack judgment.

If I tell you I bumped into my first lover who looks great and wants
to see me again, have my phone disconnected.

If I tell you my sister has asked me to lunch on Tuesday,
remind me that we already have plans.

If I tell you my cousin is coming east and wants to mend fences,
buy me a ticket to Seattle.

If I tell you how over him I am,
remind me that I cry in Pleasantville, twenty-five years later.

Someone once said that we are stronger in the mended places.
Remind me that there must be a better quote. ◇

I Can Do That

Myra Emmer Gold

Be there gratefully taking your blue-toothed calls
as you drive your superfluous Saab 300 miles
to her house, her welcome.
I can do that.

Decode your war stories, chapter by whining chapter
about women who aren't smart enough
as I sit by, sharpest mind, numbest heart.
I can do that.

Hear your rooster-proud recital of the
Ph.D lady's CV not once, but twice
and once more for bad measure.
I can do that.

Offer up my best words
to your vain, blue-penciled scrutiny
and undocumented alien rules of grammar.
I can do that.

Dive down, down
through murky waters,
once-sweet source of
earlier love,
mocking the undertow.
Today's Ophelia,
twice as mad, doubly clad,
singing, gasping, sinking, drowning.
I can do that.

But won't,
anymore. ◇

The Gardener

Gregory A. French

IT WAS IN APRIL, ON HIS WAY HOME FROM WORK, THAT WILLIAM Ernesto first saw her tugging the weeds from the rocky outcrop at the corner where the condo driveway met the street. By the time he had parked his car and taken the elevator to his twelfth-floor two-bedroom, he'd already forgotten about the old lady in the straw hat. But the next evening, a Friday when most folks in his building were throwing back cocktails, there she was again, digging little holes between the rocks and inserting begonias or impatiens or some other flower. Not being a gardener himself, William couldn't tell them apart. In the elevator, he bumped into June Hutchings, the squawky board president who seemed to poke her beak into everyone's business.

"Who's the woman planting flowers?" William asked.

"She's not supposed to do that. She's the crazy lady in 308, the one who went to sleep with a roast in the oven and hid inside during the fire alarm."

"Is she sick or something? Or maybe she's deaf?" William pulled his house keys from his suit's inside breast pocket and gently jingled them in front of June's face, as if a charm to ward off evil spirits.

"Just your typical nut job," June said. "We could see smoke puffing from her kitchen window, and the hallways were clogged. We banged and banged on her door and no one answered. Vince in 905 eventually pulled the alarm. When the firemen arrived, they banged. Still no answer. When they busted down her door, she was fanning the smoke out the window with a broom. She said she was too embarrassed to answer. Can you believe that? Too embarrassed. What did she think the fire department was going to do? Go away and let the place burn down?"

William shook his keys again, eyes fixed on the digital display counting the floors. Two more before he'd be released from this coop. June continued clucking the entire way.

"Goodbye," William said as the doors opened. "See you around." But June followed him.

"Oh, no," June said as she waddled beside William. "I'm getting off here, too. I need to talk to McIntyre about her common charges. She's late again. Oh, I'm so glad people like you, William, pay on time. You actually pay a week early. It's such a shame when people are delinquent. We have to send a letter from our attorney; then we take them to court. Eventually, we foreclose. It's just a horrible, time-consuming mess."

At his front door, William shook his keys one more time. "Well, this is me. So good to see you. I appreciate the update. I really do." June swiveled on her heels and stopped, as if waiting to be invited in. This time William shook his keys hard, hoping to convey the message that time was up. But June's head continued to flutter over his shoulder as he twisted the key in the deadbolt. When the door popped open, he considered saying ta-ta and swooshing her away, but didn't. No need to make a raptor of a whooping crane.

"June, we've had such a great chat. We'll have to continue it sometime."

She blushed; streaky red blobs, like matted feathers, erupted on her chest. "Oh, yes, that would be wonderful. How about next Friday? Would you like to come to my place after work?"

William felt the first tingles of the scratchy throat he'd use as an excuse to cancel. "Wonderful, see you then." He slid inside and closed the door quickly on June's wide eyes and pursed lips—not sure if she had been expecting a kiss, or whether she was just confused by his abrupt dismissal. Either way, he didn't want to ask her in. And it wasn't fair of her to expect an impromptu invitation. His place, like his life, was a mess.

William loosened his tie and hung his coat on the knob of the bedroom closet. He would make a quick cocktail—a Campari spritz he'd developed an affinity for on a trip to Venice with his parents before they died—and then he would change into his waiter attire of white shirt and black pants. The drink would help him relax before his second job, making him more affable and, therefore, more likely to get big tips.

William was pulling out of the building's driveway, yanking down the car's sun visor to shield the spring glare, when the rocky outcrop caught his attention. The flowers the crazy lady in 308 had so meticulously planted just a few hours ago had been yanked out and strewn across the driveway. The imbecilic teenagers across the street, he thought, had some balls to conduct their high jinks in broad daylight.

"Damn," William said under his breath. He punched the emergency flashers, pulled the car to the side of the driveway, and vaulted out. "I don't know why I'm doing this," he said to no one in particular as he picked up one plant by its delicate tip, holding his arm straight out to keep the soil in the tangled root ball from dropping onto his white shirt. He placed a plant on top of an empty hole, and then lifted another from the driveway and did the same. He didn't have time to replant them, besides he'd make a mess of himself, so he just placed them where he thought they belonged, as if they were the scattered pieces of some three-dimensional jigsaw puzzle.

He was nudging the last plant back into place when a gravelly voice behind him shouted, "What are you doing? Why have you ruined my plants? They didn't do anything to you."

William spun around and found himself face to face with the crazy lady. "Wait," he said. He held his hands to each side, shoulder high, as if he were being robbed. "I was putting them back. I think the kids across the street pulled them out. I'm sorry. I have to get to work. I don't have time to replant them."

He popped the trunk and fished a towel from his golf bag to clean his hands. The woman's head bounced back and forth between William and the plants, like a bobble-head doll. Each time her gaze returned to William, the deep furrows in her brow filled and softened just a little. After a half-dozen pivots, the creases were graceful shadows. "Oh, those damn kids," the woman said. "No worries, I'll take care of it from here.

Thank you so much for rescuing my babies." She sidled up to the flowers, petting and cooing to each plant.

William slammed his trunk closed and climbed into his car. He punched the button for the passenger window and it hummed open. "Well, goodbye then," he shouted out the window. She didn't turn her head. "Goodbye," he said again. No acknowledgment. He wanted to make a hasty retreat—in fact, he was going to be late for work—but couldn't bear to simply drive away. Instead, William unfastened his seat belt and hopped out of the car.

"I'm sorry," he said, holding out his hand. "I wanted to introduce myself before saying goodbye."

Her body whirled, but her straw hat, stubborn with inertia, resisted and fell to the ground behind her. "I didn't hear you," she said.

"I just wanted to say goodbye," he said, mouthing the words carefully. "And introduce myself. I'm William."

She snaked her hand to William's, coyly, like a ballerina. "Charmed," she said, her head cocked almost imperceptibly. "I'm sure we'll be seeing each other. My name is Grace. Grace Heart. Can you believe my parents?" Knees creaking, she sank into a deep knee bend. "It's a first-position plié," she said, whisking the hat into her arms.

That evening, close to midnight, William swung into the driveway. The rocky outcrop was bare, empty of color. On the far side of the driveway, just outside the bright shaft of his headlights, a little plant with red delicate flowers lay wilting.

"Jesus H.," William said, slamming the car into park and rushing to the plant, like a medic on a battlefield. Its stem was broken, beyond salvage. He triaged the other plants, each mortally wounded. Unable to save any, he gathered them into a pile for the super to discard in the morning. For a moment, he considered driving across town to the 24-hour big-box store and replacing them before Grace noticed, but the plants were her babies; she'd recognize the changelings come morning.

That night William tossed and turned, struggling to find a comfortable position in his sea of a king-size bed. His eyes were open wide as the first rays of light scrambled over the horizon. He was going to get

Grace's flowers after all. His day job at LayDee's Shoes started at ten. It was five now, plenty of time.

The store was empty. Despite all the TV pundits' ruminations about the economy gaining traction, people were clearly still struggling. Not too long ago, as a teenager, William would trek to one of these big-box stores with his father—usually an early Saturday morning foray before his dad's tee time—and the parking lots spilled over. Today, however, William parked near the entrance and dashed inside. He circled the impatiens for fifteen minutes before choosing a tray of mixed colors, hoping they'd match their fallen brethren.

By six a.m., after tossing gloves and a spade into the cart and checking out, he was on his way home, figuring that thirty-odd bucks was a reasonable price for improving someone's day. An hour later, as he tucked the last flower into place, June charged through the building's front entrance.

"What do you think you're doing?" she yelled.

"Planting flowers," William said, standing and removing his gloves. "The kids across the street must have pulled them up last night."

"Actually, I had the super pull them. Twice. You don't have permission to be planting here."

William shoved the gloves into his back pocket and brought his hand to his head, squeezing his temples between his thumb and index finger. "Why would you do that?"

"We can't have residents just going around planting stuff. It's inappropriate. You give folks an inch around here, and they'll take a mile."

"I still don't understand. Were you planning on planting something else here?"

"No," June huffed. "It's not in the budget. If everyone would pay their common charges, we'd have more money for landscaping. But they don't, so we don't."

"Well, how about you just think of this as a contribution, a random act of kindness." William took his hand from his temple and folded his arms in front of him.

"It's against the rules. We start ignoring one rule, and it becomes impossible to enforce any of them."

"So what are you going to do? Dig them up?"

"No, you are. If you don't, we'll fine you. It's $100. Your choice."

"I'll leave them here then." William dropped the spade in his trunk and slammed the lid closed. "And I'm not paying any fine."

June fished her phone from her pocket and started taking pictures, chewing her bottom lip the entire time. When she was done taking pictures of the flowers, she started taking photos of William's car.

"What are you doing now?" he asked.

"You're parked illegally. There's a fine for that too," June said, phone still clutched in hand, her arms aflutter.

William fished his keys from his pocket and jingled them indignantly. "I'm moving my car now." Jingle. Jingle. "And if these flowers are gone when I return, there'll be hell to pay." Jingle. Jingle. Jingle. He swung the car door open and plopped behind the wheel. After starting the car, he revved the engine, causing June to drop her phone and bolt out of the way.

William jolted the car forward. He hadn't aimed for her phone, but when it crunched under his left tire, he grinned in smug satisfaction. There's nothing like the crunch of plastic to settle the nerves, he thought. He rolled down his window and leaned out. "Sorry about that. I didn't see it. I guess that means our date for next Friday is off." He rolled up the window and drove into the garage.

Upstairs, he showered and readied for a day of slipping shoes onto women's feet. What if his restaurant clients knew he spent most days cradling sweaty feet full of corns, calluses, and bunions? He chuckled at the thought of a cross-pollinated customer base.

On his way to work, William passed the rocky outcrop. The flowers had been removed, and Grace was scratching her head when he pulled beside her.

"I thought it was the kids across the street," he said. "But, can you believe it, it was June, the board president. Something about planting flowers not being allowed in the association rules."

Grace put her hands on her hips and bowed her head. He couldn't see her face, just the top of her straw hat and the dappled hints of white hair between the loose weave. "Why do people have to ruin everything?" she said. Her words were spinning, a forceful tour jeté.

"I don't know," he said. "I drove by last night, and they were gone. I picked up some replacements early this morning and planted them. I had actually finished when June caught me. I have to work this afternoon and evening, but I have tomorrow morning off. Why don't we go to the garden center together?"

"Would you do that? That would be so wonderful."

"I don't know how to keep her from ripping them out again."

"If we keep planting, she'll stop. Trust me."

"How could you know that?"

"Life, sonny, a lifetime of experiences."

William made arrangements to meet Grace in the lobby at seven and headed to work. Her optimism must have rubbed off, like pollen on a bee, because William spent the entire day trying to figure out how to game the petty ordeal of condo politics and convince his fellow residents to support Grace and her flowers.

That evening, after finishing his restaurant shift and returning home, William found an envelope under his front door with an officially printed invoice inside: a bill from June for her phone. "Screw that," he said as he tossed it into the garbage.

It was after midnight, and William kept telling himself to go to bed, but his mind was racing. He opened his laptop and stared at the blank screen. Grumbling, he typed a few words. "Plant With Us. Sunday, April 17. 9 a.m.–11 a.m. in front of the building." He picked an artsy sans serif font, Futura bold, for the headline and added a few clip-art flower illustrations.

He racked his brain for something catchier, deleted the headline, and typed again. "Flower Power Rally." That wouldn't work either, too much hippie appeal. Only the stoners would show. The word appeal, however, fired his synapses. He had it. Appeal, as in curb appeal. "Grow Your Investment," he wrote. And, in a smaller font, he continued, "Curb Appeal Significantly Enhances Property Value. To improve our building, a group of volunteers will meet downstairs to plant flowers, and landscape." He tinkered with the wording, added his phone number, and printed 119 copies, enough for every unit in the building but June's.

It was after one a.m. when his printer stopped purring. Flyers in hand, William marched down every floor, every hallway inserting one under every door—every door except June's. He felt like a ninja Santa Claus, full of jittery mirth and stealth-like obsession. Back in his apartment, he took a quick shower and settled between the sheets.

His alarm buzzed in the muted colors of early dawn, but William woke charged, electric. He readied the coffee pot with his favorite dark roast. When the brewing cycle finished, he filled his oversized mug and turned on the TV. The usual blend of shootings, car chases, Washington gridlock, and vapid segments on fashion, food, and celebrity fluff droned in the background as he dressed. He was pulling on an orange waffle-knit, long-sleeve undershirt when the weather report began.

"We're expecting a storm front to roll through this morning," said a blonde who could have walked off a Fashion Week runway. "It'll bring high winds and severe local flooding throughout the New York metropolitan area."

William tugged his Mets T-shirt over his undershirt. Damn, it was going to rain. For a moment, he thought about canceling, but he didn't want to let Grace down. They could wander among the aisles admiring the different plants, deciding what to buy and where to put it. He'd return another day to pick everything up.

Five minutes before he was supposed to meet Grace in the lobby, he headed downstairs. At the appointed time, Grace hadn't arrived. A half hour later, he took the elevator to her apartment and knocked gently on the door. There was a rustle inside and the door creaked open. Grace's eyes peeked through the gap just under the security chain and darted up and down.

"What do you want?" she asked. Her tone was bitter, almost hostile.

"Grace, it's me, William. We were supposed to go to the garden center today. Remember?"

"I don't know you."

A flash of realization swept through William. "Remember? We plant flowers together."

"A flower can change the world. Did you know that tulip mania ruined the Dutch economy?"

"No, I didn't." It was a white lie. William remembered studying the market collapse caused by a speculative frenzy for tulip bulbs. People spent a year's worth of wages buying them, thinking they'd flip their merchandise for an even higher price. When the exuberance waned, the bottom fell off the market. Hordes were left penniless. It was used in his Wharton economics class as one of the first examples of a speculative bubble, just as the recent collapse of the housing market had sparked so much job loss, even his own.

"And there were the Wars of the Roses," she said. "But those weren't fights over roses. They were battles between white and red ones. You see, the different colored roses were important emblems between two families competing for the throne."

"That's all very interesting," William said. "I'd like to hear more. When would you like to go to the garden center?"

"I used to have a garden," Grace said, still peeking through the crack between the door and the jamb. "But we sold our home when my husband died and moved here."

"Grace, you still have a garden. It's downstairs and it needs tending. Would you like to see it?"

"I have a garden?"

"Yes, it's our present to you. Let's go downstairs."

Grace closed the door, and the chain clanked across the fastener. When she opened it back up, her purple polyester pants and a floral patterned blouse burst into the hallway. William wasn't sure, but he figured the giant splashes of orange and yellow were nasturtiums, perhaps hibiscus. She carried her straw hat in her hand.

"Where did you get that hat?" he asked.

"Oh, this thing, it's been lying around here for years."

They rode silently down the elevator to the lobby, where William escorted her through the front door. At the outcrop, William pointed to the bare spots.

"You can plant flowers here and here and here," he said. "And look here, in front of and between the rocks. This can be your special place."

Her elegance returning, Grace bowed, just slightly, at the waist. "There used to be flowers here," she said. "What happened to them?"

"You remember," he answered.

"Of course, I remember. Do you think I'm crazy or something?"

"No, nothing of the sort. They were taken away. But you told me that if you keep planting them, one day they'll stay put."

"Well, of course they'll stay put. Flowers just don't get up and walk away. And people like flowers. They take care of them. They calm the soul."

"They certainly do. What do you think? Are you up for a trip to the garden center?"

Grace agreed and William guided her to his car. Fifteen minutes later they were wandering through flowers. Grace knew all by name. She used to have dahlias in her garden, her favorite she said, and roses and poppies and columbine and purple coneflower and black-eyed Susan and hollyhock. Eventually, their cart was overflowing, and William suggested they check out and return home.

"The thing about a garden," Grace said, "is it's always changing from one day to the next, from one year to another. It's kind of like life, you see. You expect it to go one way, and it veers off course. And while you might end up disappointed because it didn't turn out the way you expected, it never ceases to thrill and surprise and give you joy. But you have to look for it. You have to keep planting."

"Grace, that's beautiful. You must speak from experience."

"Oh, I do. I do. I wanted to be a ballet dancer when I was younger. I was really quite good. But then I got pregnant and had a family. Sometimes I dream that I'm dancing so lightly, I take flight. It's my family that keeps me grounded, but they're almost all gone now. My husband passed a year ago. My son died on 9/11."

William stopped shuffling the plants from cart to the counter. One hundred and twenty units in his building, and he knew just a handful of people, usually by first name only. Everyone was curled up in a little cocoon. William, too, was snug, venturing out of his apartment mostly for work while maintaining friendships with people in the city, or a couple towns away, rather than the folks right next door. We get wrapped in our cozy little lives, he thought, not realizing that what seems comfortable is actually constricting.

"Sir, are you finished?" said the cashier, nudging her chin toward the rest of the flowers in William's cart. He resumed piling them onto the counter. When the cashier finished, the total was more than $250. He hadn't expected they'd cost so much—a big setback in his budget. From his wallet, he tugged out his emergency credit card and handed it to the cashier.

"Would you like me to pay for that?" Grace said. "I have plenty of money."

"Thanks so much," William said as he pushed the cart to his car. "There's no need for that. My treat."

"You are so kind, sonny. I can't wait to get started."

William gingerly set the trays of flowers into his trunk. When that was full, he put them on the floor and the back seat, and chuckled: his Beamer was a bee's wet dream. They pulled into the driveway after nine and the skies were sparkling blue, no sign of thunderstorms. William was hoping some of the neighbors might be waiting, but it was empty out front. He parked his car next to the outcrop and unloaded the flowers. From the bottom of his trunk, he pulled out his spade and handed it to Grace.

"Here, use this. I'll use my hands."

Grace started digging and William clawed the soil with his fingers. Five minutes later, a shadow hovered over William's little slice of earth.

"What are you doing?" June's shrill voice startled a dozen little chickadees in the bush next door, and they fluttered into the sky. "Did you hand this flyer out last night? I don't know why I'm even asking. It has your phone number on it. That's illegal, too. Handing out the flyer, that is. Simpson in 510 asked if this was okay. I've been going around all morning telling people not to come."

As June ranted, William looked over her shoulder toward the front entrance. A bald man was scanning the property. His left hand settled on his brow to shield his eyes. He spotted William and approached. "Is this the planting group from the flyer?"

It was June's turn to take flight, spinning into the air as she crowed, "You can't do this. It's against the rules."

"What's against the rules?" the man asked. "Planting some flowers? It's about time we made this place look nice." He swiveled his head toward William. "There are ten of us in the lobby. How can we help?"

"I'll have them ripped out," June said. The red splotches on her neck had returned.

"You'll do nothing of the sort," William said. "Why don't you try planting a few? It'll make you feel better. And if you can't do that, why don't you just leave us alone?

"I'll take it to the board," June said.

"Well, three of the five board members are in the lobby," the bald man said. "Why don't you take it up with them right now?"

June put her hands on her hips, huffed twice, and stomped away.

The bald man extended his hand to William.

"I'm Tony from 305. It's a pleasure to meet you. I'll get the others."

"I'm William and this is Grace. We'd love your help. But I didn't do a great job planning ahead. There's only one spade."

"That's okay," Tony said. "We all have plants on our balconies. I think we have enough tools to go around."

They finished at eleven. By the time they were done, the group was chuckling about June, association politics, and how they'd lived in the same building so long without ever running into each other. They divvied up watering duties and made plans to meet the following Sunday in the lobby to share coffee and Danishes before weeding the garden. They took the elevator upstairs in two groups. William stepped off with Grace and guided her to her apartment. This time, Grace invited William in and they chatted over tea and toast. As William was leaving, Grace tugged his hand in the doorway. "I told you a single flower can change the world."

"Yes, Grace, you were right. But I have a question. Where did you get the flowers you planted the other day?"

Grace's eyebrows rose and then settled serenely, as if pondering an impressionist painting, perhaps Giverny on a cloudy day. "Well, my son brought them. He's always bringing me flowers." She casually rubbed the back of her head and combed her fingers through her white locks. "Please call on me again soon."

"I will, Grace. I will." William stepped into the hallway, and Grace closed the door behind him. ◇

Paris Haiku

Mary O'Keefe Brady

Boulangerie

Bakery bonjours
Yeasty batons rule the rue
Baguette bliss beckons

Kiss Kiss

Perfumed boulevards
Air kisses graze powdered
cheeks
Love Parisian style

In Your Ear

Words of love linger
Wine whispers "Cherchez la
femme"
Moulin Rouge beware

A Fry in Translation

Steak frites, moules frites, frites
A hundred different ways
Got McDonald's beat ◇

Present Absence

Ann van Buren

1.

I saw you last
looking at oranges in the supermarket.

Do you remember how
before she died,
every day after school at snack time

mom unpeeled the citrus skin
in one spiral?

We ate peanut butter and jelly
on Ritz,
squeezing down the center,
licking sweetness that oozed from salt
around the cracker's rippled, circular edge.

Like a Venn diagram
we intersected with pleasure—

contentment—not understanding
the hollowness of the rind

reconstituted on the table into a sphere,
a planet, an entire universe

of emptiness now.

2.

sweet baby, you were born
an old soul
drew water from my womb
and the glistening
frozen world

one step ahead
you are what came after
all previous experience

travelling now
together in cyberspace
we sit in separate rooms
communicate
everything about love
that has ever been said

cradling you
in my arms
on my laptop
is so different
yet something feels the same

across the world from each other
we are still here

3.

there she is in this place of death
each time she wronged you

floats to sea
                    on a molecule of forgiveness
it will evaporate into the air
                                        and fall someplace else
as all things do

perhaps this time it will cross the border
from the yin to
                    the yang

depending on how you look at it

just keep things in balance
                    and the past will not consume you
use it as a flame to light the future

there is an inside
and an outside
                    forward and back

above and below

notice
          the air spinning round you
                    by and by

                      again ◇

Police Station

Ben Nightingale

When I was born in 1937, my birth certificate designated my race as white, which is how I looked. Several years later, I was issued a Certificate of Birth by Adoption that identified me as Negro. I was eventually adopted by a Negro couple in Philadelphia and brought up in a black community and a black church. But not everyone accepted me.

I STOOD IN OUR NEIGHBORHOOD POLICE STATION AND GAZED AT THE tall Negro teenager standing between two police officers. He was sweating in the overheated room and the front of his T-shirt was wet. His muscular arms were curled behind his body, his wrists secured by handcuffs. He was staring down at me and I had to lift my eyes up to see the top of his head, which seemed to touch the high ceiling. I was only nine.

"Is this one of them?" An officer was speaking to me. I looked at the policeman and pushed closer to my mother. Her hand tightened around mine.

"Mrs. Nightingale, would you please explain to your son that we want him to tell us if this one helped to attack him?"

My mother bent down towards me and glanced at the handcuffed teenager.

"Now, Benjamin, is this one that beat you up?" She looked at me.

My mother had already explained everything to me at home.

We had sat in the living room before coming to the police station. I understood we were possibly going to see one of the teenagers who had beaten me. I was scared. What would happen if I identified him? Would they let him go? Would he beat me up later for telling on him?

At the police station, these thoughts kept me from speaking. The teenager was standing right in front of me. Right over me. Glaring down at me, just as he had before.

I had seen this older boy with two of his friends on one of my walks home from school. My route seldom varied. I was a familiar sight to shopkeepers, who waved to me from their stores. Some people sitting on their front stoops would nod or say hello. I had also become a familiar sight to three others. They knew the way I walked home from school, down 19th Street, a narrow Philadelphia street. One day I heard one of them say to me, "Hey—nice coat you got there." And another say, "Yeah, you white folks dress good." My camel's hair coat and cap had caught their attention. I sped up my pace. Their voices faded away. At the end of another block, I ducked into a doorway and peeked around the edge. The street was clear. I continued walking home.

Several days later, on my way home from school, the same three stood in front of me. I tried to go around them, but couldn't.

"Where you think you goin'?"

I was speechless. To answer might bring more trouble. Yet not to answer gave them an excuse to be mad at me. I walked to the curb, out into the street, and felt a little safer with an automobile between us.

"I was talkin' to you. No use you goin' into the street."

They laughed and started in my direction. Then a door opened at one of the houses, and two people came out and stood talking on the front steps. The three teenagers began to back away from me, walking slowly down the street. I circled around the car and back onto the sidewalk and started quickly towards home.

A week went by. I was now walking down different streets each day as I made my way home. But later it was learned from the one they had caught that my changes of route were being watched. These same three teenagers were waiting and planning to get me.

Then, six blocks from home, I saw them one street away, coming in my direction. My mother had often told me, "If someone bothers you, run to a house and ring the doorbell." I looked at the houses nearest me. My thoughts raced. Should I ring the bell? No. It would be embarrassing. Besides there might not be anyone home. So I crossed to the other side of the street. The three of them were getting closer. Then they crossed to my side of the street. Panicking, I began to run towards home. I even ignored a red traffic light as I dashed across a street, never looking to see if a car was coming. I was pumping my arms as hard as I could, my schoolbag feeling heavier and heavier. Looking over my shoulder, I could see them running behind me. Another look—they were closing in. Now I was running wildly. I knew I couldn't outrun them, yet I kept on going. It was all I could do. Propelling myself along the sidewalk, arms flailing, shoes hitting the concrete as though somewhere, somehow, I would exit this scene when all my energy was gone, or some new force would well up within and I would be safe.

They were now just a step or two behind me. Why weren't they catching up? Was I really outrunning them? I flung my schoolbag to the ground and darted towards the street. I jumped off the curb and began to run between two parked cars, hoping a passing motorist would help me. But I couldn't escape. One of the teenagers had circled around to block me. The other two came up behind me and threw me to the ground between the parked automobiles. Now I was clearly out of anyone's sight.

Two of them held me down while the other one stood watch. They tore the buttons off my coat. One grabbed my shirt and tie and pinned me to the ground. He spit in my face, rammed a fist into my stomach. I began to double over, wanting to throw up. The other one grabbed my head by my hair and raised me off the asphalt to meet his fist, which blasted into my nose. Lights danced in my head.

"Let's get outa here. Some people are comin'," the lookout called.

My collar and tie were suddenly loose. Breathing became easier. From my position on the ground, I could see several pairs of feet walking hurriedly away from me. I lay in the street for a few minutes. Rising to one knee, I peered around the bumper to see if they were still there.

They weren't in sight. Slowly I struggled up and leaned on the trunk of an automobile. Streaks of blood were on my tie and shirt. I touched the back of my head. It felt wet and sticky. I brought my hand around and saw the red liquid on my fingers. I tried to close my coat but there were no buttons. I looked around, searching for my schoolbag, picked it up, and walked the rest of the way home.

At the police station, I was snapped out of remembering as my mother repeated her question—"Did he beat you up?" The accused teenager continued to look down at me. Finally I could speak. "Yes, he's one of them."

He stared at me harder, but there was nothing he could do. His arms were pinned fast by the handcuffs. The officers on each side moved closer to him as I made my identification. Then they took him through a door. It closed and he was gone from sight. But I could still see him. Still see him beating on me. Still see his hate-filled eyes staring at me.

A detective motioned my mother and me to a desk and we all sat down. "Now, Mrs. Nightingale, we're looking for the other two. Until we arrest them, we will be on the lookout for Benjamin when he comes home from school." My mother went over it all again, making sure I understood that I was to leave school at the same time each day and walk home the same way and the police would be watching for me.

The next day, on my way home from school, I saw a car slowly moving behind me. Two men sat in the front seat. They were the detectives assigned to protect me. The car would pull slightly ahead, wait, then when I had passed, begin to move again. This continued until I turned into Martin Street and was safely inside my home.

Several days later, my mother received a phone call informing her the other two had been caught. Again I was taken to the police station.

"Are these the other two?" The detective motioned towards the two Negro young men standing on the other side of a railing.

I nodded yes. My answer wasn't enough. The officer asked me to describe what each one had done. I told him all that had happened, as best as I could. The officer seemed satisfied. But my mother was not.

"How could you beat up a little boy?"

There was a moment of silence, of stillness.

"What in the world possessed you to do such a thing?" my mother asked.

Then one began to mumble apologetically, "We didn't know . . . we thought he was white." ◇

Pedaling

Mary Hegarty

pushed the pedal down, carried me
over grass, beyond pavement
to the holy land, holy water
the reservoir, cathedral of evergreens
pushed me to myself, the only one I was searching for after all
the only body that could save me
I pedaled as close to me as I could ever get
and as far away from you ◇

Gardening

Jenna Lynch

That year, we ate everything we found:

we'd wake early, the heat of the morning
rising slowly over the garden,

the warbler's song filtering through
the open window of the kitchen,

yellow-throated and perched in trees
above stones mossed and dampened

in the glaze of the morning sun.

We pulled up celery growing
wild in the yard,

crushed sage between our fingers,
chewed the ends of agoseris leaves;

we boiled clovers dipped in saltwater,
fried ostrich ferns and served them buttered

on a bone-white dish;

dried the bulbs of mariposa lilies for soup
and roasted the roots of goatsbeard for our morning

coffee. We peeled the shells off whole shrimp,
large and wet, fresh from the fish market,

threw them in a pan with olive oil and
slices of lemon.

We wasted nothing; used the shells for broth.

And later, in the first cool hour
of the evening, the sun edging below

blue mountains carved against the sky,

we sat on the porch drinking
white wine, talking and kissing,

the shadow of our house growing smaller on the lawn. ◇

Banana Peels, etc.

Emmett Shoemaker

RIGHT NOW, AT THIS VERY MOMENT, IN THE PULPY SUMMER NIGHT of an eastern collegiate hamlet, an exceedingly drunk young man is about to attempt the impossible. Before him stands a dresser, purchased earlier today at a yard sale. Said object, when measured against the slight frame of this tender lad, is much too large, and the staircase behind it—much too steep. He is alone in his newly rented house—really, upsettingly alone, except for the bugs making themselves known, and the anticipatory heaviness of his breathing, and the whiskey-gingers clicking in his ears.

Though his conscience is under assault—though his mother's voice reprimands him in a caustic stage whisper, warning him not to do the very thing he is contemplating doing—he is resolute. The dresser is going upstairs. Tonight. Right now. Having arrived home from an evening of substantial social failure (several distinct failures, if he's going to be honest) the matter has taken on no small amount of symbolic importance. So he is staring at it, really eyeing the saucy thing, and increasingly the project is getting all entwined in that odious masculinity "hang-up" of his (diagnosed, strangely enough, by three former girlfriends and just as many therapists), so, oh boy, no turning back. All this is happening right now, at this very moment, as you read this.

Right now, yes, right now he's laughing because, winning out over his mother's admonishments, the word "chifferobe" has just ping-ponged to the front of his brain, in a voice that he feels is maybe a kind of racist caricature. "Chifferobe." It's from *To Kill a Mockingbird*, he remembers, the film version. Hence, the probable racism thing. He is unclear as to what exactly constitutes a chifferobe, is fairly certain that the dresser before him does not qualify as such, but is chuckling nonetheless at the pompous little word, stopping just short of speaking it aloud, and instead flipping his tongue against the interior of his cheek in a manner self-consciously playful. We do these things when we have been drinking. But anyway, the chifferobe. Up with the chifferobe. All right.

This initial encounter, this first dance of theirs, is predictably awkward. Like an inexperienced lover (mistaking enthusiasm for technique), our guy wraps himself around the front of the object, and—skinny forearms fitting snugly underneath the lip of its surface-top, mysterious, unforeseen protuberances (the glass drawer knobs, perhaps) jutting into the soft of his pectorals—heaves. The terrific force of his exertion succeeds, not in lifting the thing, but instead (shit), in toppling it onto its backside.

There is a pregnancy right now, in that house. The kind of quiet when a barroom confrontation is on the brink of animal physicality, or someone has said something they've wanted to say for a long, long time, or a heavy wooden dresser has just fallen over. It's back to the drawing board for this young man, admittedly over-eager and, yes, drunk. He's standing there, both hands drawn through his thick curls, assessing the situation. "Disaster mode" is what his mother would call this.

The first thing now is to see whether or not the chifferobe has been damaged. The boy, for whom money has never been any source of anxiety (or even topic of thought), is half-hoping that it has passed on. Should its structure be irreparably damaged, he's thinking he could just drag the damned thing out the front door and surrender it to the afterlife of roadside scavengers, which would be infinitely more convenient than the business of hauling it upstairs.

But getting down on all fours and inspecting (a dizzying procedure, to be sure), he sees no indication of damage: no cracks, no splintering in its frame, at least not on its face or lateral panels. If anything, the wood looks richer, more vibrant, softer somehow. The grain of the wood is tighter, almost imperceptible in its uniformity. In fact, now it is spinning, and the young man is going to be sick.

Abandoning his patient, he stumbles into the kitchen, thrusts his head into the sink and, heedless of the several unsuspecting dishes resting in the basin, spews. It is, by this point, a very familiar ordeal, but still horrible. After some eons of spitting and sniffling and wiping his mouth with the back of his hand, he returns to the living room, trying to convince himself (as we all do after getting sick) that he is feeling better, invigorated even.

But something strange has happened, or, at least, something strange may have happened, he can't be sure. The dresser is standing upright. He *had* left the thing lying on its back on the floor, drawers facing up, hadn't he? He had. He had to have had; there is simply no way that, in his dizziness, he could have righted the thing and made it to the sink in time. Then again very little is obvious or certain at this hour of the night, in his condition. He is aware that in his confusion, he is fast becoming a caricature of the drunk, the one whom the universe plays nasty tricks on: banana peels, etc.

So there is no head scratching, no visible displays of incredulity, absolutely no theatricality, lest anyone be watching, be it deity or world government. He is no one's fool, and not ever one to be laughed at. So he accepts this development (the sudden liveliness of the chifferobe) with grace and tact (a feat of mental discretion certainly made easier by his inebriation) and is now trying his best to move forward. "Forward," of course, being upstairs. Now.

Aware of, but ultimately uncaring as to the fate of the newly polished hardwood flooring, this industrious miniature adult is heaving his full weight against the entirety of the piece, hoping now to simply push it the half-dozen feet to the bottom of the staircase, where he then plans (and perhaps he's getting a little ahead of himself here) to use the first step as leverage against which he might lift one end of the dresser (the chifferobe), achieve an unprecedentedly solid grip on its body, turn 180 degrees and walk backwards up the stairs carrying it. In his mind, this sequence unravels in a single, fluid, acrobatic motion, so convincingly that for a moment he forgets the miraculous, self-righting of the dresser, forgets even his drunkenness and what an ordeal this has been, and with his newfound clarity of mind manages to negotiate the formidable wooden mass to the bottom of the staircase.

Things are going well. What seemed, moments ago, a doomed enterprise is slowly edging into the realm of possibility. Having reached his preliminary destination, the hero is taking a self-congratulatory break to dust off his hands, but his mood is, this very second, right now, shattered by a phenomenal, leaden pain emanating from his right foot and pulsing up his leg. Instinctively, he jerks his foot towards him, bending his leg at the knee, but something is deeply wrong: his foot does not move; nor does the pain lessen. Looking down, he is appalled to see a leg of the dresser resting squarely on his white oxford, crushing all five toes and metatarsals. With sudden preternatural strength, he lifts the offending object enough to yank his foot out from underneath, before collapsing and rubbing vigorously, through the leather of his shoe, his injured digits.

Christ, what a night. But it had been resting. He had scooted the dresser up, flush to the staircase, and then stepped back, never once lifting the thing. It is as if it had leapt up (without his noticing) and landed on his foot. Still tending to his pulsing toes (the pain in each is hot and nasty) the young man is eyeing the dresser, suspiciously. Something, yes, something is catching his eye, something not quite right, something changed.

It's the legs; the legs of the dresser are different. He couldn't have missed them when purchasing the thing, of this he is certain. Whereas before each of its four legs existed as simple, cylindrical extensions, unremarkable in form, all of them now terminate in, well, sort of hooves: cleft hunks of wood darker and seemingly far denser than the rest of the dresser.

How. Right now is he is asking, 'how.'

A strangeness has cloaked that quiet house, and the young man inside is vaguely aware of a danger and a gravity heretofore unknown to him. More pressing than the question of 'how' is the suggestion of 'up.' Neglecting to examine the logic, he is quickly developing the theory that if only he might succeed in elevating the dresser to the second floor, and move it into his room (his domain), it would stop misbehaving. What had begun as a drunken compulsion has quickly become a matter of some necessity.

'It's a job for the knees,' he is thinking—a quote that, while entirely without context, could probably be attributed to his father, recently deceased. He is wrapping his arms around the thing now (careful of the hooves) and bracing it against his upper legs, aware of how precise and slow-going this journey must be. He is sweating; He can smell himself. The booze pours out his skin.

First step. Second step. His slow thighs, those vague pistons, pump methodically, each, at its turn, assuming the entirety of the dresser's weight. Third step. There is a creeping blackness in his periphery and he fears briefly that he might faint from the exertion, but like smelling salts, the thick hanging odor of a body at work (on a sweltering summer night) calls him back to the present. Though, truthfully, he has never smelled anything like it before. Much too strong to be the effluvium of his person, he is thinking. Fifth step. Too musky. Sixth.

Right now, several things are happening at once: the young man is feeling what is unmistakably a jettison of hot wet breath (the kind only produced by cavernous, bestial nostrils) against the crook of his forearm, where a corner of the dresser rests; he is peering over the far end of the dresser at a rather bushy foreign object protruding from its anterior and swaying back and forth; he is losing his balance. Now he is falling.

And in trying to ascertain what precisely is going on, he has contorted his body such that he is now falling *down* and *away* from the stairs, and only very briefly is he able to twist his head back to see the dresser—to see, and to think the word, 'horns.'

He is falling now. Now he is really falling. And it is all happening in slow motion. What a sad cliché. So much better to have it over and done with.

'Wildebeest, of course.' Only now does he comprehend the situation, his drunken folly.

And behind him, the dresser, the chifferobe, the wildebeest, that rough, unsanded monster is making headway. It is lurching down after him, step by step, in all its weight and glory. He can sense the force of it behind him, something suddenly holy: not just the whole thing, but the millions of singing splinters which comprise that whole, all conspiring to land on top of him, to breathe their hot breath against his broken neck.

He is thinking, 'the term hasn't even started.'

He is thinking, 'how could I have been so stupid?'

This is happening right now, and last Tuesday and next Friday. This is happening all too often. In every college town in America today, wildebeests are hurtling themselves down staircases after stupid drunk boys. It is an epidemic. Something has got to be done. ◇

Sometimes Change

M. Doretta Cornell

Sometimes the mountain yields
to magma, splits the thin
skin of Earth, pours flame-
corrosive ash
over the first pink roses.

Sometimes the road
sighs into the silver river,
sucks in the children
in their yellow bus.

Sometimes the doll lies prone
on a wooden table; almost without
a scalpel, some small part
is taken, and her eyes
fly open in their stiff lashes.

Sometimes the lock snaps off,
the cage
door does not open until
a wing grazes it
and the bird learns to fly.

Sometimes we do not know
the wall is
our own shadow,
until we lean
and it isn't there. ◇

Efficiency

M. Doretta Cornell

Flame has taken the maple this week,
drying zucchinis continue to bear
huge gold infertile blossoms
over the pumpkins, solid fruit
of last Halloween's spooks.

On my desk, the two-leaf vine now stretches
maroon and green-silver leaves toward my pen.
The coleus sprig, barely a month potted,
has ten leaves, all crimson-and-yellow streaked,
and two tiny autumn flowerets.

Even through the glass, they have
taken in the oncoming fall. What else
has fruited, colored, or last-flickered
out of sight of my efficient heart? ◇

Ubuntu

Carole Glasser Langille

WHEN THE PLANE LANDS, IT'S EARLY MORNING. MKHOKELI IS still groggy after only a few hours of sleep on the long flight. He passes through customs and miraculously finds his red plastic luggage among the first bags on the conveyor belt. He follows the other travelers out to the lobby and sees a cardboard sign with his name printed in large black letters. A white-haired woman holds up the sign. So, this is the woman. She is older than he thought, frail shoulders, lined face, but her eyes are bright. He goes up to her shyly, looks into her eyes, and smiles.

"Oh, Mkhokeli," she cries and gives him a hug. "Is that how you say your name?" She asks him to repeat it and he does.

He is in this country because of her. "An angel found you," Ayabonga said when they were kids and Esther Beckworth first came into his life. And now he is meeting her. *So many people everywhere, so many big cars*, he thinks, when they get Esther Beckworth's car from the parking lot. As they drive to her house, Mrs. Beckworth does most of the talking. She tells Mkhokeli what highway they are on—the New Jersey Turnpike going south—and later she points out Princeton, the university he will be attending.

When they arrive at her home she says he must be jet-lagged and perhaps would like to lie down. But he is too excited to sleep. He is surprised by this house. It has a pretty garden with many flowers, but it is not a large house and the paint is cracking. They passed fancy houses as they drove here and hers is not one of them. There are no servants. He always imagined Mrs. Beckworth rich, rich.

They go to her kitchen and she asks if Mkhokeli wants tea, if he is hungry. She has made a stew of beef and cabbage and potatoes and carrots. And steamed cornbread—*mm-bah-KAHNG-guh*. She knows from the letters they have exchanged for almost a decade that this is what he likes.

A big black dog comes into the room barking, excited to see Mrs. Beckworth, who pets him as he rises to meet her hand. Still barking, the dog jumps up on Mkhokeli as well, who laughs. He asks what the dog's name is.

"Ephrussi," Mrs. Beckworth tells him and explains that she named the dog after the Ephrussi family. "You'll probably be reading Proust at the university. His character Swann was based on Charles Ephrussi."

He has already read Proust, though he doesn't mention this. He liked the character Charles Swann very much. So much music in *Remembrance of Things Past*. He thinks of the song "Mbaqanga," the Mahlathini' Nkabinde song he and Ayabonga would dance to when they were alone in Ayabonga's house. *C'mon, c'mon, c'mon, c'mon, c'mon*. So much time has passed since then, and yet that moment has never left him. Time, how quickly it leaves and still remains.

She asks Mkhokeli to tell her what Cape Town is like.

"It's where the sea changes directions, wild, cold," he says, "and a mountain overlooks the sea. Cape Town is built into the side of the mountain. It's a pretty place where the keurboom and jacarandas bloom and the sugar bushes blossom with large red flowers."

But he did not grow up in Cape Town. He grew up in a village in the North West province, in a clapboard house, tin roof, seven people in three rooms, more houses every few feet. *But up in the hills there was an old shack with the remains of a garden*, he thinks. He and Ayabonga used to go there when they were sure no one would follow. Ayabonga was so skinny then. One day Cebisa, Ayabonga's cousin, came with them and put Mkhokeli's hair in dreads. It took hours, combing the hair, kneading in wax. Afterwards they had a feast of *umngqusho* and they danced till they were too tired to move. They did not have money but they had style.

HE HAS BEEN LIVING at Esther Beckworth's house more than a week before he sits down in his room to write Ayabonga a letter. He begins, *Ayabonga, I have read your letter twenty-seven times today. It is the first letter you sent me. I keep it with me, folded in my pocket. When I saw you, after I first got that letter, you put your hand on my shoulder. Do you remember? I still feel your hand. Ayabonga. My kereltjie.*

He puts away the letter he is writing.

He has taken to walking Ephrussi in the early evenings with Mrs. Beckworth. Here, dogs are treated like people. There are no *isicathamiyas*, no sneak attacks from brutal, unidentified men. Dogs are not used to hunt people.

He and Mrs. Beckworth are usually quiet on their walks. Even though he is shy, he finally asks her what he wants to know. How was it that she found him in South Africa? How was it her money ended up sending him to secondary school so that he was able to get a scholarship to a university in her country? There were many families as poor as his who could not afford to send their sons to school.

She tells him about Abuto, a man who teaches African Studies at Rutgers. He had been a good friend of her father, she says. It was Abuto who told her what was happening to people in South Africa, to people who couldn't hide who they were. Mkhokeli lets out a nervous laugh.

She tells him a story Abuto told her, a horrible, gruesome story. "But you know how dangerous it was," she says.

Now Mkhokeli lets out a sad laugh, a laugh that sounds like a sob. *Ayabonga, she knows*, he wants to tell his friend.

She says Abuto works with an organization that tries to protect students who are in danger, paying for these students to go to private schools where they are safer. She says that years ago Abuto told her what was happening, that even president Zuma bragged about beating up *ungqingili* when he was growing up because, the president explained, homosexuality was a sin against God and must be stopped. She knew she had to help. "Because, you see, in my own family . . . " Her voice trails off. And then she tells Mkhokeli about her father and he is surprised to hear her story. He thinks, *I must tell Ayabonga*. He thinks, *She is beautiful. If it weren't for her, I would not be in this country. I would probably not be alive.*

He realizes that he was chosen for this scholarship precisely because of what he was trying to conceal, that he was a *mary*, a *skeef*, *moffee*. He knew even when he was little that he was different. By the time he was eleven or twelve, he had already fallen in love with a boy in his village, even before he met Ayabonga. But who told the men and women who ran the charity that he was who he was? Did they all see so clearly what he had made such an effort to disguise?

Ayabonga told him years ago, "You know, I don't ever want to leave here. But you will leave. You will be one of the scatterlings of Africa. And you will tell your story." Ayabonga was the only one who knew Mkhokeli's other secret, that he wanted to write. And Ayabonga knew the story Mkhokeli wanted to tell.

Mkhokeli's father hated Ayabonga, forbade him from seeing his friend. *Umtathi uyawuzala umlotha*, he would say—the umtathi tree is a good tree but it turns to ash when you burn it. Which meant, of course, that a good man can have a bad son.

"He doesn't hate you. He's scared for you," Ayabonga said. When Mkhokeli's father would discipline Mkhokeli, tell him to stand up straight, to walk like a man, Ayabonga said, "He just wants you to blend in."

But Mkhokeli would not stop seeing Ayabonga. Even after he was sent away to school, he would seek out his friend when he came home on holiday.

Later he takes out the letter he began to Ayabonga and continues to write.

Ayabonga, remember we thought Mrs. *Beckworth was rich rich. So much money, she sent some to South Africa so I could go to school. We thought, a woman with so much, charity meant nothing. But she is not rich.* He tells Ayabonga, Mrs. *Beckworth's father knew the great writer* E. M. *Forster!* Ayabonga will not have heard of E. M. Forster but he will know why Mkhokeli is excited by this news. *She wanted to help a boy at risk because her father was like us. Itshoni lingenandaba*, the sun doesn't set without news.

At the private school she paid for, in Cape Town, it was not so dangerous. The uniform made a difference. He was no longer called *rent boy*, a *lisa*, names the boys would call him in his village. But Ayabonga did not have his patron or his luck.

It's cold in New Jersey. He is not used to this cold. Mrs. Beckworth tells him she hopes he will treat her home as his home when he is at the university and visit whenever he feels homesick.

He realizes he *will* visit Mrs. Beckworth. When he imagined meeting her, he knew he would feel obligated to the woman who helped him. He had always felt grateful. But now he feels more than obligation. This woman knew who he was even before she met him. He starts to feel a shift, some terrible heaviness lighten. He does not have to keep secrets from her. They share something.

It is like a warm wind that descends from the mountains and rushes to the sea, this realization. Perhaps her father did not fear for his life, as he had. But because of her father, she knows what it is to live a life that others might not understand. Mkhokeli sees, too, that she has had to make sacrifices to help him. Such sacrifices, year after year, were a way to honor her father. A father who kept his secret from his daughter until after he died. *Hayi*. No. He will not visit because he is homesick. That cannot be cured by coming to see Esther Beckworth. But he will visit.

For a moment an odd thought crosses his mind. Was his father so critical of him because he was afraid for him? He is not sure. But in his head he can hear Ayabonga whispering, *This is what I have been trying to tell you.*

He goes to his room to continue his letter. *Remember, Ayabonga, when we danced to the Mahotella Queens. How we laughed about that name. Chula, chula, chula.*

Mrs. Beckworth lights the fireplace for Mkhokeli. She thinks he may be cold even though it is late summer. When she knocks on the door of his room, he tells her to come in. He is writing a letter, he says.

"Is it to Ayabonga?" she asks.

He is surprised she should say this. He wrote to her about Ayabonga. Surely she remembers that letter. Still, she has asked him the question. He nods.

"Yes," he says. The letter is to Ayabonga. *Intaka yakha ngoboya benye*, a bird builds its nest with another's feathers. Ayabonga's love has been his only real home, no matter where he is.

She tells him she has made tea, asks will he join her.

"*Ndiyagula*," he says, "I feel sick."

But he follows her to the living room. When they sit on the couch he hands her the letter.

"Read it," he tells her. Then he says, "*Ubuntu*." When she asks what that means he says, "I am what I am because you are what you are."

When she finishes the letter, she sighs. Her face is full of sympathy as she hands it back. *It is not a distraction*, he wants to tell her, *this writing to Ayabonga. It is the whole story*. Ayabonga was his initiation, his secret, his fortune, his loss.

"In Xhosa," he says, "the past and the present are not divided. They are part of the same meal."

His voice is hardly a whisper and his breathing is shallow. He wishes, as he has wished so many times in the last year, that he could wipe his mind clean and forget. *A man says it's a good world and he ends up with his throat slit in a rented apartment in Kuruman, his tongue cut out, genitals hacked off and stuffed in his mouth*. He cannot get the image of Ayabonga's mutilated body out of his mind.

But my feeling for Ayabonga can't be killed, Mkhokeli thinks and starts to cry. *Who made me, here and why?* he wants to say.

Ayabonga Lebala Ka Nna. I will never forget you, he thinks. He gets up and walks to the fireplace. He tosses the letter in the fire and watches it flare up.

Mrs. Beckworth walks over to him. She puts her hand on his shoulder for a moment, then lets it fall to her side. They stand there together for a long time, watching the flames and listening to the crackling. ◇

Hope

Ellen Rachlin

. . . is larger than now, certainly
than angels, the heft of talismans,
any pain or truth,
and more miraculous than miracles,
the natural world that crawls
across a leaf, generosity, or illusions.

Seek no deadline for hope,
the counterpoint to time;
when placed side by side,
time becomes hope's predator. ◇

Hidden Agenda

Alan Beechey

1. Buy you flowers.
2. Name your breasts.
3. Go to a football game with you because, strange as it must sound for a guy from Jersey, I've never been to a game in my life.
4. Clean your car out for you, if only to see if that story about you losing an open can of sardines is true.
5. Cook you a meal, probably my amazing cumin-crusted lamb chops.
6. Give you the satisfaction of knowing you have a boyfriend who's the only person in the Tri-State area who knows how to pronounce "cumin" the right way. As in, "She'll be cumin round the mountain."
7. Keep sneaking that stuffed rabbit you bought me into surprising places. (I was going to ask your son to put it in your bed while you were down at the Keys.)
8. Hear the wolves howling in the Adirondacks, like you promised.
9. Bite your magnificent bottom.
10. Hear you play the "Chant d'amour" I wrote for you.
11. Hear you play the dozens of other pieces I planned to write for you.
12. Take one really good photograph of you that you will like for once and not make me delete. Good enough for you to use as a headshot, with my name in very small print underneath.

13. Have more of those long, rambling conversations in coffee shops, interrupting each other with jokes and stories and reminiscences, until we suddenly realize we're competing to tell each other the same obscure anecdote about Irving Berlin's piano.
14. Go hiking, just the two of us, somewhere isolated, and never run out of things to say, except when we stop to make love in the open air, frequently.
15. Watch a Vincent Price movie with you. I recommend *The Abominable Doctor Phibes*.
16. Dedicate my first musical to you, when it gets produced. Well, finished, then sold, then produced.
17. Be the dedicatee of your first recital CD, as long as it isn't Britten. I don't get Britten. Brahms is okay.
18. Continue to slip tubes of Preparation-H into your shopping cart when we "accidentally" meet at the supermarket, to see your face when you get to the checkout.
19. Tell you the stories that I'm too embarrassed to tell anyone else, like the time I was in a toy shop in Ridgewood and I noticed I had dirt on my hands, so it being a toyshop, I assumed they'd be equipped with some basic child cleaning supplies, and I approached the young lady behind the counter and asked her if she had a Wet One.
20. Go to more of your solo recitals and be the first to jump up for the ovation at the end.
21. Get to have lunch at that special vegetarian restaurant you love so much, and not have it matter if we run into your brother there, because by then, he'd know about us.
22. Finally hear the full detailed story about that one girl-girl (girl-girl-girl?) experience you said you had in college.
23. Swim with you.
24. Swim *naked* with you.
25. Learn to be a really good accompanist just so I can help you in rehearsal.
26. Show you that trick of getting a spider out of the bathroom with a glass and index card.

27. Then take a long, long soapy shower with you.
28. Have you with me looking like a million bucks when I collect my first Tony.
29. Convince you that I don't care when or where you last shaved if there's an unexpected opportunity to make out with you.
30. Remember how you like your coffee at the Medical Center cafe (large, dash of vanilla, half-and-half).
31. Prove that without first-night (well, first-lunchtime) nerves, guilt, haste, or a cat watching me, I'm the best lover you'll ever have. Ever. Honestly.
32. Punch out any passing wiseass who sees you struggling to get your cello into the back of a cab and asks you what it's like to perform while straddling such a big instrument. Seriously, I'd do it, even if it happens every day.
33. Believe you when you tell me I'm good-looking.
34. Persuade you that although you are beautiful and all men do want you, only one of them will ever love you as much as I do.
35. Change your flat tire myself next time instead of calling the garage, because I'd have been missed if I'd stayed any longer.
36. Buy a dress shirt that isn't white just to please you.
37. Spend an entire afternoon naked in bed, kissing and worshiping your upper torso. Feel your tongue come as far into my mouth as mine is in yours.
38. Google you regularly.
39. Let you know whenever a Cary Grant movie is coming up on TCM.
40. Tell you rude stories in my Christopher Walken voice.
41. Watch you pee, because you insisted on watching me that one time when I needed to use your bathroom.
42. Show you how I framed the scrap of paper on which you scribbled your email address, the first time I found out your name.
43. Get to know your children better.
44. Lick your armpits. Suck your toes. Kiss your new scar.
45. Meet your parents.
46. Hold you all night for the first time.

47. Wake up with you for the first time.
48. Become a vegetarian, to share meals with you. I guess that would mean those lamb chops are a non-starter. Ha, "non-starter"!
49. Assure you that I'd never expect you to turn off a recording of the Dvořák Cello Concerto that you're studying just so I can watch a baseball game with the surround sound on, like some people we could mention. Well, one person that you did mention.
50. Spank you. Harder than you're expecting.
51. Talk you through every checkup, even if it's not kosher for me to be there in person.
52. Get to meet the rest of your brothers and sisters.
53. Be the first person you want to run to when things don't go so well.
54. Have something else to talk about. Always.
55. Sit back and watch you pleasure yourself, just once. (Any more and it would mess with my confidence.)
56. Start a conversation with a stranger on the bus, because you do.
57. Watch *The Red Shoes* with you and admit finally that I've never seen it all the way through.
58. Interrupt. Without acrimony.
59. Show you how partners should truly treat each other, starting with never taking you for granted.
60. Get over my jealousy of your lifetime platonic friend Mitch, even if you assure me all the romantic attraction is one-way and you only kissed him that one time to shut him up.
61. Check you subtly to see if you're wearing underwear.
62. Have afternoon tea together whenever possible. Green, for my health. And yours.
63. Become that old couple you once pointed out to me on Broadway and 72nd—the one still holding hands in their eighties, the one you said you could see us being in fifty years. I guess that was chemicals talking.
64. Serious doggy style, in front of that cheval mirror. Also cowgirl. Remove all cats first.
65. Prove that despite the way the Princeton recital turned out, I can still be a lucky talisman for you.

66. Stop defending your husband when you want to kvetch about him.
67. Show you that after age 36, age 37 is also a good year for the woman in my life.
68. And then 38, 39, 39, 39 . . .
69. Make you realize that I'm telling the absolute truth when I say that if I can finally have you, I'll never want another woman or imagine a better one for me.
70. Convince you that you'll never want another man.
71. Defy the medical profession's current opinion and live forever.
72. Remind you that I first used the phrase "it must be fate" only five days after we started talking in the waiting room.
73. Never go to sleep at night without a kiss. God, can you kiss!
74. Lament with you that we met too late to have children together.
75. Adopt a cat together.
76. Have a partner who always knows exactly when I'm being playful.
77. Demonstrate that you were right about falling in love when you're well past the teenage years. It's rarer, and it endures.
78. Encourage you to say no sometimes. Even to me.
79. Be happy.
80. Send you more "Nice ass, Lady" texts at inopportune moments, because it is. A nice ass.
81. Get back copies of all our emails that I deleted out of caution.
82. Get back the now deleted selfie you sent me of you naked in the bathroom.
83. Get to a point where it's okay for you to touch me, hold my hand, lean on me in public places, like I had to stop you from doing before.
84. Make you keep your promise to never marry me, because marriage brings us both bad luck.
85. Actually, be outrageously happy, even if we don't deserve it, although we do. Laugh and laugh and laugh.
86. Show you that diet and exercise can improve the way I look and keep me in remission.

87. Get all of my top ten erotic moments of all time filled with memories of you, instead of just the four you currently occupy.
88. Listen to you. Hear about your days again.
89. Hear you tell me you're crazy about me again.
90. Kiss you at least once more, and not that half-hearted soulless kind of kiss you gave me the last time we met at the diner, which somehow missed my mouth.
91. Find out finally what you were planning to give me for my birthday and what you did with it.
92. Be there again for the scary times. And vice versa.
93. Ask you face-to-face if you can possibly imagine sharing with anyone else the secrets and intimacies and intimations that we've shared. Ask you if anyone could ever know you as well as I do already. Ask you why we would want to let that go without one more chance.
94. Keep my hair, since you like it so much. Or grow it back after the treatment, if it comes to that.
95. Convince you that when you fall in love for the first time in twenty years, it deserves more of a chance than just six weeks.
96. Do something in my life utterly amazing, just once, to make you as proud of me as I am of having been so profoundly loved by someone as accomplished as you.
97. Be patient. Be bold. For once in my damn life, just be bold.
98. Okay, I mean be selfish. For once in my damn life, put my needs first and screw the consequences.
99. Ask you how I can go from being, potentially, "the love of your life" to "the last man on earth" you think you should be with, in just a couple of months, after all I went through for you.
100. Keep making additions to this list, even though we both know that you'll never read them.
101.

◇

As if She Knew

for C. S. (1968-2011)

Lucia Cherciu

I wanted her scarves,
her earrings and diaries,
her hand-held mirrors,
her hair brushes, and her shoes.

I wanted to go to her house
and clean her tea cups,
the smudge of lipstick
on the rim.

I wanted to go through her
closet,
organize her camisoles by color,
even the pieces I couldn't tell
if a tube top or a bottom.

I wanted to take away her
reading chair
and haul it back to my house,
place it in front of my window
and laugh her careless laugh.

I wanted to go through her jars
of make-up, stick my fingers
in some sweet smelling goo
and spread it on my face.

I wanted to steal her sexy skirts
and wear them with high
heels—
but most of all I wanted the
books
that she bought with abandon
as if she knew. ◇

The Beacon

James H. Zorn

Surely some revelation is at hand.
— Yeats

SOMETIMES IN THE LATE AFTERNOONS IT BECAME TOO HOT TO WORK in the greenhouses, so Mr. Read would call us out under the shade of the immense oak tree by the street, where we would sit drinking cold drinks from the bottle and listening to his stories. Usually they were about ordinary things, some character he had met thirty years before in a diner in Chicago, some incident from his childhood growing up in the Midwest. There were four of us working for him, all high school boys. We didn't always believe him, but as he described to us people who had died long before we were born, places we had never been, we knew that we were being given a gift of rare importance, although we couldn't know yet how we would use it. For him, I think that his talking to us was one way of tracing back the complicated weave of events that had brought him finally to owning this little place in this small southern town, growing chrysanthemums for high school graduation, poinsettias for Christmas.

On this particular afternoon, the radio was playing on a table made of two sawhorses near the potting shed door. Dusk was not far away, the air heavy with the sense of gathering of a late-summer day, an atmosphere that at any moment might decide to storm. We had been talking, the conversation slipping into a lull. On the radio, the station announcer began reading the news, drawling his wire reports of recent and potential global catastrophes as if reading the sales list from the local grocery store chain. We were nervous that summer; the world loomed before us, threatening and threatened. As we accepted the honors of graduation and jauntily compared schemes for our lives, alone in our rooms at night we couldn't help wondering whether we would be able to accomplish all that we had bragged and whether the world might not even let us try.

Read filled one of the corncob pipes he bought by the bagful from the Bottom Dollar down the street and sat eyeing us, as if reading our minds. Suddenly he sat forward and drew a circle with his finger in the dirt at his feet. "Listen," he said.

"The town in Nebraska where I grew up was here." He drew a line out from the circle, beside it a series of squares. "Running out of town, like this, was a road. And on this road were the farms: our farm, the Eldritch farm, and so on all the way down to Aubry Bennett's place." He lit his pipe, shook out the match, and sat back. "This happened in 1919, just after the end of the first war. Late one evening out at our place, the phone went off and my dad answered it. All the telephones on this road were on one line, one single party line that connected all twelve farms. All day long, a big storm had been brewing up. Across the western part of the sky, all you could see was black clouds, no stars, and the wind was blowing like all hell. It was Aubry Bennett on the other end. 'All you men,' he said—and Aubry was a big man, heavy-set, so I've always imagined that his voice was especially deep and low on this night—'all you men come out here. Come out to my place. I want you all to see something. I want you to tell me if you see it too.'"

Read paused to relight his pipe. "I don't know what went on at the other farms. At our place, my dad hung up the phone and stood by it. Then he came back into the kitchen and told me to hitch up the wagon. Although I was just a boy, I was the only other male in the house. My oldest brother hadn't been furloughed from the military yet, and the next one above me had a job in town."

It was the wind that had blown the door off Aubry's hayloft, Read said, and Aubry had gone up there to fix it. He climbed the narrow ladder to the loft and stood in the open place where the door had been. The wind came fast and hard up there, and he had to brace himself against the doorframe as he looked out to the western horizon, to where the sky was all dark and full of clouds except for a tiny band of light from the setting sun, far out over the empty Midwestern plain. And that was where he saw it. The band of sunlight on the horizon grew narrower and finally vanished, but the light that Aubry saw did not disappear, it only grew brighter. He stood there, buffeted by the wind, his rope still clutched in his hand, watching, until it came to him, the meaning of this light and this night and this storm like no other. Then he climbed down and went into the house to call the other men.

"We all rode out there," Read said, "all the men who had answered Aubry's call. Some even brought their wives and children. I rode with my dad in the wagon . . ."

Read kept on speaking, his blue eyes flecked with gray and a sympathetic, ironic humor. His story took only a few moments to tell, and probably bore no more relationship to what really happened than what I imagined had to do with what he said. It is the product of both our imaginations, of the apocalypse embedded in every human heart, born of dread and hope. I tell it as I saw it when he told it, as I've continued to see it in the years since then, just as he had. The meaning of it for me is tied up in the image of that wagon, moving slowly across a plain dominated by rainless thunderclouds, along a rutted road towards a horizon that will never be reached.

THEY RODE OUT just after nine o'clock, the man and the boy side by side on the wagon seat. The wind came from the west in swift, sudden gusts that shook the tiny wagon and frightened the horses and then died away again just as suddenly. Far off on the southwestern edge of the sky, they saw where lightning shook the clouds in a tremulous paleness that was born, extinguished, and reborn in an instant, illuminating the plain below. Although the boy had ridden this road many times in his life, under the effects of the night and the storm, the landscape seemed changed, and he saw it now as something new and strange. The Bennett farm lay at the edge of the township and of the county; beyond that was only the next county and the endless plain. Later, he could look back and laugh at how restricted his borders had been, but then, at nine years old, the Bennett farm seemed on the edge of the world to him, the county beyond that, a mere rumor.

The last time he had ridden this road had been seven months before, when he and his mother and father and sisters had come out in the wagon to pay their respects to Aubry after the funeral of his wife and daughter. The dirt road had looked different then, the fields covered in February snow like sleeping brides, and he had been irritable, forced to dress up in his Sunday best and not really understanding why they were there except that something terrible had happened and that it meant he had to sit quiet and mannerly with the other children on stiff-backed chairs while the adults talked in low voices among themselves.

The two women had died in a tragic accident back east, where they had been visiting relatives, when the automobile in which they were riding went out of control, hit a wagon, and plunged over a steep embankment, killing them both and the driver instantly. It had been in all the local papers, and nearly half the county had turned out to offer its condolences to Aubry after the bodies were shipped home. Aubry had sat in a chair in the parlor, his hands hanging limply over the armrests, staring at nothing and speaking only when spoken to. His youngest and only remaining daughter played the role of hostess, accepting the gifts of food that the ladies brought and talking with them in a quiet, straightforward voice about the accident. The men stood on the porch and smoked, and occasionally one came in to pat Aubry on the back and shake his hand before loading up his wife and children and leaving. The big man sat quietly; he had not cried or cursed God or even gotten up and walked around, and the boy was bored with him beyond tears long before his father came in and said the few words to Aubry and his daughter that signaled the boy and the rest of the family that it was finally time to go home.

That was not the last time he had seen Aubry Bennett, but it was the image of him that was strongest in his mind as they reached the Bennett place. The turnoff was marked by the remains of an ancient ash near the point where the main road and the almost invisible track to the farmhouse met. His father called out to the nervous horses to calm them as he turned the wagon; the tree was half-dead, hit in the last season by some mysterious blight, and the branches on that side hung out dangerously over the road, swaying in the wind.

There were lights on in all the windows as they came up, and he could see women watching from the kitchen, some with small children in their arms. The men stood in a silent knot in the yard, their hats pulled down low over their faces. There was Mr. Van Doon, and Mr. Addermeyer, and John Eldritch, only a few years older than himself. He saw old man Borgsen standing beside his son. They were from the farm nearest; presumably they had been the first to answer Aubry's call. Beside them stood Eli Carroway, the Henry brothers, Carter Thompson; all familiar to him, all strange as they stood glancing uneasily up at the sky and the barn.

He and his father saw to the horses and walked towards the others. They were just a few steps away when the cluster of men parted to reveal another figure standing hatless and oblivious to the wind. It was Aubry Bennett. He turned and came towards them with his big hand outstretched and took his father by the shoulder and said something into his ear which the boy could not hear over the roar of the wind, and as the boy looked up at him, the memory of the morose victim of tragedy fell away from his mind, replaced with another memory, half forgotten, of the last time he had seen Aubry Bennett.

It had been in the beginning of the summer harvest season, when one of the traveling revival shows that were so active in that part of the country in those days had hit town. This one had somehow managed to get itself aligned with the annual country fair and had secured a tent on the corner of the fairground, where each year the people of the county came to see competitions among the men in cattle and horse breeding and the women in baking and quilting. This was the last year that the fair would be held in its traditional spot. The county had already leased the site to a Wisconsin construction firm that planned to build there a new, modern grain yard to take advantage of the rail line coming through, and a new location for the fair had already been chosen across the river.

The wealthier, more educated citizens of the county seldom attended the revivals; it was always those from out on the plain, isolated from schools and towns, who came year after year, faithfully, and were not disappointed. The boy's family was one of those who never went, but on this particular evening he had been playing a wild game of catch-me with two other boys and had run inside the stained revival tent looking for a place to hide. Instantly, the atmosphere arrested him, so different from the horsy, good-natured stalls of the men's competitions or the warm tents of the women, smelling of baked goods and starched cotton. He stopped still and began edging slowly away along the wall of the tent towards the front.

The tent was full of people. All were strangers to him, jam-packed so close together that there was scarcely room for a drop of sweat to fall to the sawdust-covered earth. From their clothes, he judged most of them to be poor farmers up from the dryer regions in the southern part of the county where nothing would grow, or hired men and their wives, the drifters that made up the bulk of the summer harvest work. The air was heavy with the smell of gaunt country people, of sweat and hay and dust. It was starting to get dark outside and small kerosene lamps had been hung from the roof of the tent; they did little to dispel the dimness and only added to the stifling heat, like being inside the belly of a whale.

The rituals had almost reached their peak. On a platform in front, a man in a dusty black suit held his hands up high, his face turned towards heaven, his eyes closed, shouting words that were by now almost unintelligible against the response of the crowd. Behind him, a thin, pimply youth in a string tie and white shirt answered his cries with "Hallelujah!" and "Praise God!" In the dim light, the boy watched the women sway, their bodies distorted with too many child-bearings. The men stood with their heads bowed, trembling, or their eyes fixed on the preacher; from some rang out shouts of "Hallelujah!" and "Bless you, Brother!" Along the edge of the wall near the door stood a few skeptics who had only come to watch, their fascination hidden under expressions of disdain or amusement.

The preacher was the center of all attention: he was the Powerhouse, the Beacon of God, the source from which all immanence of the

Almighty sprang. He moved about the little stage fixating them with his voice and his body, working the crowd in the same way that the heat at the planet's core works upon stones, until at last there is an earthquake. Behind him, his assistant swayed and moaned, his shirt stained with sweat. It was always the same, year after year, although it was seldom the same preacher and assistant two years in a row; they always moved on, somewhere east, farther out west, though there was never any shortage of them, as if the earth itself provided a constant supply to take their place.

This preacher was in good form tonight. Just when the crowd's passion was at its highest, just when he had convinced them to the marrow of their bones of the reality of God's judgment, of the coming Wrath, of the torture of Hell-fire and the punishment of the rebellious spirits, he offered them an option. They were cursed, he told them, cursed from the moment they were born, but God had left open this one slim hope: they took it now or else got ready to spend an eternity in Hell. Under the spell of his words, they could see it as clearly as if he had painted it on a wall, the angels up above and the damned souls rolling and pitching below. A trumpet sounded; a book opened; and the world split asunder.

They came. First one and two and then more fell at his feet, begging for redemption. For some, it was the first time; for others, a seasonal occurrence, which they anticipated with inchoate excitement. They pushed through the crowd to fall stricken at the edge of the platform, pleading to be free of the awful vision called up in them. The preacher gave them that forgiveness with a word, a pressure of the hand, and while some wept at their release, others fell back with joy, grasping their nearest neighbors.

The area around the stage was almost full and the boy had just pushed his way up to the very front when suddenly a man burst out of the crowd, bellowing like a bull pierced beneath its skin. He came charging through the press of bodies to the stage, where he grabbed the surprised preacher by both his ankles and stared up into his face with such a look of terrified recognition that the preacher was startled out of his momentum.

It was Aubry Bennett. For an instant, all movement in the tent seemed to stop: there was only Aubry, trembling in front of the platform, his sweat-stained face staring up into the face of the man on the platform, his mouth working but issuing no sound. The preacher looked down at the big man's face and saw in it a wild look of terror and revelation. Aubry *believed*, and for that moment, the other salvation seekers beside him seemed mere dilettantes, triflers in the face of Aubry's vision of a world created, destroyed, and remade at a word.

Then it was over. Aubry's body shook as if he would split apart. From his mouth came a single, strangled "*Yes, God!*" and he collapsed to the ground, hands over his face, sobbing.

Time resumed its normal flow; the preacher recovered and swept again into motion, resuming his rightful place at the center of attention, working his trade. A breath of relief passed over the crowd; something had just happened that frightened them even more than the preacher's vision, something too real. They pressed forward once more, seeking comfortable salvation. Aubry shrank to just another convert, and within moments, his body was hidden underneath the press of others around the stage.

Aubry Bennett had meant nothing to him then, and by the time the boy forced his way out of the tent and into the cool evening, the incident was near forgotten. He would not recall it again until that night, the night of the storm, when the big man came towards them with his hand outstretched, his eyes burning with the same conviction that the boy had seen that night in the tent, the night Aubry had been reborn.

His words were swept away by the wind, but it didn't matter; the boy didn't need to hear them. He knew all he needed to know from his father's expression, from the way he looked up at the broken barn door and then to the horizon. The faces of the men in the yard followed Aubry's pointing hand with an apprehension that could not be explained as the casual indulgence of a neighbor's mad request, while from the house the women watched, their faces pressed against the glass panes. The big man turned and began to move towards the barn. The boy, his father, and the others followed.

Two at a time the men climbed the narrow ladder to the loft and stared out over the plain to the far horizon. It was an image the boy would remember often for the rest of his life, looking up from the ground at the black mouth of the loft, the three men—Aubry, Mr. Borgsen, and his son—framed in it, hands holding their hats, wind whipping their clothes, their eyes fixed on the distance where Aubry pointed. Below stood the small knot of their neighbors, acolytes waiting their turn at initiation.

After a while, they came down. Little was said. Aubry was wrong, they all knew that. There had to be some other reason for what they saw, some simple explanation, and yet they couldn't think of it. Their place and time had provided them with an answer, one they had been taught all their lives to expect, later rather than sooner, hopefully, but inevitably, in any case. With a nod at their counterparts, the men indicated that they had seen. Those who had climbed the ladder stood a little apart from the others, a group to which newcomers were accepted only after they had climbed the ladder and witnessed. The boy and his father were the last to join Aubry. John Eldritch and Eli Carroway came down and went to join the others, and he and his father stepped forward into the darkness of the barn.

The musty quiet inside seemed unnatural, full of space, like a cathedral. A single lantern hung next to the door, its light pale in the volume of emptiness surrounding it. In front of them, they saw the ladder. The boy reached it first and began scaling its weathered wooden rungs while his father, frowning, followed more cautiously behind. The boy could hear the shriek of the wind through the open loft door and felt the cold touch of the air after the warmth of the barn. He reached the top and scrambled out onto the hay-covered floor, wiping his dusty hands on his overalls, his heart pounding.

Aubry stood in front of the opening in the wall, framed against the stormy landscape. The boy crossed the wooden floor to him, his father heaving up behind. The big man pointed and spoke—*It's been there since nightfall*, he may have said—but the words were lost in the wind. They were unnecessary. The boy could see it immediately, sharp against the tumbling horizon, bright as sunlight reflected off a shield.

It was a white light. It flashed and died and flashed again, racing across the plain like riders on hooves towards some other, distant tower. Below them, he could sense the faces of the men on the ground, upturned, watching them. The boy and his father didn't look at them; their eyes were fixed on the horizon, on the light. It defied them to explain it, impossible, enigmatic. In one part of their minds, they knew what it was; each man who had seen it that night knew what it was and trembled at the answer: a light that raced from west to east, calling forth the sunrise of the day, the last day, the Day of Judgment.

So they looked, and after a while they got tired of looking and climbed down. The men gathered around the wagons, talking about what they had seen, spitting, sheltering from the wind; but there was really nothing much to say about it, and anyway it was late and time to go. They loaded up their wives and children and boarded their wagons and went home. As the horses sought the narrow track to the main road, the boy turned back. Aubry was still in the yard, the wind blowing his hair, fists at his side, watching them, or maybe just staring at the horizon.

It was after midnight when they got home. His sisters were asleep, his mother waiting up, of course, but before he could tell her anything, his father sent him instantly and unequivocally to bed. He lay on the familiar mattress not even pretending to sleep, listening to his parents talking in the kitchen, wondering if the end of the world meant there would be no school this year. He was still awake and listening when his father came out of the kitchen and went to the front door and stood by it for a long while. Then he heard a click as, for the first time in his memory while anyone was in the house, his father locked the door.

It was four a.m. before it finally began to rain.

THE OLD MAN LAUGHED, lit his pipe, and looked at us. "But what did they see? That's the question."

For a moment he stared off into the distance, down the long quiet street lined with oaks and pecan trees still weeks away from the first hints of their autumn change of colors. Behind him, the radio announcer finished the news and, after an advertisement, the music began again. "There's two things I have to tell you before I can finish this story," Read said, looking at us. "The first is a piece of information you probably didn't know and never thought worth knowing until now: until 1919, there was no such thing as airmail service in the Midwest. That was the year the post office commissioned the first planes to fly regular routes across the Great Plains states."

He looked us in the eyes. "The second thing is this: in our town, the Sunday papers didn't arrive until Tuesday. That's how long it took them to get there from Omaha. It's a very small matter, but an important one, because you can see how this one fact, this little delay of two days, could make all the difference then."

He paused, shook his head, and went on. "So they all went home and locked their doors and waited. The next morning, Tuesday, the papers came. And they read.

"It was the beacons," he said, "the damnable beacons that the mail service put up to guide their planes across all that empty Midwestern farmland. That was all; nothing else. The storm was just an unusual late-summer storm, and those men were nothing but a bunch of ignorant farmers who saw something they couldn't explain and thought that the end of the world was at hand."

He drew on his pipe and looked at us. "Or were they? Because I've always remembered that night, through all my wanderings and all the things that have happened to me since then. All those men are dead now, the world they lived in doesn't exist any more. It's gone as clean as if God himself had wiped it away." He sat forward, his face close. "I'll tell you what I think," he said. "Those ignorant farmers thought the world was ending, but it wasn't. Of course not. Nothing ever really ends. It just . . . changes."

He chuckled, lighting his pipe, watching us. "A few days later, somebody went out and pulled that beacon down. Nobody admitted they knew who had done it, or why. The postal service put it up again, of course."

We sat quietly, he smoking his pipe, looking off down the street. Above us, the sky moved towards evening through the leaves of the tree, green but waiting. Nearby, the radio prattled on. ◇

Eden, Renovated

A. Anupama

The cries of gulls were all
        after all
        after the garden gate, still flanked by red honeysuckle
and the bare sticks that are the butterfly bushes, standing guard
in the dense mud, what stayed
        after the flooding storm. The stone
        stayed in its place, but the bench was set down closer
        to it, in the middle of the path. Look up, the gull watches you
        from the top of the lamppost. The ground sprouts eyelash ferns,
reddish-brown in the cold, waits for you to look down, touch again gently
while kneeling. ◇

Eva's Ocean

Susan Moorhead

OUT FIRST THING WITH THE DOG ON THIS COLD MORNING, THE good thing about dogs, getting you out when you wouldn't be otherwise. Like last night during a late walk, houses asleep beneath a star-grazed blue light, the underneath of bushes and low trees dark with a slight menace even though you are forty-something and should not harbor illusions about the night.

Just past dawn, your breath patterns the chilled air with lacy fog while the dog, invigorated, prances down the driveway ignoring your slogging feet, and at his first pause and sniff you realize you are thinking about Eva. You haven't thought about her in a detailed way for several years. When you drive past her house, sometimes your husband will mention, "Boy, those new people sure fixed up Eva's old house," though they are no longer new people three years in. But now, towed down the street by the eager dog, you notice the leaf-stripped trees have once again ceased to muffle the sound of the parkway, the cars on it making a continual whooshing sound day or night. Eva lived half a block down from your house, her yard backing up to the tall barrier fence of the parkway.

You asked her once if the sound of cars passing bothered her. "No," she said, shrugging ancient shoulders, "I am deaf enough that it sounds like the sea to me. Tide in, tide out, I like it."

She would try to join you on walks, tottering on ninety-three-year-old stiffened limbs, a critical word for every yard you passed at a snail's pace. *They hog up the street with their big ugly car, they raise brats, their yard looks like a dump.* You were not spared when she stood in front of your driveway saying that your children were like wild creatures running around your yard, your little dog yipping in joy at the chaos. These things enraged her.

The sixty-something widow with the Maltese who lives in the house with the yellow shutters claimed Eva drank huge amounts of scotch starting midmorning. The stay-at-home mom who walks the enthusiastic Golden Retriever chimed in that Eva's behavior was alarming and that her dog did not like her.

Her next-door neighbor, a difficult man who insisted on parking his car in front of someone else's home in the daytime instead of his own driveway, said all that birdseed laid out in pans brought rats. He called the health department that year before he moved to Florida.

You had to warn your children never to go into her home, no matter how much she insisted, after you helped her carry in groceries and your seven-year-old son lifted what looked like an antique firearm off her coffee table and Eva waved a casual hand at him, "Put that gun down, it's loaded." You helped her unload heavy sacks of birdseed that she had no business purchasing since she could not lift them from her car that she had no business driving since she could barely see. Hearing the clack of her cane on the asphalt, neighbors were known to flee into their garages or duck back in their front doors.

You disliked her as well, annoyed at her waving down your car to constantly ask for your help, annoyed it was always you roped into her needs because you were the one stupid enough to stop your car and say, "Yes, Eva?" You attempted to avoid her after particularly vicious remarks about your expanding waistline and how she thought you had no sense of what was appropriate to wear when expecting. During the next storm you relented, made sure she had a flashlight and your phone number. Later, to thank you, she left some old *National Geographics* in your car that you had forgotten to lock. She left the door wide open, killing the battery. She told your husband when he mentioned it to her that she had no time for stupid.

She walked through your kitchen door uninvited the evening after the funeral waving withered arms at your startled friends, "Why?"

she demanded to know, "are these people here?" She had never been inside your house before, but the lineup of parked cars signifying some neighborhood event she was not privy to ignited a great agitation in her. Your friends tried to calm her and shield you from her shouting as they explained about the infant's death, how she must not carry on so. Finally, you came over and soothed her, offered her something to eat, explained they were here after the funeral, and all was as well as could be expected. She nodded then, silent. That level of suffering she seemed to understand.

When she died they found her house packed with empty scotch bottles and huge sacks of birdseed, the sacks nibbled open, seeds spilling out on the floor, mouse droppings in liberal doses embedded in the once-fine oriental carpets. A family of distant relatives came to close up the house, full of stories about how difficult she was and how she kept herself isolated. How after her only sibling died, a brother, no one had really kept in touch. "Really?" you say to their surprised faces. "We were all so fond of Eva. She always had such interesting things to say. She will be missed. The neighborhood just won't be the same."

You had never seen any of these people in the decade you lived on this street. You watched them paw at her things, lifting a clock off the mantel to feel its heft. Appraise an oil painting with dollar signs in their eyes.

The dog tugs at the leash, interrupts your thoughts. She didn't like the dog but that was your other dog who is dead now, like Eva. Although she wouldn't have liked this dog either. You turn towards home under the pearled morning sky as the dog sniffs the wealth of the ground, as the whoosh of the parkway sings in your ears like ocean waves rolling in. ◇

Old Croton Aqueduct

Resa Mestel

Walk along the double arch bridge
to the weir house, descend its cast
iron steps to a mastery of construction,
madness of engineers whose nod
to the Romans led a gravity-fed tube
along a gentle gradient, 13 inches per mile,
through the hillsides of the Hudson Valley,
to bring water to a thirsty, parched metropolis.

In the tunnel, root tendrils from unseen
trees above claw at mortar, adorn porous
angled brick like a widow's veil, flakes
of rust drop from the ferrous gate
stuck upright in a lock of time.
Gear teeth will not turn in this century.

Breathe trapped air like a humidor preserves
a fine smoke, wipe the mud of history off
our gaiters, bat guano off our scalps, shield
our eyes from top-down sunlight of the

vaulted roof, swat cobwebs from our faces,
sniff the turbid pool that rests where
immigrant workers threw their cigarette ashes,
stale lunch pail dregs, humus to be carried
with the flush at the end of a thorough scrub.

What will keep the flood waters back?
We drown each day we turn the faucets on,
drip into the flow of fever tide, pour into
plastic bottles that roll on the river's skin,
a massage wand as we ride with the dauntless
crew of the Croton Maid on her singular voyage. ◇

Fusion

Lee Waxenberg

BRETT OFTEN SAID IF HE HAD TO BE IN THE WRONG PLACE AT THE wrong time, at least he was with the right girl. He embraced this philosophy with the unwavering fervor of a true believer, a fanatic follower of the private religion of me. I was nothing less to him than a personally delivered gift from a higher being.

I found my husband's devotion harmless, even a bit endearing, until a random family he spoke to in a coffee shop charged into Dr. Corbin's office at the hospital I worked at and demanded that I be a part of their mother's treatment team. I had been working under Dr. Corbin for only a few months, and interns like me were interchangeable. Patients rarely bothered to learn our names, let alone ask for us specifically. Yet Brett had convinced this family that I could somehow graze my magical fingertips over their mother's severed spine and heal the unhealable. No matter how many times I had told him otherwise, Brett believed I had made him walk again. Now, these four other people clung to the fantasy that I could conjure up a miracle for them as well.

In truth, Brett would have recovered regardless. That's how injuries work. If you can recover, you do. If you can't, you don't. Love won't cure a spinal cord. I understood that. Brett could read about it over and over again, yet he'd still tell you it was the powerful synergy of God and me.

"Somehow you always find a way," Brett had said that morning, picking up his cane from the side of the couch and placing it so he could easily hoist himself up.

"I think it's out of my hands this time."

"Did you try kissing her?" he asked as he lifted my chin and gave me a kiss on the mouth.

I'd never admit this to him, but I did try. When no one looked on and after all rational medical protocols had been exhausted, I pulled the curtain around the patient's bed and put my lips upon her ashen forehead to kiss her ever so gently.

My kiss didn't save her. I could still feel the pungent sting of her skin on my lips. Dr. Corbin let me pronounce her death—my first time as the physician of record, an inevitable rite of passage for every doctor since the beginning of time. Even a phony messiah like me couldn't overcome statistical certainty.

I called Brett to tell him of the patient's death before I left work. He responded in his habitual social-worker voice: "It was God's will . . . not your fault . . . luck of the draw." But his string of canned responses soon spiraled into a soliloquy on the unconventional ways of that newly discovered God of his and the inevitable blending of medicine and belief that will carry us all to a new threshold of healing. By the time he let out a full, twenty-second sigh of unspoken disappointment, I had bitten off every nail on my right hand.

"You know I couldn't just serve up a recovery like a package of frozen chicken," I said.

"Maybe, but sometimes you find things the rest of us can never see."

I knew I should go home to comfort him but my famous bedside manner had abandoned me. I felt our world resetting once again and I didn't want to be there to discover which version of normal I would be living by the time I reentered my house. I reached my right hand to the button that set off my own pager. It was my first lie of our marriage.

It was a Thursday night and I tried to imagine what the other interns did when they weren't working. I pictured them frolicking down Boylston Street, flaunting their scar-free, fully toed feet in open sandals. They probably met friends at a gastropub and drank pretentious cocktails with peach- and pear-infused vodka. I hadn't made a genuine friend yet since we moved to the city. I could no longer touch a drink, and the other interns always cringed at the sight of Brett limping toward me when he came to visit—his bulky arms over his frail, spindly legs, like the top of one Lego character stuck on the bottom of another.

I headed to the only place I was truly comfortable: the basement cafeteria, where, from behind the counter, Doris could always be counted on for a joke and a dose of sympathy.

"Why so glum, my child?" Doris said.

"Lost a patient."

"Those first ones are the toughest," she said.

The guy next to me in the chili line interrupted. "First. Second. Hundred and fiftieth. I like to think my doctor's gonna sob like a baby when I go."

I had seen this guy in the cafeteria every night that week. He was the soccer-playing kind, with a graphic T-shirt and over-developed quadriceps and slightly bowed calves that were too big for his small frame. He had the kind of legs that could pull off explosive plyometrics and jump five feet in the air.

"I'm Eli," he said. "Seems like a crazy time to eat alone, no?"

"It's okay," I said. "She wasn't mine to grieve."

"I'm not sure there are rules about that," he said.

He motioned for me to join him at a table. It was the music's fault that I sat down. Cheery instrumental sounds piped through the speakers to allegedly brighten families' moods. The administration had been experimenting with this nondescript, upbeat jazz with a dancing saxophone far livelier than the situation called for. I blame the bounce of the piano coupled with the untethered lightness in Eli's voice as he told me about his mother's pending release, his recent change in career plans, the quirks of each of his friends, and where his last relationship failed.

In turn, I told him the most ridiculous lines I had ever heard in the hospital, giggling a little while I did so, like a nervous idiot who had never been flirted with before. Not the kind of flirtation that the old men do when they come into the hospital and try to get themselves half an erection by brushing their hand against me. Eli was full-on enjoying my company: his chest high, his face leaning in, his eyes locking in on me. By the time he instinctively reached for my hand, we had established more of a connection than I had with anyone since medical school.

Eli stopped as the fluorescent lamps above reflected off the diamond on my finger, beaming Brett's presence around the room like a bouncing shadow puppet.

"I'm married," I said.

"How married?

"I honestly don't know."

I'D BEEN MARRIED long before my legal wedding, fused together with Brett like the bones in his sacrum. The people of our hometown rewrote history and claimed Brett and I loved each other long before the accident, but that was just part of the legend. For the better part of our senior year of high school, our relationship consisted of one hour each Tuesday afternoon, during which Brett begrudgingly allowed me to help him with physics at his mother's request. He spent half the time calculating speed and velocity and the other half trying to convince me to give him a blowjob, simply to see if he could get a geeky kid like me to follow along. He asked me to go to his hockey game one Friday night in some futile effort to upgrade my popularity. Lord only knows why I agreed. I was the kind of girl who could tell you just how fast the spitball they shot at my head would travel or how long it would take a whisper to accidentally reach my ears, but I had no clue how to negotiate the hallways of high school with any dexterity. Yet, I reveled as the kids' heads turned toward me when Brett waved from the ice. When he scored that first goal and sought out my face amid the howls in the crowd, I realized for the first time that he wanted something more from me than what all those hockey fans could provide.

I remembered the joy of that hockey game for years to come: the sheer force of Brett's legs, the skates cutting through the ice, spewing an arc of shavings toward the rink wall like a fierce weapon. It's difficult to reconcile the grace with which he glided and sped, twirled, spun, fought, balanced, and even fell on the ice with the man he became.

We stayed in the parking lot long after the game before heading to a post-game party. He directed me in that first awkward attempt at oral sex he had begged for so relentlessly. I apologized immediately afterwards for my lack of experience, mortified by my clumsy performance, but he brushed it off and kissed me as he started the car. "You didn't hear me complaining," he said, "but you're welcome to practice all you want."

Perhaps he was still distracted from our encounter in the car. Maybe if I hadn't been embarrassed by the silence or petrified of a party I had no business going to, I would have seen the other car come over the line sooner. Perhaps if I had still had a shred of confidence left to scream, he would have pivoted the wheel in the other direction.

I had eleven fractures in all, from my toes to my pelvis. No rhyme or reason dictated why some bones broke while others stayed strong. I exhausted all logic trying to recreate the accident to understand it in terms of the speed at which we were traveling, the position of objects on the floor, the weight of the steel car, and the probable position of my limbs at the point of impact. The void in my memory left corresponding holes in every formula I tried, so my injuries remained a scientific mystery to me. Four of my toes on one foot were smashed. My pelvis cracked open like a lobster claw, and my ankle had to be reconstructed with two pins and a small plate. Just the right amount of metal to send even the laziest metal detector into a fit of rage.

Lucky, the doctors called me. They liked that word.

For thirty hours, Brett was lost. My mother would walk to his room and come back with updates. Unable to move much more than my fingers, I lay in the bed thinking Brett would never resurface in the conscious world. His brief connection with me had sucked the life straight out of him.

Brett called for me when he first regained consciousness and insisted on proof that I was alive. A nurse held the phone next to my ear. Brett's voice, weak and raspy, still percolated with confidence. I had imagined that he no longer had any part of himself that was recognizable, but each inflection was uniquely his.

"If we make it through this," he said, "you better at least fuck me."

"Seriously? I'm not even sure there's still a hole under here."

"I promise you, I'll find it."

Stupid kids, we were. We still believed he was a hockey star. We thought if we didn't die, we would live. We never realized there was something in between.

My love didn't part the Red Sea. Every explanation for Brett's recovery was firmly based in science. His L3 fracture didn't penetrate the cord. The doctors performed the first surgery to remove the fragments and alleviate the pressure on the cord with minimal delay, which most likely prevented the long-term paralysis they had predicted. Complications from Brett's second surgery, a mistake by all accounts, resulted in the permanent damage that compromised his movements on his left side. The surgeons completed the subsequent operations on his legs and back with miraculous skill.

I, however, was no hero. I simply questioned the forgone conclusion.

The doctors of our small town stuck to their static notions of diagnosis: spinal cord injury equaled permanent paralysis. Even Brett's parents limited their hope to nothing more than a high-end wheelchair, but with a little help from the medical librarian, I stumbled upon the Baskov Method and the Movement Project. It was still an experimental rehabilitation program, but like me, the founders refused to believe in the inevitability of paralysis.

All I did was obsess over the right treatment. I didn't create it.

Brett didn't buy into his miracle alone. I fed the entire town their very own human-interest story. They believed I conquered my own pain by squeezing Brett's hand, but in reality, I took painkillers. An ever-changing cocktail of Vicodin, Percocet, and OxyContin.

When Brett decided he had to put on a show at a charity dance, I went along for the ride. He had his friend help him out of his wheelchair to meet me on the dance floor. Brett held his own weight for a step or two and I supported him with my better side, but I was fresh off my own cane and had limited strength on my left side. I whispered that I couldn't hold him up for very long and he nodded, but suddenly a crowd had gathered around us, rooting us on as though the Lord himself had made a public appearance to prop Brett up and install a new pair of legs.

Brett got cocky, as Brett tends to do. He swayed ever so slightly back and forth. Did he really think he could dance?

"I just wanted to see if I could," he said.

He couldn't. And I couldn't. The unexpected twist, coupled with the weight of his body, shot that all-too-familiar pain through the top of my pelvis and hip and up through my spine. I dropped Brett to the floor. The crowd around us grew silent, so I did the only thing left to do. I inhaled deeply to dull the pain and climbed right down on top of him on the dance floor. I forced a smile and kissed him hard on the mouth like a raunchy porn star.

"Don't you dare make us look like a bunch of pathetic cripples," I said, insisting he kiss me back.

The crowd roared again as if this was all just par for the course. I didn't tell them that it set back my physical therapy six weeks to get in that position or that I doubled my dose of Percocet for the next two months to give them that thirty-second show. To them, we made handicapped look sexy.

INFIDELITY IS EASIER than it should be. You'd think there would be some forty-eight-hour waiting period, but it didn't take long until I was climbing the stairs to Eli's apartment. It felt familiar, as if Eli had ordered items A through L from a single page of an IKEA catalogue and positioned them in his apartment just as they were placed on the page. Eli could take off and set up the exact same apartment in another city in a matter of hours with nothing more than an Allen wrench.

As soon as the door shut, Eli grabbed at me as if he'd been depriving himself for years. I pulled back and reminded myself that this was nothing more than a standard physiological reaction. I tried to excuse myself to get to the bathroom to let both the somatosensory and olfactory stimuli pass. I understood the physical changes better than anyone out there and I assured myself they could be conquered.

Then Eli picked me up. He picked up my whole person. He lifted me up with his hand under my butt and carried me toward his bedroom as if I were made of a light plastic. Not quite sure how to respond, I wiggled too much and began to fall out of his grasp. He bounced me back up until my torso was straight again. "I'm sorry," I said. "I've never done this before."

"I realize that," he said, but I knew he didn't truly understand.

I had never been with a man capable of doing anything like that. I had never had someone able to sweep me off my literal feet and into his arms. I had never had a man able to balance in a dominant position, throw me down on the kitchen table, or do it in the shower standing up. There was so much I had never done. At some point, Eli would figure that out.

I lost my virginity before Brett recovered the full use of his legs. The logistics were unromantic, but we were both so excited by the mere possibility of the maintenance of an erection that we went for it. Technical penetration occurred about a year after the accident, but only for a split second. Even if he could have performed longer, spreading my legs wide enough to climb on top and avoiding hip flexor issues was no easy task. By eighteen months, we could manage it for a full two minutes. It was year two before we were able to add a few new positions to our repertoire and year three before I had a full-fledged orgasm.

I didn't get much advice. Visuals no longer made Brett hard and my capacity for endurance was more like a geriatric than a teenager. Doctors were completely unwilling to discuss the matter with someone my age, so we learned all of the tricks on our own. I knew just the spot on his earlobe that needed to be touched to elicit an erectile response and he learned how much pressure my barely healed pelvis could withstand before I screamed out in something far different than ecstasy. What we lacked in ability, we made up for in camaraderie.

Eli had no reason for such a sense of caution. At first, it was thrilling: this graceful, muscular body throwing me down on the bed and balancing on his knees, on his toes, flipping from one side to another. But in his manic rush to consummate our relationship, he stretched my leg just an inch too far and crashed his entire body weight into the tender spot where my pelvis attached to my leg. His hands grasped and tugged at whatever was available to him until he finally plopped down on my leg in a way that bent back my ankle and I squealed.

"Are you okay?"

I said yes, although it was a shallow lie. I prayed he would finish up quickly without great fanfare while I could still pretend to perform. The familiar aches in my bones flared up a little more with every rhythmless movement that Eli thrust my way. Soon enough, I felt nothing else.

That's the peculiar thing about injuries. You think you're all healed up. You think you're a success story. You think you can do things the way the pain-free live. Then, no matter what, you realize the injuries are still there, as inflamed and brazen as ever.

Eli smoothed his finger over the scar on my ankle. He stopped right at the point where Brett's scar lined up with mine. Sometimes as a joke, I'd position the scar on my ankle next to the scar on Brett's leg and we looked just like the map of Rhode Island, right where Route 146 meets I-95.

When Eli's finger reached the spot where Brett's scar should have been, I swatted his hand away and scrambled to find my underwear. "I can't," I said as I fished around under the covers for my clothes.

"I think you're a little late," he said as he pulled me back to bed, but I wriggled away.

Eli watched as I got dressed. I may have been the first woman to leave him lying there, but I had no further explanation for him, no apology or justification. I returned home in the rain, the humidity settling into my sore ankle. I stopped outside my apartment and, through the ground-floor window, I watched Brett lounging on the couch and shouting at the referee on the television. He raised his arms up over his head, and although I couldn't hear him, I knew a goal had been scored. He caught me looking through the bars on the window and blessed me with that hockey-star smile that made me believe I was the only fan who mattered.

I knew I'd tell Brett the truth. If nothing else, our relationship always commanded a certain level of honesty. He'd ask me why I did it and I'd tell him I just wanted to see if I could. He'd have to understand that. The state of Rhode Island couldn't be divided. ◇

Rondelays

Richard Kostelanetz

Excerpted from an upcoming book, whose dedication reads, "In memory of Dom Sylvester Houédard (1927-1992), who introduced me to 'concrete poetry.'"

ARTARTART
TARTARTAR
ARTARTART
TARTARTAR
ARTARTART
TARTARTAR
ARTARTART
TARTARTAR
ARTARTART
TARTARTAR
ARTARTART
TARTARTAR
ARTARTART
TARTARTAR
ARTARTART
TARTARTAR
ARTARTART
TARTARTAR
ARTARTART
TARTARTAR

EROSEROSEROS
ROSEROSEROSE
EROSEROSEROS
ROSEROSEROSE
EROSEROSEROS
ROSEROSEROSE
EROSEROSEROS
ROSEROSEROSE
EROSEROSEROS
ROSEROSEROSE
EROSEROSEROS
ROSEROSEROSE
EROSEROSEROS
ROSEROSEROSE
EROSEROSEROS
ROSEROSEROSE
EROSEROSEROS
ROSEROSEROSE
EROSEROSEROS
ROSEROSEROSE
EROSEROSEROS
ROSEROSEROSE

EVILEVILEVIL
VILEVILEVILE
EVILEVILEVIL
VILEVILEVILE
EVILEVILEVIL
VILEVILEVILE
EVILEVILEVIL
VILEVILEVILE
EVILEVILEVIL
VILEVILEVILE
EVILEVILEVIL
VILEVILEVILE
EVILEVILEVIL
VILEVILEVILE
EVILEVILEVIL
VILEVILEVILE
EVILEVILEVIL
VILEVILEVILE
EVILEVILEVIL
VILEVILEVILE
EVILEVILEVIL
VILEVILEVILE

ALLUREALLURE
LUREALLUREAL
REALLUREALLU
ALLUREALLURE
LUREALLUREAL
REALLUREALLU
ALLUREALLURE
LUREALLUREAL
REALLUREALLU
ALLUREALLURE
LUREALLUREAL
REALLUREALLU
ALLUREALLURE
LUREALLUREAL
REALLUREALLU
ALLUREALLURE
LUREALLUREAL
REALLUREALLU
ALLUREALLURE

STORESTORE
RESTORESTO
STORESTORE
RESTORESTO
STORESTORE
RESTORESTO
STORESTORE
RESTORESTO
STORESTORE
RESTORESTO
STORESTORE
RESTORESTO
STORESTORE
RESTORESTO
STORESTORE
RESTORESTO
STORESTORE
RESTORESTO
STORESTORE
RESTORESTO
STORESTORE
RESTORESTO
STORESTORE
RESTORESTO

Negatives

Michele Zimmerman

August 17, 2010

L,

I need some time.

Love,

Ben

Today is August 15, 2011 1:18 p.m.

Lately I've had the desire to take photographs. To solidify my surroundings, as if I fear memory will betray me in the end. The compulsion comes on suddenly and at the strangest times. I watched Bernie climb catlike onto a windowsill, and felt in that moment all would collapse if I didn't capture her there. One foot was on the ledge, the other swinging wildly. But I don't have a camera.

I sat on my front step yesterday and watched as the sun swept across the chimney of my neighbor's stone house. Just as the light slid off, leaving the stone cold for the rest of the day, I wished again to cage the image. The urgency to do so was nearly overpowering. It must be the knowing that there will never again be another today that makes me feel this way. I want to pour concrete over my life. Harden myself into permanence.

That is not to say I truly want to live forever just as I am, or that I fear death. I simply mean that I am afraid of the moment when things in life come to an end. It's a hard fear to articulate. I tried explaining it to Bernie yesterday, but she didn't quite understand the concept. It's okay though, because I probably don't understand the concept either. At first, all she could think to say was, "What's the difference between an ending and a death?" She smoked two cigarettes, one right after the other, before she concluded, "Besides, things never really end."

I am enraptured with the notion of forever. But I have trouble believing in it.

Today is August 17, 2011 6:23 a.m.

I have work today at Thomson's. My shift starts in about an hour. Usually I don't have to go in so early, but the warm months are the busy months. Like I said, today is August 17. Rain is pouring self-destructively, and as I slid my heavy boots up my calves, I didn't have any sympathy for the day.

I really hope that today I am left to stand behind the cash register and smile placidly at customers. Mr. Thomson knows he can ask me to finish the odd jobs he's gotten too old for; once an almost-daughter-in-law, always an almost-daughter-in-law. I don't mind helping out, but today I don't want to climb the ladder in the back to reach for boxes too heavy with ripe fruit. I don't want to pull the old awning back into place when the wind blows it askew. I want to wear my apron and my nametag and forget that Ben's newest letter is hidden under my bed, unopened. There are many of his letters under there. I've opened them all, but I've never been able to answer. Maybe this time he wrote to tell me that August 17 means a year since my fear of endings first appeared.

His second letter, sent a few weeks after the first, reverberates now in the raindrops. Plink. *Dear L.* Plink. *I miss you.* Plink, plink. *I miss your clunky rain boots. I miss the way you used to touch the back of my neck when you thought no one was looking. I miss the scar across your left thigh.* Plink. *Ella, I miss you.* Plink. *But I love it here. New York City is so huge, and open, and unlimited. So different from home. Right now I'm working as a waiter in some fancy Italian place until I get on my feet. I hope you know that's why I left—I wanted to learn how to stand on my own.*

I know I should be concentrating on that, but instead I seem to have found Jessie. Plink, plink, plink. *She's the hostess at the restaurant. She's quiet but has lots to say; she wants to be a writer. She reminds me of you. That's probably why I was drawn to her. I realize this changes everything. It may be asking a lot, but I would love for you to come out here.* Plink. *See the city, see my life. Maybe even meet her.* Plink, plink.

Ella, you've always been, and will always be my closest friend. Being here without you is difficult. Not hearing from you at all is worse. Plink.

So please, L, forgive me. And please write back, or call, or something. Plink.

Love, plink

Ben plink

I hate the rain for the flood and regurgitation of those lines. But I hate myself even more for allowing them to bubble up and muddy the surface like a broken sewer system.

Today is August 19, 2011 11:34 a.m.

There are pros and cons of letter writing. Pro: It's like receiving part of a person. Con: It's like receiving part of a person. Less gruesome than, say, finding a finger stuffed in an envelope, but it's somehow more trying. The intimacy of knowing that their fingertips smoothed out the paper, and left their prints in the words intended only for you, is undeniable. Wonderful when you want the intimacy. A beast of a burden otherwise.

The beasts living under my bed breathed heavily last night.

7:46 p.m.

Part of me must enjoy losing sleep over this. That must be it. Why else would I even keep the letter? Keep all the letters? I fear this ending so much that I would rather live in perpetual postponement.

11:19 p.m.

The new letter could say, "I'm marrying Jessie." Or it could say, "There are no trees in the city." Or it could say, "I have totally lost my mind, please come help me find it." I don't know what it could say and I don't know what I want it to say. Maybe I want silence.

3:43 a.m.

I sat holding the new letter for a while. Instead of putting it back under the bed, I placed it on my nightstand.

Today is August 21, 2011 3:51 p.m.

I feel good today. Like I'm breathing. I can't explain it except to say that this feeling came on without warning. The spider crawling along my ceiling this morning was allowed to live.

The palm reader was in Thomson's today. She's small and bizarre. Always buys three lemons. I wish I knew her name. She's so out of place in this town. She spoke to me today as I was bagging the third lemon. She said, "You'll know when you're ready."

She picked up her bag and walked out of the store.

I've never believed in palm readers and psychics. Then again, I'm feeling good today.

Today is August 22, 2011 2:13 a.m.

Bernie and I went to The Dice tonight. Around 5 p.m. I got it in my head that I wanted to go, so I called Bernie on the phone and told her to get dressed. She asked, "The Dice?" and I said, "Yes, The Dice." Again she asked, "The Dice? Are you sure?" and again I said, "Yes."

I drove. It was a clear night, no rain. When Bernie lit her cigarette though, I saw our first time at The Dice billow up in her smoke the same way I'd heard Ben's letter in the rain. Bernie had lit up a cigarette that night too and she had passed it to Nora in the back seat. They were only together for three more days after that.

The guy I worked with after school had invited me, and whoever else I wanted, up to The Dice to hear his friend's band open a concert. He said it didn't matter if we were underage, the bartender would let us in if we said we knew the band.

"What if he needs proof that we know them?" I had asked.

"Tell him Chris, the guitarist, only has four fingers on his left hand," he said. I thought he was joking, but it got us in the door.

I didn't know much about Ben back then. I knew that he was Mr. Thomson's younger son and that he was two years older than me. I knew that he always had a five o'clock shadow. I knew he sat with me on work breaks and that he was allergic to peanuts. I knew he had invited me to meet him at a bar with a stage on a Friday night. I was seventeen, that's all I needed to know. So, I took the chance.

Standing in the pit below the front of the stage, the three of us looked up toward the security guard at the microphone. He reminded us of the band's name, reminded us to thank them for coming out, and reminded us that all beer was on tap. He wore a black shirt with three diagonal white dots down the front.

With the first song from the opening band, I learned Ben was a drummer. With the last song of the headlining band, I learned I enjoyed it when his five o'clock shadow scratched my cheek.

I was still feeling good when Bernie and I walked into The Dice tonight. But I would be lying if I said that I was living in the present. When the headliners got onstage, I took Bernie by the wrist and headed for the pit. We danced. And I pretended to forget about everything.

Today is August 24, 2011 5:27 a.m.

Woke up with tear tracks on my cheeks. I hate when I cry in my dreams and wake up to find that it's real. Then again, it's my fault for going back to the beginning.

Today is September 4, 2011 4:43 a.m.

I think about the night Ben and I sat on the docks far more often than I would like to admit, even to myself. It was a humid day and we had both sweat through our shirts. The mosquitoes bit hard. Hair stuck to the base of my neck uncomfortably and Ben's curls had expanded in the heat.

"Let's play a game," Ben said. "One of us asks a question, any question, the other answers and then asks one in return."

"What kind of game is that?" I said.

"My kind."

"Okay, you start then," I said.

"Ladies first." He nudged me with a shoulder.

"Hmm. What's it like being nineteen?" I asked.

"I don't know, what's it like being seventeen?"

"I don't know either."

"Fair enough," he said.

"Your turn," I said.

"I know, I'm thinking. Gotta make it good." He sat for a minute looking out at the water, drumming his fingers against his thigh. I swatted away another mosquito. "Sun or moon? Go."

"What's that, like, Pepsi or Coke?" I asked. "Um, moon."

"Why?"

"I don't know. How about you? Sun or moon?"

"Sun," he said.

"Why?" I asked.

"I don't know." He laughed. "Your turn."

"Why drums, and not guitar, or something?"

"I do play guitar."

"Really?"

"Yeah, just not for the band."

"Why not?"

"Chris is better than me."

"Do you play anything else?"

"Violin," he said. I hadn't expected that. "My turn, what's something you want to do? Anything—it doesn't have to be anything that you'll actually do—it doesn't have to make sense."

"Oh, that's a good one. Hmm. Okay, this is kinda embarrassing, but roller derby." I giggled and hugged my knees to my chest.

"Roller derby? I never would have expected that! Don't they have different names—like game names or something?"

I nodded. "Yeah, they do, and they are always so cool. And badass."

"Do you know what your name would be?"

"Hella's Bells." I laughed at hearing myself speak a fantasy out loud. He laughed with me.

"I see what you did there—Hella—Ella, I get it." Our eyes met, and we burst out laughing again. I elbowed him lightly and he draped an arm around my shoulders.

"Ugh, it's so hot out, we could die of heatstroke." I made as if to shake him off.

"I can take it," he said and gripped a little tighter.

That was a good night.

Today is September 16, 2011 5:19 p.m.
Bernie met someone. A redhead with a pixie cut. The three of us got Mexican food last night. The redhead is nice, but I didn't pay too much attention to what she said because I know she will be gone within three months. I wonder if that is a mean thing to think. But the truth is that Bernie is a flighty human being. Inconsistent. I don't know how she has managed to remain a permanent fixture in my life. Through crunchy bites of tortilla chips, Bernie asked me how I want to celebrate. I forgot that my twenty-second birthday is coming up.

8:51 p.m.

I remember one of Ben's birthdays. We were in the back of Thomson's, standing among the crates of food not yet priced.

"Hey you," he said.

"Hey!" I wrapped my arms around his neck. "So tell me, how does it feel to be twenty-one?"

"I'll tell you after I finish my beer tonight." He smiled. His breath was sweet, like he had been eating chocolate. He untied my apron and bruised my neck with his teeth. "How does it feel to be nineteen?"

"Pretty damn good."

Today is September 17, 2011 2:29 a.m.
The new letter is still sealed. But I moved it farther from the bed and off the nightstand. I didn't know where it should go, so finally I wedged it between the frame and the reflective glass of my mirror. Maybe I'll sleep better now.

Today is September 18, 2011 2:13 p.m.
Bernie says we can go out and do whatever, that she'll pay for everything on my birthday. I told her all I want to do is order a pizza and rent a movie. Have a night in. Be comfy. She says she'll buy us matching pajama pants to make things more festive.

Today is September 21, 2011 8:39 a.m.
I woke up. I brushed my teeth. I put on my clothes. I turned to the mirror to slide my earrings smoothly into my earlobes and I had to stop. I

didn't think of this when I put it there; the letter is literally staring me in the face now.

4:22 p.m.

I can do this.

9:01 p.m.

I have to do this.

9:45 p.m.

I can do this.

11:14 p.m.

Bernie called. She talked to me about the redhead. I love Bernie when she starts a new relationship; it's funny hearing her laugh like a small child while I know she's breathing in tobacco.

I feel light after talking to her. I'm sick of being heavy.

I can do this.

Today is September 22, 2011 3:51 a.m.

Ella,

Talk to me. I know you've received my letters. I know things are a mess. I don't know why you won't answer. My father mentions you over the phone. He says that you look like you're disappearing. Honestly, it feels like you are.

I would like to know where we stand. You owe me that, at least.

Ben

3:17 p.m.

The last Christmastime he was still home, it snowed and snowed and snowed. It piled up and the sanitation department made more piles. Eventually the tops of the piles glazed over, crystallized. Ben and I went out walking late one night. The streets were quiet; our faces were red from the wind.

I can't remember why, but I know that I had this overpowering desire to touch the top of a snow pile. To make sure that it existed. I removed my glove and slid my fingers over it. Wet. Sleek. I spread my fingers and pushed, palm down, into the hard surface. A perfect print was left behind. If I could go back, I would take a picture of that handprint.

Ben and I looked at each other and simultaneously we each raised a heavy, booted foot. When the surface cracked, it did so quickly and satisfyingly. Made a fantastic sound. High pitched enough to make you blink, and then the wind carried it away.

We slept in the back seat of his car that night. Parked on his street. Our bodies stung.

Today is September 23, 2011 12:01 a.m.
I'm twenty-two and displaced. A picture couldn't lock me in. This is where I stand, Ben. This is my letter to you. ◇

The Joy of Writing

after Wisława Szymborska

Maceo J. Whitaker

You smell like last week's sushi.
No spray, no rinse, no scrub would
free you from your chains of funk. You?
You're burnt hair plus curdled Yoplait.

Much can be crammed into a carnival
of flesh. Mutton rots your meaty gums.
You could impart the meaning of life, yet
ears would shun you. Serves you right.

You're a swept stinkbug on its back
after tumbling to the floor with a click.
You may douse the tile with cologne, yet
you're duped by the resolve of bones.

Your drool tastes like Omaha Beach
water foam. Or rubber bands flicked
from braced teeth. All lies, I know, but
this poem, these words, make it so. ◇

Polar Bears Asleep in Trees

Anne Graue

Sugar maples bend low without breaking—
the ground, covered in grass and leaf clippings,
browns mixed with greens, mouse skeletons, ashes,

weeds, and dirt. Their bulk suits them on the ice
and, as it turns out, on the thin branches—
crouching tentative and unreachable

by most conscious humans. Their eyes, like mine,
closed, serene, possibly dreaming; branches
holding them like china cups, and a fog

of a breeze caressing their white eyelids;
sleep uninterrupted by vertigo
or nightmarish visions. Unblinkingly,

bark-encrusted bulwarks stand beneath, hold
their great weight, and remain still, cradling
the polar giants in their creaking boughs. ◇

You Can't Reach It

Giulia Mascali

You are granted another day, but you're not sure why. The high-pitched pulsing noise is back. You try to put your mind somewhere else but the sound is inescapable. Finally, you get out of bed and cross the narrow studio apartment to turn off the stereo. After a few moments there is silence. It's interesting that a quiet home still comes as a surprise to you. You've had so much time to grow accustomed to it.

You shower, shave, and brush, thinking they'll appreciate the extra effort. Today you decide to go with the gray suit, complementing it with the beautiful green tie Diane bought you a few years ago for your forty-fifth birthday. You place the nicotine patch on your arm and walk into the kitchen wondering if you'll ever get around to decorating. For some reason the bare walls are getting to you today. Noticing the time, you quickly eat some cereal straight from the box. You're running late.

At the Rhinecliff station you park your car in a twelve-hour spot and enter the old brick building. Alan is selling tickets today.

"Hello, Alan," you say.

"How are you, Andy?"

"Doing well, and yourself?"

"Good. So where is work taking you this week?"

"New York City."

He prints out your ticket. "Oh, the city is great this time of year. And not too long a ride. You must be happy about that."

You smile at him. "Yes, looking forward to it."

An electronic ad for *Full House* stares at you while you walk down the steps to the tracks. Last night you were flipping through channels and you caught an episode where Michelle calls Joey "Da-da." Danny, her father, is so busy working that Joey spends more time with Michelle than he does. For a moment you felt bad for Danny, but then you remembered that he's a fictional character and that his life isn't real. Your face merges with Danny's, unsettling you, but the uneasy feeling melts away with your reflection as you step further and further down.

On the train you see a man reading the newspaper and ask if the seat next to him is taken.

"No, please."

He's also in a suit. His briefcase is on the floor. He seems to be going on some sort of business trip. Leaning over slightly, you discover that the man is reading an article about a Yankee game.

"Hell of a game this week, no?" you say.

"They keep playing like that, the World Series is ours."

"Here's hoping. I'm Andy." You offer him your hand.

"Jeff."

You get talking. Jeff is a lawyer and is heading down to the city for a business meeting. He asks about you.

"Business as well, in the city."

You tell him that you're also a lawyer and that you work for A&E Henderson, although he's never heard of that firm before. You learn that his favorite baseball team is the Yankees, his favorite player is Don Mattingly, that he played baseball in college but quit after he tore his ACL his sophomore year, that if he settles this deal in the city today he'll get a raise.

When the train pulls into Penn Station, you say goodbye to one another and part ways. Every time you reach the concourse, the environment overwhelms you. With each step you take and each food stand you pass, a new smell presents itself. Even more chaotic than the odors are the sounds. The passive-aggressive spinning of wheels on suitcases as their owners jerk them along. The scattered chatter undermined by unceasing announcements. Welcome, Amtrak passengers. Please sit in designated areas while awaiting the departure of your train. Thank you for choosing Amtrak services. The announcements that you've heard so many times are now a part of your brain.

After using the bathroom in the station, you grab a burger and then wait on the ticket line. Alice is behind the counter.

"Hey, Alice."

"Hi, Andy."

"When's the next train to Rhinecliff?"

"Thirty minutes."

"One, please."

While she waits for your ticket to print she asks you how your business trip went.

"Great. I'm getting a raise for settling a deal."

She congratulates you as she gives you your ticket.

You sit alone while waiting for your train, sipping from your water bottle as you observe the people around you. They're either rushing to get onto their train to see someone they love or rushing to get off their train to unite with someone they love. Your desperate eyes continue to scan the room.

Once you board, you look for a place to sit.

"Is this seat taken?"

"No."

"Hi, I'm Andy," you announce when you're seated. You wait a few moments before speaking again. "I'm Andy."

"Look, Andy, I don't really feel like talking." The man turns to look out the window.

"All right, no problem." *He's one of those*, you think to yourself.

All the remaining seats are taken except for two together. You're not going to let your money go to waste, so you move to a different car. Eventually you stumble upon an empty seat next to a woman. She's an older woman, definitely a good twenty years older than you are. She has luscious dark brown hair, sort of like Elizabeth's. But it's the familiarity of her eyes that fascinates you. They're Diane green.

"Is this seat taken?"

"No, please," she says.

When you settle in, you put out your hand. "I'm Andy."

"Ellen."

A pile of pictures lies on her lap. An easy in.

"Are those your kids?"

"Grandkids," she says, smiling, her eyes still fully invested in her grandchildren's beauty. "You flatter me, believing I'm young enough to have teenagers."

She asks if you have grandchildren, and you nervously laugh, telling her that your girls are only seven and eighteen and are too young to have kids.

"My granddaughter Genevieve is also eighteen. I'm on my way back from seeing her at college. She goes to Columbia and is taking some summer courses there now."

"You don't say! I'm on my way back from visiting my daughter Elizabeth at NYU. She's also getting some credits out of the way. But wow, Columbia is an amazing school. You must be so proud."

She nods her head and goes on to talk about how intelligent her granddaughter is. You decide to jump in and brag about Elizabeth. You talk about all of her possible successes: how she was student council president in high school while being in all AP classes, how she volunteers every weekend. You say pretty much anything you can think of that might seem within Elizabeth's reach. For all you know she's taking over the world. She was always so smart.

She asks about your other daughter so you tell her how adorable Alyssa is. When Alyssa was a toddler, you say, she used to sing a song and fall on the floor. You and your wife never knew why. She would jumble up the words, sometimes screaming "Roses! Roses!" before falling over. It took a year for you and Diane to figure out she was playing "Ring Around the Rosie."

Ellen seems amused so you go on to tell her about singing the "Goodnight" song to Alyssa before she goes to sleep, and how she refuses to close her eyes otherwise. It's the song you made up one night when she was a baby, out of desperation to make her stop crying. It's not much of a song, you tell Ellen, but Alyssa loves it so much that she makes you sing it to her every night. Although with that anecdote, you need a moment before you can continue.

After you calm down, you offer to show her some pictures of Elizabeth and Alyssa from your trip to Florida five years ago. But as you stretch to reach your attaché case, your sleeve is drawn back and her eyes are riveted to the scar on your wrist. She tries to look away but you know it's the color of it, the intensity of the red that captivates her. She politely asks what happened. Before taking a sip of water you decide to tell her that it was from a cooking accident.

The rest of the conversation consists of memories of your kids and her kids and grandchildren. She has three grown sons. Each of them is married with kids: the oldest has a girl, Genevieve, the one who goes to Columbia, and a boy; the second has a girl, who just won a piano competition. The third has a baby girl, who just learned to walk.

At home, you eat some cereal from the box you left out in the morning and then prepare for bed. Today was a good day. You decide not to shower but instead just to wash your face. You walk towards your dresser, turn on the stereo, and play the CD that permanently resides within it. The tenderness of Louis Armstrong's voice fills the room. The stereo is programmed to repeat the song for four hours just in case you have a hard time falling asleep. But by the third time the song begins, you surrender to the night ever so gently. You only cried a little tonight. Today was a good day.

You hoped that if you were to wake up to another morning, it would be in peaceful silence. But there it is again. That sound. *Don't let it control you*, you think to yourself. You get up and turn the stereo off, shower, put your patch on, and get dressed for the day.

At the station, the person at the ticket window is not Alan, but his backup, Sam. After greeting him you purchase your ticket. Because of your good mood you've decided that a short ride to Albany will suffice. You get on the train and look around for an empty seat. You see a woman with the same Prada bag that Diane wanted a few years ago.

"Is this seat taken?"

"No, it's not."

"Sorry, but is that the Prada Saffiano bag?"

"Yes it is." You've impressed her. "Are you some kind of Prada collector?" she jokes.

You laugh and explain how for months you would only hear, "Andy, Andy, please, this is the most beautiful bag in the entire world, please, our anniversary is coming up." And you would say, "Di, it's either food for the next month or your bag, you can't have both." Of course you were lying to Diane, the bag was actually sitting in the attic waiting to be unwrapped in a few days for your anniversary. From the woman's reaction she seems to be the sentimental type, so you go on to tell her that you gave it to Diane with a CD of *Louis Armstrong's Greatest Hits* bundled up in tissue paper inside the bag. "Wonderful World" was your wedding song.

"That's so sweet," she says.

A girl sitting in one of the seats facing you is staring. Ignoring her, you continue talking.

"Yeah, but man, it cost me an arm and a leg."

The woman tells you that her husband bought her the bag for her birthday, and when you ask what he does, she says he works for Bank of America. You tell her that you also work for a bank, although she's never heard of Henderson Corp. You stop talking for a moment; you're distracted. The girl is still staring at you, maybe even more intently than before.

When you regain focus, you tell the woman that you don't regret buying the bag for Diane. She wears it everywhere, even places it's inappropriate to wear such an extravagant bag. Last weekend, you go on, you and Diane went grocery shopping with your kids and she wore her bag. Every woman in the store kept coming up to her and asking about it. She was like a celebrity or something. Now your older daughter asked if you could buy *her* one, and you told her, "Elizabeth, it's either your college tuition or that bag, you can't have both."

You and the woman both laugh at the second attempt of your joke. Before you can continue the conversation, the girl who trapped you in her gaze is leaning towards you.

"Mr. Henderson?" she inquires in a soft voice.

You're hesitant to answer, but you do. "Yes?"

"I thought you looked familiar. I heard you talking about Mrs. Henderson and Elizabeth, so I knew it was you. I don't think you remember me, or recognize me, but I'm friends with Elizabeth."

"Oh."

"Look, Mr. Henderson, I know it's none of my business or anything, but I was wondering if you were maybe thinking about coming to our graduation? It's next Sunday. I know it's not my place to ask, but I know Elizabeth really wants you there. She hasn't been able to get in touch with you for so long, so when I noticed you, I had to say something."

The woman you're sitting with looks confused. *Say something, anything*. But you can't. You hear that noise again, the noise you wake up to every morning. *Just move to another car, just move to another car,* you tell yourself. But it's different this time. Everyone is staring at you. They know.

Your face becomes damp. You drink your water and take deep breaths, but nothing is working. It's screeching, shrieking, louder than ever before. You need to escape.

You grab your attaché case and start walking up the aisle.

"Mr. Henderson?"

The next stop is at least fifteen minutes away and you can't get off this train until then. People are still staring. Their images blend together as your breathing becomes heavier and sweat drips off your nose. You make it to the bathroom and drown your face with water to escape the heat. Standing is difficult so you crouch over the sink, cup the water into your hands, and begin to slurp. But nothing is working. Nothing is taking the heat away. You sit on the floor and do your counting to steady your breathing.

"One. Two. Three," you whisper. "Four. Five. Six."

The noise won't stop. It's reverberating against the bathroom walls, louder and louder. But you can't reach it. You can't reach the source of the sound.

Alyssa, Daddy's tired, and it's time to go to sleep. But I don't wanna! I know, sweetie, but Daddy's tired from work and Mommy is out with Elizabeth. You leave Alyssa's room. Bathroom. Cigarette. That's a nasty habit, Andy. I know Di, I'll quit soon. I promise. Daddy, Daddy! You put the cigarette down. Yes, Alyssa? You forgot the "Goodnight" song, Daddy. I'm sorry, how could I do such a thing? Goodnight my sweetheart, goodnight my dear. Don't you cry, Daddy's here. "Thirteen. Fourteen. Fifteen." I love you to the sun and back. Please don't you ever forget that. You leave Alyssa's room and fall asleep in the living room.

You wake up with your face coated in sweat. The heat is excruciating. "Twenty-two. Twenty-three. Twenty-four." A strange man with a mask stands above you. You see his coat and gloves coming closer. Behind him are flames, smoke. Goodnight my sweetheart, goodnight my dear. Daddy, Daddy! Alyssa! You need to come with me, sir. Don't you cry, Daddy's here. My daughter! I love you to the sun and back. We'll get her. You need to come with me. "Twenty-eight. Twenty-nine. Thirty." He pulls you up and forces you past the flames towards the door. Please don't you ever forget that. Dadd-ee. Dadd-eee! You extend your arm back to Alyssa's voice and a tongue of fire licks your wrist. You can't reach her. Eeee. You can't reach the source of the sound.

Lying on the bathroom floor of the train, tears escape from your eyes. You look at your scar with blurred vision and smash it against the wall, wanting to hurt yourself as badly as you hurt your daughter. When you close your eyes, all you can see is the image of her in the hospital, discolored, disfigured. You forgot to put out your cigarette. You left it on the hallway table near her room. You're the reason she has nightmares. You're the reason that you can't look at your own daughter. The scar on your hand disgusts you. It's an eternal reminder of what you've done.

As you lie curled on the floor, your body suddenly shifts forward, slamming your head against the wall. The train has stopped. Finding the strength to stand seems impossible, but you know that you can't stay on this train any longer. You force your body up.

Once you get some air, attempting to relax, you take another train home. As you sit alone, your mind wanders into the world of what your life should have been like, the relationships you were supposed to have with your wife and kids, the memories you imagined you'd share. You were living that life. You were living your dream. You were.

While walking up the steps of the station, you're forced to face

Danny Tanner looking down at you. You get into your car, but you don't drive home.

When you arrive at your destination, you contemplate what to do. During your previous attempts, you were at least able to make it out of the car. But here you are. Stuck. The last time you were here some of the shingles still needed to be painted after the repairs. But now the house appears to be perfect. There's not a single mark left to reveal that any harm had been done at all. You envision Alyssa standing in front of you on the lawn while Diane watches from the door. You hold your little girl in your arms and tell her how sorry you are. How much you love her. You sing her song while gently rocking her, telling her that you're here and will never leave again. You want to, more than anything, but you don't. You can't.

On the first Sunday in June you're not sitting in the seat reserved for you at Pierson High School, but outside the train station, finishing your cigarette. You could have seen Elizabeth win the Principal's Award, you could have seen her receive her diploma, you could have seen her throw her cap in the air. But instead you see Alan.

"Great to see you, Andy."

"How are you, Alan?"

"Doin' good. Where to?"

"Chicago."

"That's a pretty long trip. Wouldn't it make more sense to fly?"

"I got a good deal on this ticket."

"You won't mind the ride?"

"A long train ride is just what I need right now."

He hands you your ticket and wishes you a good trip.

When you get on the train, every seat is taken except for one next to an elderly man. You sit down beside him.

The man sticks his hand out. "Hi, I'm Liam."

"I'm Jack." ◇

Prayer

Michael Patrick Collins

Thank you for this sacred gull
swooping and circling against
the noon blue sky, so my eye

might trace in his air-shaded wake
the shape of wind, spirit through spirit,
for it grew thunderous as

it drew near to me, then transfigured
its visage into a model plane,
robbed me of the obvious god-

image I comprehended, returned
the distance across which I speak to you,
the between within which I listen. ◇

Fall

Michael Patrick Collins

I am one of the leaves floating on the harbor

this morning, detached from mother, branch roots, ripples

holding me, dancing, delighted, spinning into decomposition,

grateful blithely hazed with terrified.

The wavelets spin me forever, seconds; I

embrace the gracious freedom I never saw coming. I sink in;

I allow it to sink in; this was the best year of my life. ◇

Constitutional

Michael Patrick Collins

Soon I will have to return
from my reprieve in the harbor
breeze to shuffling fractions
of myself in emails and meetings

in between Facebooking and tweeting
as-if snippets of a Cubist self-
portrait, yet, in the momentless
strolling moments, I permit

the soul I live within to cruise
my body like a borrowed car
around our water, her mirror,
currently quite tranquil. I am

improving by and by at being
unconfined by duty, performance,
ambition—letting my soul live
herself though me. Today, in fact,

I've lasted almost half an hour. ◇

Kissing

Mark Benedict

It was the last day before spring vacation and Mrs. Nealand was talking about humping. Yesterday it was the female reproductive system, today it was premarital sex. Mrs. Nealand seemed openly and happily distracted, her expression amused, almost liquored, and Ethan suspected that she was wondering, impishly rather than uneasily, how many of the twenty or so students present had firsthand knowledge of the topic.

Ethan was wondering himself. Ninth grade, it turned out, was a new era: people were definitely doing it, and not just a few people, either. Still, it wasn't strictly clear who these people were; some of the things you heard were hard to rule on, seemed at once like truth and just talk, and no doubt there were plenty of true things that you didn't hear, that were secrets. In fact, Rick Mueller excepted, the only person here that Ethan was positive about either way was himself. Unless it had somehow happened without his awareness, it hadn't happened. Not even close. Rick Mueller, in contrast, had done it ten or more times, verified: not only did his locker-room narratives sound, stirringly, alarmingly, like actual true-life accounts, but he had printed out and circulated an e-mail exchange between Katie Welch and himself that squared with his hump stories about her and so conferred added legitimacy upon his hump stories about others.

Mrs. Nealand, slim, pretty, not young but not ancient, paced slowly back and forth at the chalkboard, lecturing them on the very serious consequences of sex before marriage and meanwhile looking like she was about to crack up. Ethan liked her puckery mouth, and her serene voice and crisp enunciation. Still, she was a big come-down from Ms. Tucker, the previous Health teacher. Ms. Tucker had reportedly brought so much pep and enthusiasm to Sex Ed that she often seemed on the verge of picking a volunteer and favoring the class with a demonstration. There would have been plenty of volunteers to choose from: Nealand was well preserved, no doubt a fox in her day, but Tucker was glowing, busty, a fox still on the hunt. Alas, she had switched junior highs last spring; Ethan felt almost hurt when he heard, as if she had stood him up personally.

At the desk on his right, Amanda Mixler was scribbling away in her notebook. She was a cheerleader, a member of the yearbook committee, and almost definitely a virgin. Today as always she had a pink smell to her, faint but sweet, as if she had dabbed each side of her neck with cotton candy; Ethan wasn't sure if it was perfume or just her own sweet self. Outside, through the windows on his left, morning dimness was giving way to noontime brightness. He suddenly realized that he had a fifth-hour math quiz that he hadn't studied for. His fists clenched automatically; he hated math.

"Psst! Ethan," Amanda whispered.

He turned to her. She was holding up her notebook at a low angle, and smiling. *???Would you have premarital sex with Mrs. Nealand???*

Ethan shrugged uncomfortably. He'd rather have premarital sex with Amanda. She was short and cushiony, and bongo-boobed, with a small pug nose and dimpled cheeks and shiny pert lips. She was all curves and liquid softness—you wouldn't so much hump her as sink into her, and you might just sink forever, never reaching anything that was quite solid. How soft was it down there, anyway? Sex Ed was a colossal flop when it came to the details you actually wanted. Today Amanda wore a tight pink T-shirt with the word Sweetheart cursived in red across the front; her black hair was piled on top of her head, with thick strands hanging down like ribbons. She'd probably lose her virginity to a jock. Jocks were jocks partly because they liked sports and partly because they wanted to land girls like Amanda. Ethan had tried to be a jock almost entirely because he wanted to land girls like Amanda, and it wasn't near enough; back in the fall, he was one of only a handful to be cut from the ninth-grade football team.

"Ew! You would," Amanda mouthed.

Ethan went back to half-listening to Mrs. Nealand. Maybe at lunch he could ask Amanda if she could spare a minute to help him with math; she was in his class and was pretty good at all this negative-integer crap. What he hated about math was it was so inhuman. There was nothing to connect to, just a bunch of numbers to crunch, and the story problems weren't very relatable either. The characters had no attributes except name and gender and no lives beyond their intention to trade some oranges or take a train ride. And Mr. Camden taught in a dry, all-business style. His attitude seemed to be that a job was a job, that he was paid to teach math, not to entertain. He was like a character in a story problem. He had no life beyond his obligation to bore you and give you C's.

Mrs. Nealand had just said something about *promiscuous*. Ethan's stomach zinged; it was one of his favorite sex words. It sounded like dirty silly-slang, a word in a porno scripted by Dr. Seuss, but at the same time it had a slightly clinical ring that made it legitimate: promiscuous girls weren't just rumor but fact. Their existence increased the likelihood that one day you would have sex; it stood to reason that they would be less choosy than regular girls. Also, *promiscuous* contained *prom*, and so you pictured the promiscuous girls in shiny cleavage-baring dresses with hair rippled like frosting and wrists that sprouted gardenias, as if *promiscuous* were an occasion and everyone was invited. Still, there was a downside to *promiscuous*. After all, though a promiscuous girl was more likely to give you a tumble, she was also less likely to think of it as a big deal or to consider it the start of something. It was an occasion for you, not for her.

The bell rang, cutting off Mrs. Nealand. She smiled sheepishly; one never quite got used to teacher interruptus. "More tomorrow," she called after the scattering students. "Or, well, after break, that is. Have a great week everybody."

Out in the hallway, Ethan made his way toward his locker to drop off his books; he had lunch next. His friend Dave Edwards came up alongside him. "Hey bro, you got a couple of bucks I can borrow? For lunch?"

"I don't know, maybe."

"I forgot my—ho, what's this? Fight? Fight!"

A crowd had formed in the middle of the hall right across from the cafeteria. Ethan and Dave pushed to the front of the crowd. The fight, it seemed, was between Pete Conklin and Pete's locker. Amanda Mixler stood on Ethan's right, but she merely glanced at him and inched away to give him room, as if he were a stranger.

"He can't get it open," Jason Richter explained. "He's tried his combination twice but it's jammed or something."

Pete karate-kicked the locker, then tried but couldn't lift up the latch of the built-in lock. Changing tactics, he slammed his shoulder against the locker, and again, but nothing happened. "Bastard," he muttered. "I'll getcha, though." Huffing, he stared at the floor, apparently considering his next move. Other guys stepped forward to assist, but Pete waved them away; this was between him and the locker.

"Maybe he's got the com wrong," Ethan suggested.

Jason shook his head. "He's double-checked it."

Suddenly, Vice-Principal Burke was part of the crowd. "What's going on here? Let's move it along, you're blocking . . . Holy hell! Conklin, are you looking to get suspended? That's school property you're abusing!"

Pete froze, then grinned. "Aw, man, I ain't abusing nothing."

"Oh, no? So I *didn't* just see you punch that locker?"

"Well, but you've got it all wrong, Mr. Burke. *It's* abusing *me*. Damn thing won't open. I ain't into beating things up, as a rule, but if you give us crappy—"

"Christ alive! Are you stupid, boy? I don't want to hear it!" He took a deep breath, calming himself. "Okay, Conklin, here's what you're gonna do. You're gonna shut that excuse-machine you call a mouth and march your ass to my office. Got it? Good. The rest of you, get to class. Pronto!"

Ethan whispered, "And the locker lives to fight another day."

Amanda gave him a sidelong look and smirked appreciatively; this stranger wasn't so bad. But then she quickly wandered off.

At Ethan's own locker, he and Dave stood around talking idly and watching girls go by. There went tan and trim Tamara Davis, calling hello, then short and mousy Emily Burnett, pretending she wasn't aware of them. And now blond and bosomy Carol Lifford, actually not aware of them. Ethan loved their names—so classic, so pungent, like the names of the female characters in the old novels they read in English class. English was so much better than math. Here came tall and cream-complected Susan Wilbur, slowing down, coming toward them. She was wearing her trademark white cashmere beret, Ethan's scraggly Michigan State sweatshirt, and a plaid skirt.

Dave gave Ethan a winking look. "Whoa, gotta split. See you in the caf."

Ethan grinned awkwardly as Susan sauntered over to him, her high-top sneakers squeaking against the floor. She had borrowed the sweatshirt over a month ago, for gym class, and had worn it to school at least once a week ever since. Her not returning it was supposed to be some big joke on him, but the joke was on her: he *loved* that she wore it.

"Ethan," she said, sharply, her voice breathless as always. She slouched down to his level, regarding him slyly. Her sleek blond-brown hair oozed out from the beret and down to her shoulders like melted butterscotch, and she had puffy red lips that were so sexy that sexy didn't even begin to cover it. Like her outfit, her features were somewhat mismatched; her hair and lips were goddess-hot, but her crooked nose and boobless body were strictly wallflower. He had no idea if Susan was a virgin or not. It seemed equally likely that she had done it dozens of times or that she had never even kissed anyone.

"Susan," he said, equally sharp. It was their routine: she made out as if there were some bad history between them, and he went along with it. In truth, though, unless you counted the sweatshirt thing, they had no history at all. He had never even exactly *met* her; one day a few months ago she had simply started talking to him, already adversarial, sniping at him familiarly as if picking up from the day before. In fact, well . . . who the hell was she, anyway? None of his friends had her in a class or knew anything about her. And if she herself had friends, she was keeping them out of sight. He wasn't complaining; these mysterious hallway encounters left him buzzed, even gleeful. Sometimes, though, he wished that things would evolve with her or with Amanda, even if only into a more conventional kind of friendship.

She sighed heavily. "So? What's new?"

"Nothing much. What about you?"

"*Uh.*" She cocked her head and squinted at him. "Not that you noticed, but I just got here. I missed the bus and had to have my psycho mom drive me in."

"Well, that sucks."

She bobbed her head forward. Her nose this close up was even crookeder; her person smelled sugary and musty, like candy corn from a hundred Halloweens ago. "Oh, yeah," she muttered. "I can tell you're all broken up about it."

It was thrilling and so awkward; if she came just a little bit closer, they would be kissing. Humping her would be intimate and intense, not anything like the eternally sinking experience of humping Amanda. Susan would be on top, for one thing, bolt upright, smiling slyly, and right when you plugged into her she would stop and stare into your eyes until she had you good and hypnotized, and then, just when you couldn't take it any longer, she would start rocking slowly, her fingers lacing through yours. Her set-the-mood music selection would be late-era Beatles, vinyl. Amanda during sex would be a good sport but not a particularly active one; somehow, she'd fulfill her part just by letting you hump her. With Susan, it would be some sly, mystical communion and you wouldn't even be quite sure that you were the one doing the humping.

She retreated and broke out into a friendly smile, her deep-blue eyes twinkling. "Hey there. You look a little done in yourself. Rough morning?"

He was startled that his discomfort was so transparent. "What? No. I mean, I'm just nervous about a math quiz, is all."

She smirked. "Or maybe you're just preoccupied with Sex Ed. Maybe all that carnal knowledge is corrupting your innocence."

Ethan grinned awkwardly and looked away. Carnal was another

word that stirred him up. So close to carnival, and wasn't that perfect? He pictured the inside of a carnival tent, where a dark-skinned mystery woman, with hair down to her butt and huge thick-lashed eyes, was strip dancing within a circle of satin pillows. Satin pillows, like lit candles, were signifiers of humping about to happen. And even without a freaky carnival girl, sex was still bound to be a carnival of sinful pleasures. A real, live girl, willing to be kissed, explored—that was a carnival in itself.

"So what's the dirt? Learn anything interesting today?"

"In Sex Ed? Just that premarital sex is bad and that girls are tramps."

She gave him an annoyed look, then took a breath and closed her eyes. Good lord, Ethan, are you really this stupid? Or are you just pretending cuz you don't like me?

"What's going on?" he asked. "What're you doing?"

Think I'm pretty. Think I'm hot. Look at me the way you look at fat little Amanda Mixler—want me like that. I'm not positive that I love you, but I'm pretty sure I do. I want you to take my flower, except I have to be your first or it's off.

"If you're mad about something, why don't you just say so?"

"I'm telepathing, stupid. Can't you hear me?"

"Oh! No, but I wasn't ready. Try it again."

I won't wait forever.

"Uh, you want me to lend you another sweatshirt?"

"Oh, forget it. Just forget it!" She stomped off, but then turned around and shot him an evil look. "Maybe you should worry less about math and more about Sex Ed."

"Huh? What does that mean?"

"It means you're gonna flunk—forever! You'll never have anyone."

Ethan watched her swoosh off down the hall. He'd offended her with his tramp comment, probably. He turned and started back toward the cafeteria, wondering if he would ever land a girlfriend. What he really wanted, though he would never admit it to anyone, was just a girl to make out with. Smooching was where it was at. He had made out with a few girls during Spin the Bottle at Karen Wilks's birthday party, but also once, in the best two minutes of his life, with Tonya Spaulding of her own free will at a roller rink. The soft puffy lips and thick swirling tongue, the tart perfume, the boobs pressed against your chest—making out with a pretty girl was so close to heaven that you might as well call it heaven. In fact, sometimes he could hardly believe that making out *wasn't* sex; it was that great. If there was something even better, and there was, because the existence of Sex Ed and pornos proved it, then truly it was a wonderful world.

Still, as much as he wanted to go all the way sometimes, when it came down to it, he would be scared. Maybe even *really* scared. In fact, he was pretty damn nervous just making out sometimes. Oh, sure, he would do fine with some anonymous promiscuous girl or some stripping carnal Amazon, but it was sure to be more nerve-wracking with a girl you knew and worshipped. And what if no one ever wanted to have sex with him? But that was just stupid: sooner or later, almost everyone got to have sex. Ethan rallied for a moment, then crumbled. Almost everyone wasn't the same as everyone. Almost everyone had made the ninth-grade football team.

"Ethan! Hey!" It was a pink voice, pitched rhythmically, like a cheer.

He turned around and there was soft, bongo-boobed Amanda Mixler. "Oh. Hey."

She frowned, her eyes squinching with concern. "What's wrong?"

"Nothing." He forced a grin. "Just hungry, I guess."

Her eyes popped. "Yeah, me too. My stomach's like, *Fill me, fill me*. Hey, listen. I meant to ask you, did you study for the quiz?" She waved her math book.

"Actually, I forgot about it until this morning. What about you?"

"I studied a little last night, but I could use a refresher. I'm gonna go grab a salad, but let's sit together and study-buddy, okay?"

"Yeah? Okay, sure. I'm pretty lost, though."

"Oh, that's okay. It helps me understand it better when I explain it to someone. And remind me to give you my cell number so we can text over break. I mean, we've been pals for so long now, and we've never even texted! Ooh, there's Tina, I gotta go talk to her." She rushed off, calling, "See you in there!"

Ethan closed his eyes and shook his head. Oh, these girls! They were so classic, so dazzling; their eyes sparkled like sequins. He of course realized that at any other school there were girls just as pretty, and no less mysterious, but at the same time he knew beyond all doubt that those other girls were counterfeit copies and these girls here were the originals, and that he should always remember to be grateful that through sheer dumb luck he was here too. Would he ever sleep with one of them? Would they still be in his life five, ten years from now? Would he always know them? He wanted to hold them so badly, forever, but mostly he just hoped he would always know them. ◇

A Middle

D.B. Levin

I live in the asphalt valley
of Brooklyn, just beyond the mountain
Manhattan is, canyons and caves
and holes full of badgers
in blazers in beer-soaked
sootways and moneygutters.
I have brought back gifts from
nightlessness, this 13th hour of my youth.
Here's the bitter tunnel of my throat
full of lights and grinding hopes.
Here's the $17.50 toll to get in
and out of my soul. ◇

Conversation About Perspective

D.B. Levin

"Manhattan is great, sure, but like anything
you have to get the right perspective.
You have to see it from a distance,
so that it starts to look inanimate.
Like something totally vibrant and virile
that died suddenly. An ant colony calcified,
someone wearing incredibly tight pants
hit by a car, frozen in mid air.
Like waves on the ocean
which look like clouds from high above.
What I'm trying to say is, with enough activity
and distance, there is stillness. So the universe
is a photograph. That's why
I'm climbing this building,"
King Kong said to the fighter pilot.
Though from the pilot's perspective
it sounded more like,
"mmgRRAARRad...whiiRRAARssoo." ◇

Jokes

D.B. Levin

A serial killer walks into a bar and kills everybody.

A horse walks into a bar and the bartender doesn't even like horses because of something to do with the length of their faces but his daughter is there and giving him 'those eyes' and he groans like, "not 'those eyes!'" and when the bar closes they take the horse home.

A rabbi, a priest, an imam, and a diabetic walk into a bar and complain about their diets.

In this one dimension, the big bang occurs in such a way that the universe is a bar and everything walks into it.

A boy, a bear, a piglet, a tiger, a rabbit, and a donkey all walk into a bar, are rude to the bartender, get into a big fight, and pay only in honey. In another story the bear wanders back and steals all the honey or gets stuck in a wall or something.

A woman named Alaska and 49 of her imaginary friends walk into a bar.

A woman named Alaska walks into a bar and the bartender falls in love with her and she falls in love back and they get drunk together and have sex and it's decent.

Alaska is the bartender's imaginary friend but he always forgets that.

God walks into a bar and Jesus is already there and there's this Awkward Silence.

A bar walks into a bar.

A bar walks in on a bar and it's uncomfortable and the first bar doesn't know what to say and just closes the door.

A bar and a bar are together for years until the bar finds the other bar in another bar.

A man and a woman walk into a bar and then later out of a bar.

Sisyphus pushes a bar all the way up a hill and when he is about to walk into the bar it rolls back down again.

The bartender has a dream in which everything is beer except beer which is clear, tasteless, and various degrees of sobering.

A psychotic maniac charges into a bar but is very well spoken and makes a lot of friends. Later they're all into regime change.

God commits suicide in the bathroom of a bar and all of time is piecing him back together.

War walks into a bar and never leaves because of a deal with a genie and a bottomless glass.

This one guy in a bar keeps talking about his penis.

Everyone in the bar is on drugs.

The bartender can't remember ever going outside and wonders if his life is some sort of joke.

A bomb goes off in a bar and destroys everything and philosophers sift through the rubble wondering, "Well, what is 'a place'?"

The loud hum of everyone talking walks into a bar. Bewildered, you stare around the empty room.

The wind blows into a bar and Dawn is in the back spinning a Frisbee on her fingers. ◇

Premium Vantage Points!

Evan Crommett

ARE YOU A DIRECTOR? OR FOR THAT MATTER, ANYONE INVOLVED in moviemaking whatsoever? Well have we got news for you! We know you're getting tired of working with the CGI of yesteryear, toiling all day to create jaw-dropping onscreen explosions (we're looking at you, Michael Bay). Well go ahead and toss all that simulated garbage in the trash, and look no further than NASA's upcoming expedition, Europa 43!

For the past decade, billions of dollars have been funneled into this project, which promises to land a rover on Jupiter's fourth largest, frost-covered moon, Europa. The plan is for the rover to collect samples of ice and silicate rock, thus determining if the frigid orb might harbor life. Sounds pretty cool, huh? Well what's even cooler is that if this painstakingly researched, revolutionary mission *doesn't* work out (i.e. the rover's launch fails, due to any number of technical errors, resulting in combustion of epic proportions) there's a golden opportunity for <u>you</u>. At long last you'll be able to capture the explosion you've dreamt about since you were just a Terminator-loving tyke!

Before we say anything further we want to take this opportunity to make it clear that we at Premium Vantage Points™ support the Europa

43 mission wholeheartedly. We 100% hope it is a success and would be the first to celebrate its completed voyage.

But in the extreme likelihood that the rover's shuttle detonates upon launch, we want to be prepared, and more importantly, we want you to be prepared. We feel it would be a shame for no one to find a silver lining in the tragic, probable event of Europa 43 exploding. That's where you come in!

What better way to get the attention of movie critics than to include a real life detonation in your film? How many moviegoers, in their right collective mind, could pass on the sort of cinematic masterpiece that boasts government funded pyrotechnics? I'll tell you how many: zero, zilch, diddly-squat.

That's why we're so happy to be able to offer you (current/future directors, special effects guys, Kubricks of the future) a Premium Vantage Point™ less than forty yards from the Europa launch site! For three easy payments of $998, you ensure yourself a spot in our open-air, luxury facilities the day of the launch. Not only that, you also get a Premium Vantage Point™-certified license to film, and a complimentary "I ♡ NASA" T-shirt upon your arrival. Our team has been working tirelessly to prepare the facilities: clearing glass bottles from the pavement, laying down picnic blankets, even setting up a refreshment stand so you can stay hydrated during the shoot!

Don't wait until the last minute to book your spot! Other savvy filmmakers may have already leapt on this opportunity by the time you get your butt off the couch! Call or click in today at:

1 – 800 – VANTAGE
Premiumvantagepoints.org

DISCLAIMER: Premium Vantage Points™ is responsible for absolutely no refunds in the event that the Europa 43 launch is a success. However, in the case of said success, each and every "I ♡ NASA" shirt must be promptly returned to its respective vendor. Failure to comply will result in immediate and decisive legal action. ◇

Contributors

A. Anupama is a poet and translator whose work has appeared in several literary publications. She received her MFA in writing from Vermont College of Fine Arts in 2012 and is currently a contributing writer at *Numéro Cinq Magazine*. She lives in Nyack, New York, and blogs at seranam.com.

Jacob M. Appel is the author of the short story collections *Einstein's Beach House* and *Scouting for the Reaper*. He practices medicine at the Mount Sinai Hospital in New York City and divides his time between Scarsdale and Manhattan. More at www.jacobmappel.com.

Susan Hunt Babinski, a nurse and psychologist, worked for many years in a children's psychiatric hospital and now works part time with elderly residents in a nursing home.

Alan Beechey was born in England and now lives in Rye. He's the author of a series of comic mysteries and coauthor of a nonfiction book about American culture. Alan thanks the Sound Shore Writers Group for their help in shaping "Hidden Agenda," a different kind of mystery story.

Mark Benedict is a graduate of the MFA Writing program at Sarah Lawrence College. Recent publications include short stories in *Bird's Thumb*, *Catch & Release*, and *Swamp*. Mark loves loves loves music. Camera Obscura's My *Maudlin Career* and the Gaslight Anthem's '59 *Sound* are among his favorite CDs.

Mary O'Keefe Brady's debut chapbook, *Time Out*, was published by Finishing Line Press in 2015. Her first novel, *Mourners and Other Strangers*, is making the rounds. She is a member of The Hudson Valley Writers' Center and the Poetry Caravan. She lives with her husband, Brian, in Briarcliff Manor.

Max L. Chapnick grew up in White Plains and now lives in Washington, D.C. In 2014, Max studied creative writing in Wellington, New Zealand on a Fulbright scholarship. He graduated from Washington and Lee University in 2013 with degrees in Physics and English.

Lucia Cherciu is a Professor of English at SUNY/Dutchess in Poughkeepsie, NY, and the author of two books of poetry in Romanian, *Lepădarea de Limbă* (Editura Vinea, 2009) and *Altoiul Râsului* (Editura Brumar, 2010). Her poetry appeared in *Paterson Literary Review, Cortland Review, Connotation Press, Memoir, Connecticut Review,* and elsewhere.

Michael Collins' poems have appeared in more than 40 journals and magazines, including *Grist, Kenning Journal, Pank, SOFTBLOW,* and *Smartish Pace.* His first chapbook, *How to Sing when People Cut off your Head and Leave it Floating in the Water,* won the Exact Change Press Chapbook Contest in 2014. A full-length collection, *Psalmanadala,* was published later that year.

M. Doretta Cornell is a member of the Poetry Caravan. She taught at Pace University and has given poetry workshops at HVWC and Good Counsel. Her poems have appeared in *Earth's Daughters, Inkwell, Third Wednesday,* and *Commonweal,* among others, and in the anthologies *(en)compass* and *Literature* 5th Edition (McGraw-Hill).

Evan Crommett is a student at Bard College, and is majoring in creative writing. He was born and raised in New York City, where the rest of his loving, incorrigibly artistic family resides.

Bonnie Jill Emanuel lives and writes in Scarsdale. Her poems have appeared in *The Westchester Review, Chronogram,* and *Podium,* the virtual journal of the 92nd Street Y. She is working on her first chapbook.

Gregory A. French is a freelance writer based in Mount Vernon. He is a graduate of Northwestern University's Medill School of Journalism and has studied fiction writing at The Writing Institute at Sarah Lawrence College.

Herb Friedman is a pilot and a corporate lawyer. He lives in New Rochelle. Together with Ada Kera Friedman, he has written several nonfiction articles on aviation subjects.

Brooklyn-born **Myra Emmer Gold** lived, worked, played, and wrote in Westchester County for the most formative decade of her life. Her first published poem appeared in the East New York Savings Bank *School Bank News,* and earned her two inscribed pencils and a thirst for poetry that has never ceased.

Anne Graue is a poet and writing instructor living in New York. She has studied poetry at The Hudson Valley Writers Center, Columbia, and Barnard. Her work has been published in *Ginosko Literary Journal, Compass Rose, The 5-2 Crime Poetry Weekly,* and *New Verse News.*

William A. Greenfield began writing poetry in college, and thanks his daughter for inspiring him to start writing again. After a long career with the Federal Government, he is now semi-retired and resides in the Catskill Mountains of New York. His poems have appeared in *The Front Porch Review, The Storyteller Magazine, The East Coast Literary Review, 2 Bridges Review,* and other publications.

Mary Hegarty grew up in the beautiful hamlet of Valhalla, where she currently resides. She's been writing since she was ten years old. Nature deeply informs her writing. Mary is a watershed and storm water specialist; writing and hiking are her favorite pastimes.

Amy Holman teaches poetry at The Hudson Valley Writers' Center, and was a guest poet at the Ossining Weir for The Masters School juniors. Her books include *Wrens Fly Through This Opened Window* (Somondoco Press, 2010), *Wait For Me, I'm Gone*, the 2004 Dream Horse Press chapbook prizewinner, and a writer's guide.

Helen Kellert was born and raised in South Africa. Retired after teaching French and English for twenty-two years at the Bronx High School of Science, she studies creative writing skills in Westchester County. This is her first published story.

Individual entries on **Richard Kostelanetz's** work appear in various editions of *Readers Guide to Twentieth-Century Writers, Merriam-Webster Encyclopedia of Literature, Contemporary Poets, Contemporary Novelists, Postmodern Fiction, Webster's Dictionary of American Writers, Baker's Biographical Dictionary of Musicians, Directory of American Scholars, Who's Who in America,* NNDB.com, Wikipedia.com, and Britannica.com, among other distinguished directories.

Carole Glasser Langille, author of four books of poetry and a collection of short stories, lives in Nova Scotia and teaches creative writing at Dalhousie University. In the early '80s she lived in Ossining and worked in the Community Development office. "Ubuntu" is from a manuscript of linked short stories.

D.B. Levin is a young poet from New Jersey. He received his undergraduate degree at Sarah Lawrence College, where he was awarded the 2013 Lipkin Poetry Prize. He has been previously published in the *Sarah Lawrence Literary Review* and *Provincetown Arts*. He currently lives in Brooklyn, New York.

Katharine Long is a playwright member of the Ensemble Studio Theatre, where many of her one-acts have been produced. Her work has been published by Samuel French, Broadway Play Publishing and included in Ramon Delgado's *Best Short Plays*. Kate lives in Larchmont and serves as a Teaching Artist for the Manhattan Theatre Club.

Jenna Lynch lives in New York and teaches at The College of New Rochelle. She holds her MFA in poetry from the University of Oregon. Her poems have previously appeared in *Stirring, Sundog Lit,* and *Construction Magazine*.

Leon Marks writes fiction that explores darkness, crime and identity. He holds a Master of Fine Arts in Creative Writing from Fairfield University and teaches writing and communications at the City University of New York. More at www.leonmarks.com.

Giulia Mascali is currently a student studying Written Arts at Bard College. She was raised in Sag Harbor, New York. This is her second time being published.

Matt Matros is the author of the non-fiction narrative *The Making of a Poker Player*. His writing has appeared in *The Washington Post*, *CNNMoney.com*, *Mental Floss*, and UCSB's *Spectrum*, among other places. Matt received his MFA from Sarah Lawrence College in 2004. He lives in Brooklyn with his wife, Ivy.

Resa Mestel is a poet, weaver, community-based volunteer, and Family Nurse Practitioner living in Ossining. She has studied writing at The Hudson Valley Writers' Center, Poets House and Bread Loaf Writers' Conference. *The New Verse News* published her poem on Darwin Day. This is her first print publication.

Susan Moorhead's writing has appeared in *Lowestoft Chronicles*, *JMWW*, *Woman Around Town*, and *Crab Creek Review* among others. Nominated three times for a Pushcart prize, she holds an MFA from Manhattanville College. She is a librarian in Westchester County.

In addition to winning competition prizes from the *Avalon Literary Review* and *Eye on Life Magazine*, **Claudine Nash's** recent work has appeared in a number of magazines and anthologies including *Asimov's Science Fiction*, *Star*Line*, *Foliate Oak*, *The Lullwater Review*, and *The MOON magazine*. Her chapbook, *The Problem with Loving Ghosts*, was released by Finishing Line Press in December 2014.

Ben Nightingale's publishing credits include "Fragile Winter," a short story published in *Mendocino Review*; "Now I Lay Me Down to Sleep," a short story published in *Obsidian*; and "A Terror of Knives," a short story published in *The Jewish Magazine*. His website is BenNightingale.typepad.com.

Lisa Olsson is a poet, musician, artist who grew up in Hastings and lives in Dobbs Ferry. Formerly a Design Director for Pearson Education, she currently teaches cello in a private studio and at Hudson River School of Music. Her poems have appeared in *Ginosko Literary Journal*.

After studying Japanese literature at Stanford University, **Peter Porcino** spent his mid-twenties working in Japan and traveling to each continent except Antarctica, which he has saved for last. In late 2013 he returned to his native Ardsley, New York, to work odd jobs and write fairy tales, fables, and other fiction.

Ellen Rachlin is the author of *Until Crazy Catches Me* (Antrim House Books, 2008) and two chapbooks, *Waiting for Here* (Finishing Line Press, 2004) and *Captive To Residue*

(Flarestack Publishing, 2009). She serves as Treasurer of The Poetry Society of America and works in finance.

William Seife of Larchmont studied Astrophysics and Cinema Studies at the University of Pennsylvania, where he wrote a full-book musical comedy that was performed in Philadelphia, New York, Boston, San Francisco, and Los Angeles. He is currently working on a feature-length film. This is his first published short story.

Emmett Shoemaker hails from the sunny wilds of Los Angeles, California. He is in his senior year at Bard College, studying the written arts, and has recently begun work on a collection of ghost stories.

Ann van Buren lives in the Hudson Valley, where she works as a poet, educator, and activist. She teaches poetry workshops in the U.S. and Europe and has been published by *The Blue Door Gallery, THE*, and other journals. Her poetry book reviews can be found in *The Rumpus*.

Lee Waxenberg is a freelance writer who lives in Irvington, New York. Prior to turning to writing, she received a law degree from Fordham Law School and spent many years working on Wall Street.

Richard Weiss is an internist and gastroenterologist, a member of The Hudson Valley Writers' Center and The Cleveland House Poets of Martha's Vineyard, whose poetry has appeared several times in *Pulse*, an online journal of prose and poetry, and in *Let the Poets Speak* as a finalist. He lives with his wife, Maggie, in Armonk.

Maceo J. Whitaker is a Creative Writing teacher whose poems appear or are forthcoming in journals such as *Poetry Magazine, North American Review, The Common, Rattle*, and *The Florida Review*.

Fred Yannantuono has published 356 poems in 85 journals in 30 states. His work has been nominated for a Pushcart prize in 2006 and 2013. His book, *A Boilermaker for the Lady*, can be browsed on Amazon. Was featured Poet in *Light Quarterly*. *To Idi Amin I'm a Idiot–and Other Palindromes* and *I Hate to Second-Guess Myself, or Do I?* are due out in 2015.

Michele Zimmerman received a BA from Sarah Lawrence College in May 2014. Her work appears in Issue 48 of *Sugar Mule*. Two of her short stories were Top-25 Finalists in *Glimmer Train's* Short Story Award for New Writers. She is a fiction reader for *Slice Literary* and *Post Road Magazine*.

James H. Zorn's work appeared in *The Westchester Review 2013* and *2014, The Seven Hills Review, Third Flatiron*. He was named among the Top 25 in *Glimmer Train's* Very Short Fiction Contest 2013. He lives in Irvington, New York, and is currently at work on a number of fiction projects.

SUPPORTERS

We gratefully acknowledge a generous grant from a Westchester family foundation.

Mary and Steve Borowka
Sandy and George Gottlieb
Ann and Paul Spindel
Jonathan Terdiman
Mika Varma

Anonymous

BOOKSELLERS
Anderson's Book Shop
Larchmont, N.Y.
Arcade Booksellers
Rye, N.Y.
The Village Book Shop
Pleasantville, N.Y.
The Voracious Reader
Larchmont, N.Y.
Womrath Book Shop
Bronxville, N.Y.

OTHER MERCHANTS
Amazon.com
Beehive Designer Collective
Mt. Kisco, N.Y.
Candy 'N Cards
Scarsdale, N.Y.
Designer One
Larchmont, N.Y.
Futterman's Stationery
Larchmont, N.Y.
Silver Tips Tea Room
Tarrytown, N.Y.
Standing Room Only
Scarsdale, N.Y.